Faceless

DUSTIN SANCHEZ

DEDICATIONS

For Katherine

For Lynda

Table of Contents

Chapter 0: Prologue

Experiment 1343 sat in the dark Parisian alleyway. He looked at his collar on the ground; his tracker blinked rays of light that cut through the harsh darkness. He had pieced it back together, just enough to work again. Its frayed wires and its cold steel belied the world to which he knew he would be going back. The night air chilled him, but not as much as his cold, lonely cell.

"I don't want to go back," his voice cracked; if he had he tear ducts, he would have cried. The child turned away from the electronic harbinger on the ground; as an unspoken defense, he curled away from the mocking device; his eyes rested on the girl.

1343 looked at her. He didn't remember even telling her his name. To her he would simply be some boy that held her hand while the sky cried.

So 1343 closed his eyes and inhaled deeply. Cold or not, the time he had left was precious. It wouldn't be long before he was shoved back into isolation. The prison waited for him like it had every day of his life. He thought it was childish, for him to think that he could escape from it. He was only seven, though; he still believed in childish dreams. He gazed at the girl in front of him – the one whose age matched his own. She looked back through her black-rimmed glasses; her big, smoky-blue eyes had welled up with tears.

"You're going to call the Monsters?" The Girl in the Rain asked, weakly.

"I'd face the Monsters for you," he said and looked at her. He remembered what she had said; she needed something called insulin.

She kept looking to him for guidance, but it was that she was looking at him at all that surprised him. He thought about how she wouldn't look away; she didn't grimace, or wince at his lack of face. He looked back, at her rain-matted, snow-blond hair. He studied her, remembering all of her that he could. She shivered and nuzzled into him. The action brought him back to reality.

He took her by the hand and led her to a spot in the alley more protected from the sky-tears; a place that was more protected from the taunting of the collar. She seemed so fragile; he was genetically perfect, but she seemed porcelain. She was beginning to drift, falling asleep on his shoulder.

He knew they wouldn't be together when they woke up. He touched his lipless face to her cheek; it was his way of a kiss, before she drifted off to sleep; it was a memory he wanted for both of them. The sound of a helicopter cut through the quiet, Parisian night. The Monsters had arrived.

"They're here," 1343 whispered, closing his eyes. Those words were for himself; the next were for her. "Don't forget me."

The helicopter landed on the roof above. 1343 looked up. The Monsters rappelled down the roof with their guns and dog collars to take him away.

~Arc I: The Boy in the Rain~

Chapter 1: 1343

Experiment 1343 groaned in boredom. He knocked his head against the tile wall of his cell. The rear of his helmet would protect it, like its opaque front did his face. It protected NightCard's hundred-million dollar investment. He bounced the helmet again; it made an echo in the ten by twelve room. As long as he was chained to the wall, the dull knocking sound was his only entertainment.

He looked around the dark room. It had the sterile reek of a room that was too clean. There was a loud dripping sound coming from the faucet in the corner, where he drank and showered. He was in a Kevlar bi-weave straightjacket weighed down with lead. The genetics engineering company couldn't afford him to escape.

The once-incessant sound of the water droplets' plop and metallic "ring" had become so constant that his brain more or less tuned it out. The mask was what was really bothering him. It shielded his face, so it did its job – but it itched. Inside the opaque helmet front was a rough material, like unfinished leather. His sole desire at that moment was to scratch his nose. Not that one could see his nose; only his clear blue eyes peeked though.

The clear blue eyes scanned the room like they had thousands of times before; they looked at his most valuable possessions – his paintings. Originals of Picasso, Rembrandt, and Da Vinci adorned the walls. 1343 had argued that he wasn't inspired by copies and needed the original if he was going to refine his craft. His original Keeper, the nurturing type that she was, had agreed with him. She had convinced NightCard, and was the first to call him Faceless.

While 1343 loved classical paintings, right above his head were his favorites. They were stills of comic books from his childhood that hung from nails that had rusted from the humidity. All of the artworks had grown to have a mildew smell to them.

Faceless leaned his head back against the wall, bored of bouncing. He rolled his head to the side and looked at the paints he used during his weekly one hour of "free" time. His face was still sore from his latest workout session. It hurt him, after all, to keep ripping his face off. He started humming Beethoven.

The giant metal door 1343 was facing had three two-foot diameter steel tumblers that locked him inside. They were bulletproof, absorbed energy, and taunted him with the reminder that there was no hope of escape. Faceless looked at the tumblers, every day hoping that they would open – hoping for any sort of interaction. It had been a forever since he had seen his Keeper.

"Open," Faceless said, although the leather mask muffled his sentiment. "Open. Anyone, I would see anyone. Even that fat-ass, Giffin."

The gears ground and the tumblers tripped. 1343 watched, waiting.

* * *

Kevin Giffin stood outside 1343's room. He hated this part of the job. The routine inspections were only once a month, but even then he had decided to skip the last two. He swiped his card, and the tumblers sounded and the door slid open. He braced himself. Half of the time 1343 would greet him with a "good to see you, you ginger fat-ass."

The insult didn't hurt in itself; what hurt was how true Giffin found it.

The rotund man crossed the room and was out of breath by the time he had made it to Experiment 1343. He would have to start working out. There was a gym the employees could use for free; he'd been meaning to go. Giffin took a rag out of his pocket and used it to wipe the sweat from his brow. Afterwards, he threw it at 1343 – that ought to teach the bastard. The genetic experiment turned his face as best he could, but the sweat-drenched rag smacked the helmet. It left wet streaks across the front as the rag flopped off. It hit the ground with a wet splat.

"That's going to smell for a while, now," 1343 said. "Although it smells better than when you were on your Indian food binge."

"Let's have a chat, shall we?" Giffin said, taking breaths between each word, still recovering. He knew he needed to stop by the gym tomorrow. Maybe next week.

Kevin Giffin flipped a switch next to 1343, pulling the bastard higher up the wall; Giffin wanted him eye level. Giffin unhooked the facemask; his own face stared back at him.

"Damn it, I told you to stop doing that!" Giffin shouted. He tore 1343's face off.

Giffin looked at what lay beneath. It had been just under a year since he'd gotten the job, but what he saw still unnerved him. 1343's face – if one could call it that – was a kind of pure white, slick, and glistening surface. His face was a translucent jelly that glinted light off it. His clear eyes and mouth free-floated in the jelly; the entirety of it glistened with a wet, slick texture as it waited for his command. Then 1343 breathed out and Giffin saw the eyes slowly start to move in the jelly; the mouth's opening shifted further down in the jelly and the gunk itself retracted slightly, forming a different jawline.

Patterson watched; his disdain for the abomination suspended itself for a second. Even after a year, he was too preoccupied with what he was seeing. Starting from the ears, skin branched out like veins across 1343's face; the different bands of flesh found each other and melded together. The bands expanded, crafting themselves into a mask; 1343 became another man. After a few moments, Giffin stood there, looking at his boss. It was John Patterson's thin face, complete with a graying goatee, and sharp green eyes, but it was 1343's expression.

"Stop messing with my favorite experiment, fat-ass," the experiment said, mimicking Patterson's voice; his practiced, patronizing tone reflected the original perfectly.

Giffin drew his hand back and punched 1343 as hard as he could in the face, which he was sad to say, wasn't all that hard.

"Heh-heh. You shouldn't punch a face worth forty-two million dollars," Patterson's face mocked, the impact causing his face to rip. It hung there, halfway attached.

"Screw you, you genetic abomination. When I came to work for NightCard, I didn't think they'd stick me with some test-tube abortion like you."

"You should apologize quickly, Kevin," 1343 said in a singsong voice then gestured with his chin behind Giffin.

* * *

Not again. John Patterson was trying very hard not to look like he was concerned. If he ran, then people would start to think he gave a shit about Faceless.

No, it was 1343. Faceless is what the damn thing wanted to be called. Property didn't get a say on its name. Patterson looked down at the cell phone in his hand. The alert was yellow. That meant Giffin was in the cell alone. Giffin had been suspended from that privilege after losing his cool last month.

Patterson quickened his pace even more. 1343 was a hundred million dollar experiment. He would get his ass handed to him if Giffin fucked up. Patterson would have to deal with Red. The blood drained from Patterson's face at the thought of bringing any kind of bad news to the President of NightCard. He broke into a run.

When Patterson approached the doors, he looked at the two guards standing outside of the room like jackasses. "What the hell?" Patterson said, slightly out of breath. "Why the fuck are you two jackasses not in there stopping him?"

The guards looked at each other like the military rejects that they were. The fact that they hadn't yet shot themselves with their stun guns surprised Patterson.

"Giffin said he wanted some alone time with 1343."

"What did you think he meant?" Patterson growled.

"I think what he's attracted to is his business," Jackass Two said.

"That's not… you're a dumbass," Patterson said. "Open the door."

The gears ground again, and the door to the room opened up. Patterson saw Faceless smirk. Technically it was his own face; the little bastard was just wearing it. 1343 saw Patterson's angry look over Giffin's shoulder.

"You should apologize quickly, Kevin," 1343 said in a singsong voice.

Giffin turned just in time to see Patterson's fist coming at his face. Patterson only put forty percent into the punch, but it still lifted Giffin off his feet. The surprised Keeper crashed into the Mona Lisa. He slid down the wall, the broken picture frame coming with him, the impact itself leaving a crack in the wall. Damn it; Patterson knew he'd have to pay to fix that.

Patterson watched Giffin lay there, stunned; the bastard was only barely hanging onto consciousness. "You damn idiot! He's worth more to this company than you could ever imagine!" Patterson shouted, his spittle flying everywhere.

"Yeah Giffin, I'm more important than you," 1343 stuck out his tongue, angling so it came out of the torn, half-hanging Patterson face.

Patterson walked up to 1343, tearing off the mutilated copy of his face. The action made Faceless grimace.

"Just because I can do it doesn't mean it feels good, John," 1343 said with a weak chuckle.

"Shut up," Patterson said. "That thing was giving me the creeps. I'm way more handsome than that."

Patterson held it up for a second, then with a grimace flung it to the ground. The discarded face landed on top of a growing pile of others; some were of important politicians, others of rock stars, but most of them were of Patterson.

"Really? Here I thought I was being generous. Especially with the wrinkles," 1343 said looking away casually.

"Shut up. I have to deal with this, then I'll get back to you," Patterson growled.

"Do your thing, old man," 1343 chuckled. Patterson fought the urge to punch the experiment; Patterson knew that Giffin's punch was puny and had no strength, but his own would have completely crippled 1343.

Though the idea had appeal.

Patterson turned to reproach Giffin. "Do you know how hard it would be to recreate him: his face is a bed of hyper stem cells – hell, his entire body. His motor functions are faster than humanly possible. We made the perfect spy with photo-kinetic reflexes. There's a lot riding on Project Morph."

"Too bad I'm such a pain in the ass, right daddy?" a little girl's voice said from over Patterson's shoulder.

Patterson sighed. He recognized the voice; he knew Giffin would too. Patterson watched the Keeper's body tense up. He saw Giffin's frame begin to tremble with rage. Giffin looked past Patterson; Patterson turned too see as well. Giffin's daughter was staring at them from the head of the straightjacket. The red-haired curls framed the face. The eyes were the exact shade of green that Patterson had seen from Giffin's wallet pictures. The freckles were even in the proper placement; this was a well-practiced face.

"I blame it on my parenting," Project Morph said in a little girl's voice; 1343 tried his hardest to look cute with his tongue sticking out of his pre-adolescent face.

Patterson could feel it with his practiced instincts; the air shifted in the room. A roar left Giffin as he charged 1343. Patterson stuck his arm out; his forearm caught Giffin by the neck and knocked the Keeper down.

"You didn't get 'most-important-to-NightCard?'" Patterson growled down at Giffin. He lifted Giffin up by the neck and flung him across the room into the door; the Keeper bounced off and crumpled in a heap. Patterson crossed the room, opened the door, and scooted the heap of broken bone and disappointment out of the room.

The door shut, the tumblers tripped, and there was silence. Patterson sighed and brushed his thumb across his nose.

"Ah, so time to turn the cameras off then, Patty?" 1343 asked, familiar with the gesture.

Patterson calmly walked up to 1343 and drove his knee into Project Morph's abdomen. The impact drove 1343 into the air; his chains rose for a moment, and then as 1343 slammed back downward they caught. Patterson heard the breath catch at the back of 1343's throat; he knew that even through the Kevlar, it would hurt. Patterson was getting old, but fifty-six years old or not, he still had at least half of the strength he used to have.

"Ow," 1343 said, keeping his little girl voice. "I didn't think you'd hit a girl." Patterson pulled up a chair and sat across from 1343. "Then again," the redhead said with her best princess voice, "maybe you get a sick thrill from hitting little girls. It's okay Patty; your secret is safe with me."

"You know, this is the thirteenth Keeper you've had me forcibly remove from this room," Patterson said, pulling out a cigarette and ignoring 1343's comments. He took a match and lit it by dragging it across 1343's face. The action tore a line through the little girl face. He leaned back and took a drag. He exhaled and glared at 1343 through the smoke.

"Smoking isn't allowed in my room, Patty," Faceless said. "It's bad for my health."

Patterson took another puff from the cigarette and then blew it at Faceless. "I'm beginning to think there's no reforming you. I mean mentally, of course. Your physical reforming is fine," he chuckled at his small joke and took another drag.

"Uh! Well I never. I happen to think I'm perfectly fine, Patty," the little girl face said haughtily, turning her nose up and letting out the frustrated sigh of a typical teenage girl.

"Okay. Let's talk, 1343. Yes, your real face is nothing but stem cells. Yes, we've taken the time to train you in our own personal brand of mixed martial arts, and sure, you've been given tutors, art lessons, lessons on philosophy, technology, and medicine, everything we could fit into that little brain of yours. You're valuable, you little bastard," Patterson said, distracted; he spared a moment to look at him, "but, in my personal opinion, we've spent enough on you."

He was looking for the ashtray he knew Faceless's – Patterson shook his head – 1343's Keepers hid in his room. 1343's Keepers tended to want a smoke after five minutes in his company – usually more than a cigarette. Patterson found it and put the cigarette out.

"However, even though I think we've spent enough on you, the President of the United States wants you. And whatever Madam President wants, Madam President gets."

Patterson saw Faceless shudder. Patterson shared the sentiment. They'd both met the President of the United States four years ago in 2012 right after she had been elected into office. As soon as she could, she had come by to start to bid on experiments. NightCard had happily obliged. The United States kept the United Federation of Nations off their back. Well, the United States and their ally, the U.S.S.R.;

NightCard also did transactions with the U.F.N. in secret. Sweden even permitted NightCard's main base of operations, Fati, to exist within their capital.

"It's the beginning of the month, and since it's June thirtieth, tomorrow it's your birthday. Happy birthday, but we need to run another field test. So here's the deal, you little bastard. Don't cause any trouble, and I'll resist the ever-present urge to shoot your ass full of the 'happy juice' for the next three months," Patterson smiled. "Happy juice" was one of the only ways they could control the little bastard. Patterson had grabbed the drug from their pharmaceutical department; it was one that left the victim with no control over his body and heightened pain receptors; for someone with a lot of receptors in his face, this was torture. This treatment was particularly effective against Faceless; with it he couldn't control what faces he made. They always looked twisted and disfigured. "Unless you want me to do that?"

"No…" Faceless bowed his head; he kept the little girl's voice, refusing total submission. Patterson tried to ignore it.

"Good. Then get some sleep because the field test is early tomorrow," Patterson said. He rubbed his nose again and the film started up once more.

As John Patterson walked out, he saw an eavesdropping guard standing watch in the hall; the guard trying very hard to make it seem like he wasn't just listening in.

"And that," Patterson smiled, packing another cigarette, "is how you deal with 1343."

* * *

Faceless sat in his room and looked at the walls again. They were covered with paintings; he had copied each of them from a different artist; he had replicated every brush stroke. He remembered being a kid sitting with his first Keeper, Joan Saint; the twenty-two year old had been his favorite. Faceless remembered that she had been kind. She was just doing her job; she had helped him refine his abilities by improving his imagination. She was his surrogate mother, and she was certainly the closest thing to one that Faceless had ever had.

Faceless looked at one of the tumblers on the door; it had a small little smiley face on it drawn in permanent marker, a goodbye from Joan; it had a little bit of fresh Giffin blood staining it. He wanted desperately to wipe the blood off. The smiley face was thirteen years old; that fat bastard's blood didn't deserve to touch it. Faceless looked closer to the smiley face. The smallest little imperfections were in its mouth's smile; if one really squinted, they could see it shaped Joan's favorite animal, the dolphin.

His attention went back to his face; it hurt. It hurt to keep ripping off that face he was born with; he didn't think of it as really being been through. He knew he had been one of five test tube babies. It was necessary; his face had glands that excreted stem cells. He knew he was special; the first four hadn't made it, and he almost hadn't either. He looked at the corner with the finger paints.

Then his eyes moved to the table. He saw its finger-paint stains. Faceless missed Joan, ever since she had been reassigned. He gazed across the wall at his favorite painting. It was the only painting Joan had ever painted; it was only for him, of a woman without a face.

"She's out there," Joan had said. "You'll find her someday."

He told himself that the field test was his chance, to finally escape and be free. He had promised a friend a long time ago that he would get away; he would start his own life – a challenge, how the friend had put it, and one to which he was determined to rise.

Faceless hummed Beethoven until he sang himself asleep, still wearing the little girl's face and thinking about tomorrow.

Chapter 2: Field Test

Faceless could hear the chains that bound him clinking against each other as he walked blindly out of the mouth of the corridor. He was wearing a blindfold as he was being led out to prevent any attempt at escape. He could still feel the change. The practice arena was open air and he took a breath. The stark contrast between the stale, recycled air that he was used to and the fresh air was enough to let him know he was outside. He could smell the forest on the other side of the coliseum walls; it beckoned to him. Then the guard took off his blindfold and the flood of sunlight made him blink; the unfamiliar sun overwhelmed him for a moment. He wasn't able to raise his hands to shield his eyes; he tried, but the manacles were tethered to the chains on his legs. The most he could get was a resistant clinking sound; it was the only evidence he had tried. When his eyes adjusted, Faceless looked around. The morning of the field test was cloudy and humid. For Faceless it was only the fourth time he had been allowed out of his room, and it was only the third time he was allowed outdoors.

Anyone else would have seen it as another slightly overcast day with high humidity, but for Faceless it was the best day of his life. If things worked out the way he wanted, it was the day he would finally join the world.

Faceless looked around the practice arena; it had been years, but the arena looked different than what he remembered. Steel walls had been set in place for the exhibition; they crossed each other and cordoned off different parts of the coliseum making pathways. It was a maze, Faceless realized. Patterson walked in front of him, cutting off his studying. Faceless looked up at Patterson.

"All right, 1343, here's how the test is going to work," John said, nodding at the shackled experiment to be sure he was paying attention.

"Go on," Faceless said. Today he was wearing the face of Patterson's son.

"This field test will check your response time, and your ability for hand to hand combat," Patterson said, packing his cigarette box against his wrist.

"Okay. Yeah, dad, I know," Faceless said, sighing through Patterson's son's mouth.

Faceless saw Patterson hesitate for a moment. Faceless knew Patterson thought he had called him dad just to get to him. What Patterson probably didn't know was that Faceless really meant it.

Faceless saw Patterson's head give a sharp nod; a NightCard agent came walked in front of Faceless and held a gun to Faceless's head. Another from behind held one to his back. Faceless felt the gun in the back of his head and looked at Patterson.

"We don't want you trying anything," Patterson said, shrugging.

"We don't want you trying anything," Faceless mocked Patterson like a five-year-old child.

"Bitch."

A third agent unshackled Faceless; they all slowly backed away. Faceless's skin was illuminated with hundreds of lasers.

"Really?" Faceless said, raising his arms and showing off all the dots on them. "This was necessary?"

"Ask David's balls," Patterson grunted and pointed at one of the snipers on the wall. "You took a shot to them the last time we did this without the dots."

"It was a paintball gun, and I was young," Faceless said defensively.

"Try not to make us shoot you. David was really happy when I assigned him to the wall," Patterson called behind him as he walked toward the bulletproof glass partition at the edge of the field.

As Patterson walked away, Faceless saw him gesture over at one of the gunmen on the wall. The sniper waved at Patterson. Then Faceless noticed the marksman point at him. The next thing he saw was a middle finger; it was one of the issues of having superior vision.

"Begin test," Patterson said over the loud speakers. Faceless looked out and saw three agents. He looked at the closest one and then at the paintball gun in his hand. Faceless had an idea. He ran for the maze freestanding in the training ground. Faceless tilted his head thirteen degrees toward the right for his peripheral vision and hyper reflexes to insure nothing was going to hit him. He fired paintballs at the agent closest to his rear and charged into the maze.

* * *

Patterson was worried. He very much did not want this to go as bad as last time. He took a cigarette out of his freshly packed box and lit it. Sometimes he wished the damn U.S. Government had gone with nukes instead of genetic manipulation in World War II. If they had, he wouldn't be here, but no, they had to go look into freaking genetics.

Portly NightCard agent Ted Dixon looked at Patterson. "I thought you quit smoking?" Dixon asked, probing.

Patterson took a drag and looked at him. He enjoyed the drag and then let it out slowly.

"I smoke to calm my nerves," he said, with a sigh. "It just so happens my nerves need calming when hundred-million-dollar experiments go into field tests with forty-seven high powered rifles trained on them."

"So... every Monday?"

"That's what I said, isn't it?" Patterson grunted as he shoved the cigarette into his mouth again.

"Yeah, you'll quit smoking," Dixon said, rolling his eyes.

Patterson wouldn't ever admit it, but he was a little worried about Faceless too. He didn't know why, but that asshole seemed to grow on him.

Patterson knew 1343 was the best marksman that NightCard had, even if they weren't willing to admit it. He saw Faceless use the walls as a makeshift stair-step to flip into the last agent following him. The agent was caught off guard. He lost his footing as Faceless leg-swept him, then Faceless pushed him into a shadowed area.

Patterson tensed. He looked around at the monitors. He didn't have a camera in that area. He waited in anticipation. This was exactly what he didn't want to happen.

Forty-five very long seconds passed, and then the agent came stumbling out; paint was smeared on his visor. He held his hand up to the control on his helmet and paged over to Patterson and the Conductor. Patterson noticed that even though the gun holster was on the right side of the agent, he used his left arm. His right arm hung uselessly at his side. Patterson knew that look; it had probably been pulled out of its socket.

"He uh… he escaped boss," the agent said, wincing in pain.

"What do you mean he escaped?" Patterson asked. It wasn't a question, not really. He was just daring the agent to say it again.

"I mean I think he's trying to leave the facility," he said it cautiously; he recognized Patterson's tone.

"Shit," Patterson said leaning back; his face had turned pale. The Conductor looked at Patterson. Patterson knew everyone was waiting for his response. "Pull the guys back in and then arm them with real bullets." Patterson rubbed the bridge of his nose. He took another drag of his cigarette. "Shoot to kill," Patterson said.

"Are you sure sir?" The Conductor asked.

Patterson waited another second. "Yeah," he said. He unconsciously started packing his cigarettes against his wrist again.

Fucking nukes wouldn't have had this problem.

* * *

The agent with the paint-smeared face handed his paintball gun to the armory clerk. He hurt very much. His body was aching; that had been an embarrassing ordeal.

"You really let him get away," the clerk said with a scoff.

"Well, not intentionally," the agent said. The clerk scoffed again and gave the agent a handgun. The agent walked over to the medical tent and had his shoulder popped back into place. In his opinion, it didn't particularly feel very good. After a sharp hiss of pain, the agent looked at the medic. "Tell Patterson I got to take a leak and then I'll head out," the agent said as he headed off to the lavatory.

In the restroom the agent took off the armor and ripped off the vent cover with an almost inhuman strength.

"Those dumb-asses," Faceless said as he dove into the vent.

He smiled as he disappeared from sight, crawling toward freedom.

Chapter 3: The Trudge

Faceless eventually made his way out of NightCard's ventilation system. It was hot in there; winter was close, and Patterson had cranked the heat. Faceless leaned against the side of Soul, NightCard's building that had been his prison for years. He looked around him; he saw nothing but forest. It seemed as though Soul was isolated; it was the only evidence of man in sight. His attention turned back to the gun in his hand. He had hopes of never using it. Still, he slid the gun into the side holster the guard had so graciously given him.

The most important thing was figuring out where he was. All he was able to gather from being trapped in that room for years was that he was in France. After the War, the entire landscape's change had given the people of Paris beachfront property. He smelled the air. It had a hint of salt in it. He was near the ocean. He ran to the tallest tree nearby and climbed it. He looked past the treetops; in the distance he saw something that he had only seen in books and pictures. Along the treetops of the forest surrounding NightCard he saw a tower of bent steel and metal. It was the Eiffel Tower. A slow, cautious smile spread across his face. He remembered her. He was closer to the Girl in the Rain than he thought.

He began the ten-mile hike to the highway. After that, it was a twenty-mile drive to Paris, but one of the things that unnerved him was the scary bedtime story that Patterson told him as a kid. The story was a scare tactic, to get Faceless to obey, that way Faceless knew what was waiting for him if he ever tried to escape. He did know. Standing between himself and the highway was The Trudge, NightCard's name for the woods between itself and Paris. It was more dangerous than any other woods. As soon as Patterson found out Faceless was in The Trudge, he'd have the Tens after him. The Tens were famous for their ruthless and usually fatal practices; they didn't have a single recorded account for bringing people back alive. The Trudge was their playground, where they knew every rock, every tree. The Tens wouldn't stop until they found him.

Faceless looked at the Eiffel Tower again, and he thought of the woman of his dreams waiting for him. She was more of a beacon than the Tower was. Then he thought of the Tens.

"Let them come," he said.

* * *

Patterson was walking in a hurry towards the interrogations room. The damned security guards had somehow managed to fix their initial screw up. They'd caught 1343 and tied the experiment up in a chair. They'd just let him know. Patterson thought back to the last time they had used the interrogation room. It had all the fun interrogation methods, including the less legal ones. He thought about how it had been David that had caught 1343. He thought about all the sharp instruments in that room. Then he remembered what had happened to David's balls.

He quickened his pace.

He needed to get there fast. If anything happened, the Black Joker would not be happy. He thought about how their interrogation room paled in comparison to Black Joker's Playroom in the Fati building. He thought about the Black Joker's nipple clamp jumper cables and his device simply referred to as "The Unicorn," Patterson had seen the Unicorn in action once. He didn't want to disappoint the psychopath in charge of Experimental Development.

Patterson was pissed the building was so damn big.

He saw Bill the Intern on his right.

"Patterson! I need to run these numbers by you about the Kings—" Bill started.

"Not now, ass-wipe!" he said, blowing him off with a wave of his hand.

"But Spade is getting restless!" Bill shouted after him. "He's asking for more romantic visual novel games!"

"Handle it!" Patterson roared back.

Patterson finally reached the door. He opened it and after a moment of composure, entered.

He knew 1343 couldn't see any of them. The room was dark, with a single beam of light that shone down on him. It cast shadows on Patterson's face that were deep and ominous as he walked out into the light. 1343, whose face was cast in shadow and hidden by the light, was almost pitch black, but the face was Patterson's son.

"Okay, 1343. You gave us a run for our money, but we caught you."

The imprisoned experiment looked up.

"I told you, Patterson: it's me, Roy," he pleaded one more time.

The irritating sound of his voice had given Patterson a headache.

"Shut up," Patterson said, and grabbed the corner of 1343's jaw. He ripped off the face of his son and saw Roy's face underneath. He tugged on the new Roy face.

"Ow."

It didn't budge.

"Oh crap," Patterson groaned.

"I told you. He disarmed me, took my clothes, and ran," Roy said.

"Damn it," Patterson said, his headache was getting worse.

He thought for a second. The most rational course of action was to call the Tens. Patterson didn't want to do that; they'd assuredly kill him, but they were the only ones that stood a chance of catching Faceless in the Trudge.

"Damn him for making me do this," Patterson grunted as he walked over to the side of the cell and paged the Conductor. "Send the Tens."

In some small part of his heart, he hoped Faceless made it.

The rest of his heart was pissed.

* * *

Faceless was about halfway through the forest before he heard the rustling sound behind him. He turned just in time to see one of the Tens lunge at him. Faceless, born with hyper reflexes, grabbed the Ten by his combat vest and redirected him into the tree trunk. There was a crack as the Ten's head made contact with the foliage.

"Well, that was stupid," Faceless said as he removed the Ten's helmet. He ripped out the transmitter and raised his eyebrow at the unconscious Ten. He figured the best way to fight the Tens was to go on the offensive; he stripped the Ten of his vest and his sword. Tens didn't use guns; they were silent killers, trained in the arts of hand-to-hand combat. Faceless thought that apparently this guy had missed a few lessons.

Faceless belted on the scabbard and sheathed the sword. He swiftly disappeared into the forest; this time with the Ten's body heat goggles on.

In the distance he noticed the outline of a Ten. Faceless chuckled; the Ten was pissing while his partner stood guard. Faceless climbed into the nearest tree and jumped swiftly to the next, making his way to the pair of Tens.

When he reached the tree above the pair he jumped, back flipping onto the peeing one as he drew his sword. The Ten's head hit the tree he was watering and Faceless turned to confront the other one that had drawn his sword to fight him.

Each of their katana clashed as they came together and separated. Faceless looked at the Ten in front of him; he gave the Ten a closer look this time. Faceless's eyes observed the Ten's body language: every tick, every subtle change of the body. Faceless's eyes recorded them all. He was constantly learning, even now. The eyes were stealing the moves from the enemy.

The Ten shifted and as soon as he moved forward with a lunge, Faceless parried the sword and, desperate to end the fight quickly, kicked his opponent in the nuts. The Ten fell, as any man would. Faceless wasn't proud, but he had done what he had to.

The Ten began screaming for help. Faceless kicked him square in the jaw, but the Ten continued shouting. Faceless couldn't let him continue alerting his squad.

He held the sword and ran it through his heart cleaving the muscle in two.

The Ten sputtered.

"I'm sorry," Faceless whispered to the Ten.

The Ten lay silent and Faceless slid the katana from the body. The sickening sucking sound rang out in the silence. It caused Faceless to shudder.

Faceless claimed the Ten's sword and attached it to his back.

He began to walk again towards freedom. He didn't know, but his distance from the highway was four miles.

* * *

Faceless ran swiftly through the forest; he preferred to run on the tree branches when he could. The bark on the branches, unlike the soft and wet ground, left more subtle footprints. After running two miles, he sat down on an especially high branch for a break. The sun was getting ready to set; he wanted to admire his life's second free sunset. The colors danced along the sky; as it set, it threw hues of purple, orange, and red. The colors faded into stars as Faceless cast his gaze upward. He watched; he was mesmerized as the first stars he had seen since his night in Paris began to light the French sky.

A dart came into his peripheral vision. He jerked his head back instinctively; the dart stuck harmlessly into the trunk. He jumped to his feet and pulled out a sword in each hand. It had to be the last Ten, and he used guns. What he saw next confused him. It was a Ten, but one with curves. He squinted to be sure. Yes, it was a woman; she was a rather big-chested woman at that.

Faceless saw her cock her head to the side and look at his swords. He saw the faint-outline of her lips smile under her mask; she holstered the gun and drew the two swords she kept on her belt, yearning for the challenge. Faceless could tell she was well trained. She held the blades like a practiced martial artist. He looked at her stance, the way she held the swords, and the guarded stance that still remained loose and receptive. It was something he found funny, actually. This woman was trying to fight with the same style as he was.

Chapter 4: On the Disadvantages of Night Vision

Faceless looked at her body language. She had the same style, but she wasn't built like him. She couldn't be as effective.

He was born with an innate ability to read the body movements of a person, as well as to memorize them. It wasn't super heightened, not to the point where he could read people's minds, but he could tell how dangerous a person was. The twinge of fear from her that he had experienced at first had disappeared. No matter how hard he looked at her, she didn't seem that much of a threat. He waited thirty seconds or so to confirm she wasn't. Faceless decided to be merciful and finish her fast. He wouldn't kill her, but he'd knock her out for a couple hours.

He swung at her with the backside of one of his blades. She parried with one of hers and almost took his head off with the other. Faceless noticed just in time to avoid it. She was almost as fast as him.

Faceless saw the woman let her body language slip enough to show she was impressed with herself.

"Interesting," Faceless said. She was able to fool his eyes.

"I wouldn't underestimate me because I'm a woman," the Ten said.

"Are you telling me that you're as powerful as I am? The great 1343?" Faceless asked, puffing up his chest.

"1343? Psh," the Ten let out a scoff, "I'm by definition better than you are. Stronger, faster, more agile."

"Well, I'll tell you what I'm going to do about that," Faceless said, squinting hard at her, raising his swords and letting off an aura that made the Ten involuntarily take a step backwards.

"What's that?" she said, cautiously looking at him, but trying to remain courageous.

"Run away," Faceless said, sticking his tongue out.

He jumped back and ran into the forest. There was a half-second where the Ten stood still, shocked. Then, almost immediately, she chased after him. When he heard her coming up behind him, Faceless turned to run backwards. He needed to keep his full attention on her, because if he looked away even once, she'd kill him.

He didn't find it the least bit surprising when his back ran into a tree. He parried blades with her into a corner. As his back pushed against the tree trunk, he felt something attached to the back of his belt. It pressed into his back.

"Well, milady, I'm afraid you're going to lose," Faceless said as he noticed her night vision mask.

"I'm superior to you in every way imaginable, 1343. What makes you think you'll win?"

"I've got a flash grenade," Faceless smiled, pulling out the flash grenade hidden behind his back. The pin had already been pulled.

Faceless looked away as the grenade went off.

The woman covered her face with her arm, and Faceless took that moment to slam the butt of his sword between her sternum and stomach.

Her breath labored for a second, then she passed out.

"My win," he said, smiling.

He grabbed her by her shoulder and lowered her gently to the ground. He was completely satisfied with his win. It was one of the few times he wasn't as observant as he should have been. Part of her costume was torn in the fight; on her upper shoulder blade was a black bar-code tattoo. *1344,* it said.

Faceless never saw.

Chapter 5: Naked Hitchhiking

Faceless crouched in the bushes outside of town. He wasn't exactly sure what his next step was. He didn't know anyone outside of NightCard. He looked down at his clothes: blood-and-sweat-stained body armor. He frowned. He wasn't really dressed to go walking into town. Bulletproof vests and assault rifles didn't mix well with the general populous.

His stomach growled. He couldn't remember the last time he ate. He actually missed being fed his meals. Then he remembered the only reason they were being fed to him was because his hands were tied to the wall.

Looking around, he decided the best thing to do was to pretend to be a normal hitchhiker. Unfortunately, since he was wearing bloodstained armor, he doubted anyone would pick him up. With a sigh, he realized he would have to do this naked. He never really had any shame anyways.

A smile crept onto Faceless's lips as he unbuttoned his pants.

A naked, scarred version of John Giffin wandered out of the bushes, onto the highway. The smiling man waved down the first car that headed down the highway.

* * *

Faceless waited for what seemed like forever to find a ride. He didn't particularly find this surprising; he wasn't well experienced in the outside world, but he had to imagine no sane person wanted a stranger's naked ass on his or her car seat.

Eventually, a passing trucker pulled over. Faceless told the driver he was robbed and left for dead. The man took pity and offered Faceless a ride. Faceless was convincing, as only a naked man could be; the portly trucker gave him trousers and a plaid shirt, which swallowed Faceless's frame. The gentleman even told Faceless to help himself to the remnants of the trucker's graham cracker stash.

"This is like, my first food since I escaped from that cell," Faceless said aloud, enjoying the precious graham cracker crumbs dissolving on his tongue. He looked at the truck driver that had picked him up. The old man was heavyset.

"Cell?"

"Did I say that?" Faceless said, realizing that probably wasn't the best sentence. "I meant… the cell that was the concept of walking the highway naked after being robbed. I'm not sure, actually. I'm traumatized; don't listen to me."

The old man gave him a satisfied, dismissive grunt and returned his attention to the road. Faceless turned his attention back to the graham crackers.

It tasted sweet, and it tasted like freedom. That was something he had never tasted before. So after clothes and a ride into town, his priorities became finding his next meal. After that was looking for better clothes. Preferably ones that weren't grease-stained.

The clenching pain of hunger reminded him of food, as well as the need for money. He walked down an alley and grimaced. He picked up the remains of a croissant from a trashcan.

His lip curled as he held the already half-eaten bread up to his mouth, but his stomach made an audible growling noise. Ashamed of himself, he stuffed his face. Soon the hunger passed and all that was left was a large amount of shame in himself. His cheeks were still puffed out like a chipmunk as he looked down the alleyway and out onto the street. He saw a suit store with a sign. *Now hiring*, it said.

Faceless looked at the croissant and chewed thoughtfully. Inspired by these thoughts, he walked into the suit store.

"I'm here to apply for a job," he told whom he assumed was the store manager. The store manager was wearing a suit that was a half size too small. On top of his thick neck and rotund head sat a toupee that looked like misshapen animal fur.

"We're not hiring right now," he said; his nose turned up slightly, showing off the pretentious snob that he was, "to those who haven't showered. Ever."

"You're kind of a dick," Faceless said. With that, Faceless memorized his face and walked out the door.

* * *

It was later that night; Faceless sat in the alleyway outside of Toupee man's store. He peeked his face around the corner of the window and saw one employee sweeping. The strength and aggression that the employee was using made Faceless conclude Toupee Man had left the young man to close up shop. The boy froze mid-sweep. He looked back to the back of the store, threw the broom down on the ground, and then walked to the back. Faceless turned and looked in the alley around him. There was a children's clothing store next to Toupee Man's shop. He looked at the dumpster behind him; the one that belonged to the children's

49

clothing store had clothes that had been thrown away. Faceless gave a sad smile and walked toward it.

* * *

Toupee Man's part-time worker was closing up shop again. Jimmy, the young worker for Toupee Man, returned from the back room with a plate of microwaveable crepes; they were already half eaten and he had slight burns in his mouth. He couldn't believe that his boss was giving him yet another closing shift; the asshole never seemed to close for himself. Jimmy was startled when he looked up to see Toupee Man staring at him.

"Laugh and you're fired," Toupee Man said; his eyes were just slits.

Jimmy looked down and noticed what his boss was wearing. He wore a rather ratty pair of pants and plaid shirt that was three sizes too small. It looked, to the shop clerk, like clothes that had literally been found in a dumpster.

"I was robbed by that asinine bastard from earlier today," he growled at Jimmy.

"Boss? Really?" The worker said, trying really hard not to smile at his boss' impressively large man-boobs.

"Really. Now go home. I'll finish closing shop; I've got to borrow a suit anyway," Toupee Man snapped at his underling. Jimmy found it strange; the snarl on his face seemed like it almost had a smile hiding under it.

"Right boss," Jimmy nodded and rushed out the door. He wanted to leave before the boss changed his mind. The thought that was on Jimmy's mind was heading to a strip club. It was something for which Toupee man's chest had set him in a mood.

* * *

Toupee Man watched Jimmy leave. He looked out the window and as soon as Jimmy had rounded the corner, his man-boobs deflated. He thought hard and the hair on his head grew full again; suddenly the shirt he was wearing fit him again.

Faceless looked around the store; he smiled through Toupee Man's lips.

"Now, which of these is the most expensive?" he said; rubbing his hands together, he looked around for the most expensive brand.

* * *

Faceless had found the most expensive black suit and tie that fit him. His old clothing sat wrinkled in a pile on the floor by his feet. He looked at himself in the mirror. More so, he looked at Toupee Man's face in a mirror. He curled his middle-aged lip when he saw his reflection. Fake or not, it was repulsive.

To his left he saw a stack of suit catalogues. Their spines were crisp and unbent. Some of them still had the delivery address sticker on them. He picked one up; the smile of a handsome cover model gleamed at him. He nodded appreciatively as he flipped through the pages.

Hours passed; Faceless was standing in a small pile of trial-and-error faces; the skins were test runs of models' faces blended together. Faceless finally picked one that he felt was enough of a mix of different faces that it had its own character. The face he had was a strong jaw, with classically handsome, semi-long jet black hair, and piercing brown-and-black eyes. Then he cocked his head to the side as he looked at his work of art once more.

"Maybe I should tone down the handsome," Faceless said aloud, trying out a new voice, then he tried out its laugh. "Nah, why let women suffer because I don't want to look good?"

He chuckled and walked out the door, three or four suits in a bag slung over his shoulder; he had intentionally left the door unlocked.

Faceless chuckled as he walked off, leaving the store's contents to the Parisian night.

Chapter 6: An Art Museum

It was the next day, after the first night Faceless had spent on a roof. He stretched; his back popped as he tried to loosen up his frame. The roof had been cement and cold; although the cold had been inconvenient, it was the cement's texture that had left speckled divots in Faceless's back that had yet to smooth out. He was happy, back divots or no, with walking around, free and handsome in the streets of Paris.

Out of the corner of his eye, Faceless saw an art museum that just seemed to call to him. Faceless could hear the Beethoven when he walked in. Faceless would have found the museum moderately sized, had Faceless known museum sizes. However, as he had no point of reference, he thought that this was the grandest museum on earth. It was modestly furnished, and the walls were of the smoothest porcelain finish. Gold trim decorated the halls, traced along columns and banisters that he had seen in coloring books. The floor was polished marble scuffed with the marks of the heavy foot traffic.

Faceless walked around the art museum and gazed at the pieces; they were all sculptures and paintings from contemporary artists. There were those here and there that interested him, but none of them impressed him the way the Renaissance paintings did that hung in his old room.

A woman walked up to Faceless as he was busying himself looking at a painting.

"Ah, I see you have a good taste."

Faceless looked up. It was a woman dressed in a white long sleeved ruffled shirt; the clothes looked out of place when accompanied by her short, purple hair.

"Who painted this?" Faceless asked the woman.

"Ah that would be the great Monet, an Impressionist artist; it's the oldest print we have in the museum," the woman said. Faceless looked at her again. This time he noticed, under one of the shirt's ruffles, a name tag. *Janet*, it said, *Museum Director*.

"Can I be honest with you? You seem to be the same sort of person I am."

Faceless maintained his composure, but allowed himself a mental scoff. He himself was basically a walking stem cell; he didn't see much in common. "How so?"

The director showed an almost physically pained look on her face.

"Art has died," she said; with a sigh, she pitched himself backward; she leaned against a support beam. "The world has no talent anymore, and I crave the work of the masters, the Renaissance."

"Ah, that's what you meant. I guess we're a little similar then." Faceless gave Janet a begrudged shrug.

"Oh, I found a kindred spirit that appreciates the golden days of art," Janet smiled. "What's your name, stranger?"

"My name is Aedon Saint," Faceless said.

"Saint? That's a lovely name."

"Family name," Faceless said smiling.

"Well, as you're so well dressed, I wouldn't assume you were looking, but we have an opening at the gallery. If you wanted to apply, I'd be more than happy to interview you; personally, I mean." The look Janet gave him left an uncomfortable lull in the conversation.

Faceless wasn't wanting to find out just how the director was planning on interviewing him. "Well, in all honesty, I don't have any papers; I'm sort of what you'd call drifting around Europe. I haven't even got a place to stay, and as nice as these clothes are, they aren't very warm."

"Oh, well, in that case I can offer you a temporary job if you wish, something to tide you over while you stay?"

Faceless inwardly grimaced, he wasn't really wanting to make this rather eccentric woman's company a regular occurrence, but at the same time, he did need a paycheck, and attaining one where he was surrounded by art wasn't the worse choice.

"Well thank you; I'd be happy to accept," Faceless bowed slightly.

As the woman returned the bow, however in a more of a hybrid curtsy/bow, Faceless felt he should make something clear.

"Yeah, I can't wait until I return back home to my girlfriend and tell her about all the experiences I had in Europe." Faceless watched the woman's face go crestfallen; Janet shrugged and winked at Faceless.

"Well, in my opinion you don't have to tell her all your... experiences. You can stay in the attic, I guess, as long as you don't mind sleeping with art staring at you."

Faceless could barely suppress his grimace.

"Oh when I write her, I'll definitely leave some of my more distasteful experiences out." Faceless looked at Janet's face. Janet's smile told Faceless that the museum director had missed the hint.

Chapter 7: Spade

Patterson was sitting across from his superior. Had he not been nervous, he would have been pissed off. Two weeks had passed since Faceless – 1343 had escaped. Patterson softly shook his head. That was almost a bit of humanity; humanity wasn't something to have in front of Morgan. Patterson had done everything he could in that time to get 1343 back; he hated meeting his boss. He had to fly to Sweden within the hour of the call; President Morgan wasn't a patient man by anyone's standards. As it was, Patterson had very low standards set for the people he worked with at NightCard.

They were sitting in Morgan's office on the 101st floor of Fati, NightCard's main office building. A building of sleek black metal and glass that towered above everything else in Stockholm. Morgan was sitting in his armchair and sipping blood-red wine out of a glass. The room was dark, just the way it was every time Patterson sat in with Morgan; it was how the President preferred it.

"You see the problem with this, what you've made me have to resort to, Patterson?"

Patterson lit up another cigarette. He had a feeling a large sum of money was going to be involved. More than likely, it was probably going to be a sum that would come out of his budget. It was alright; he reasoned that he would just fire Giffin.

"I have to send in the Kings," Morgan said. Patterson choked on his cigarette. "Your dumbass field test has my nuts in a vice. I have to send in four people I really don't want to. Well, three. One is still on assignment."

"Sir, you can't be serious. They're not stable enough to send on this mission, Morgan!" Patterson exclaimed.

"Patterson, I know you're not talking to me like that," Morgan said coolly, sipping more of his wine.

Patterson looked down.

"1343 was expensive, President Morgan," he mumbled, then took another drag.

"Patterson, let me put this in very simple terms. My procedure is only halfway done. I have another fifty sessions left. You see my wine, Patterson?" Morgan held up the blood-red wine glass. Patterson could see the look in Morgan's eyes through the glass and wine.

"Yes, President Morgan."

"This is the last guy that failed me. You don't want to be involved with the next glass, Patterson. Go fetch the Kings."

Patterson's face paled; he remembered the last time they used the Kings. The entire western half of Russia had been taken out. Patterson saw a silver lining; the Kings operated on their own budget; his was safe.

He chuckled as he walked down the hallway towards the elevator. He decided he'd fire Giffin anyways.

* * *

"You know, you picked a good time to call on them, Patterson," Bill the intern said to Patterson as they walked out of Fati's elevator.

"Why's that, Bill?"

"They were getting a bit stir crazy, and you know how the Kings are when they get antsy," Bill smiled.

Bill had led Patterson into the lower levels of Fati. Patterson looked around; the colors changed as one went to different levels of the Fati building. These were black, a dark, almost wet-looking black, as though the air was kept humid to keep something growing. Patterson had heard of this place: the research and development lab. This was the same part of the building where Faceless's creation had happened.

Patterson looked back at Bill's unnerving smile.

"Would you like to meet them?" Bill asked.

"Don't be all mysterious about it, Bill. I have to give them their assignment."

"You just ruined the one fun part of this job, Patterson."

Bill let out a sigh and slid his ID badge. There was a buzzer as the door opened. A minute later the Kings Patterson was waiting for still hadn't come out.

"Well that's anticlimactic," Bill frowned, twirling his pencil in one hand.

"Bill, what the hell, man? I'm in a hurry."

"I swear that I let them know you were coming. Hold on, I'll go get them."

Bill walked through the door. Patterson waited, looking at his watch. Five seconds had passed on the watch hands when Bill flew back through doorway and crashed through the doorway. Bill's body made a solid, wet sound as it hit the wall. Bill had hit upside down; his body was already dead and broken. The upside down Bill slid down the wall, leaving a red impact spot and trail that contrasted sharply with the black of the walls. He had a distant look in his eyes, and he wasn't breathing.

"Bill," Patterson breathed. He tensed for a moment; he cracked his knuckles in his right hand, preparing for a punch if one needed to come. Then he looked behind him as he heard movement.

"Stupid bastard interrupted our game. Do you know how hard it was to find the secret warp tube? Now I'll never rescue the princess, and this one was sexy, dude," a man's voice said through the doorway. Patterson looked in the direction of the voice. Then the man who had spoken walked through.

He was dressed in a black suit splattered with drops of red. The left sleeve was ripped off. The man was wearing a black dog collar, and he had an average look about him. Physically he was fit; the most abnormal things about him were his eyes and his hair: long black and brown hair, and eyes so brown they were almost black. What was special about him was his aura. He radiated power and dominance unlike any other man Patterson had met. He had even more of an aura than NightCard's President.

Patterson remained poker-faced. He knew the King was looking for a reaction from him or for a sign of weakness showing he was the dominant one. Patterson knew how these things worked.

The King used one hand to pick up the broken Bill by his skull; then the King looked at Bill's dead face. Patterson felt there was an almost perceptible look of disgust on his face. Then the King brought Bill to Patterson. With the other hand he grabbed the base of Bill's jaw and ripped it off.

"Finally! All that damn yammering has stopped," the King sighed with relief. The King flung Bill over his shoulder and leaned back with a happy sigh.

"Bill has interrupted my poker game before; I get your frustration," Patterson said, looking at the splatter mark and the crumpled body that was once Bill. Interruptions in games were annoying, and Bill certainly had a tendency to butt in, though Patterson thought this was a bit extreme.

The man looked up at Patterson and scratched his face with the torn sleeve. There was a tattoo of a Spade on his forearm.

"I take it you're Spade, then?" Patterson said.

"Who're you?" Spade said as he walked over to Patterson.

"I'm the guy about to give you your next assignment," Patterson said evenly.

"I just told you, I'm in the middle of saving a sexy princess. I don't interrupt your meals, do I?"

"I'm not sure how the two connect."

Spade almost flew to Patterson and stuck the wet, bloodied hand, the one that had just ripped a man's jaw off, an inch from Patterson's face.

"Do you know what my power is...?" Spade trailed off, leading into a question.

"Patterson."

"Thank you. Do you know what my power is, Patterson?"

"Kinetic Amplification," Patterson said.

"That's right, but do you know what that means?"

"Not particularly."

"It means that I can supercharge the molecules in your body, make them burst with kinetic energy, until your cells become so over energized that they just explode, violently."

Patterson didn't respond. He trusted his training.

"All of this, I can do with one finger," Spade put his index finger to Patterson's forehead, shaping his hand like a gun. Patterson had to fight the unyielding desire to cringe, as he felt Bill's gore touch him.

Patterson smiled. "You'll really love this job, then."

Spade and Patterson looked at each other, the same smile on both of their faces. The smile of an alpha male. Spade put down his finger. Patterson held out the file and Spade snatched it. Patterson felt the wet blood still on his forehead; he had to fight the urge to wipe it off.

Spade whistled. "Damn, this bastard is sick. I can understand why you want this guy roped up quickly. He isn't something you'd want to let run around."

"President Morgan doesn't need Faceless alive," Patterson said as he lit another cigarette. "He said if you and the other Kings can only bring in ten vials of BloodWine, that's fine enough for him."

"You're not the soft type, are you old man? It's 1343. Don't humanize the garbage."

Patterson pursed his lips. "Fine, Morgan doesn't need 1343 alive, but I would consider it a personal favor if you can bring him in breathing. I have… a lot of my budget invested in him."

"Haha!" Spade laughed. "You may not know Hearts, but restraint isn't exactly her strong suit."

"So tell me, is your file correct, Spade?"

"Oh, you mean the looking-for-the-short-term thing?" Spade said dismissively, playing with the dog collar around his neck.

Patterson looked at it. Every one of the Kings had a robotic tracker on. It looked like a dog collar. It was how NightCard stayed in control, how they tracked the King's movements, and if need be, how they killed them. Patterson had just gotten his off two years ago.

"Yeah."

"Yes, Patterson, it is. I'm kind of a dick like that. I was born that way, since I took the BloodWine back in the trial phase."

"Any other of the Kings like you?"

"No. Which is why Bill here is dead. He interrupted my feeding. Which isn't even really feeding. It's just a damn stop-get measure."

"So they let you go out once a week to get yourself a real meal right?"

"Yeah, and that's why I love assignments. Always manage myself a little strange on the sly," Spade smiled.

"Well, this is your assignment. Take care of it, and if you happen to 'manage yourself a little strange,' then all the better."

"I want this damn collar off, Patterson." Spade hooked his finger under the collar. "It is incredibly hard to pick up women while wearing a damn dog collar."

"Consider it done, but keep it on your person," Patterson said. "If you run, we send the Kings after you next."

Patterson walked off, and waited until he was sitting in his office before he allowed himself the shiver that had been waiting to crawl down his spine.

Chapter 8: Clubs

Spade went to go wake up Clubs. He looked around at the sanitized, quiet hallways. The Kings' Quarters were cold, always cold, and he hated it. It just gave his world one more level of sterility and distance.

Spade knew that Clubs probably didn't feel the same way as himself. Clubs wasn't like Spade. Instead, Clubs was, as he himself put it, a Blood Feeder. He lived off the pain and death of others. It was literally in his blood.

Spade approached the frozen, lifeless body of Clubs. Since Clubs was a little more deadly by his own nature, NightCard had its scientists create a way to suspend Clubs in cryogenics, to stave off his condition; it made more sense only to thaw him out when there were missions. Fewer people died that way.

Spade flicked a few switches on the chrome switchboard next to Clubs's ice coffin. He put his hand against its cold, icy metallic surface as he heard the machine start to whine, coming alive.

"Hey there, bud. It's been two months. You know what that means. I get my wingman."

The response was a low, audible hiss. Cold, twirling steam came out of the sides, and the door opened. Fingers came from the fog and curled around the coffin's edge; they were blue, stained with marks of red as the blood flow returned. From the fog came a man with a short buzz-cut and two-day-old shadow on his decidedly handsome face. He walked out, stark naked, with a body stolen form romance novel covers, chiseled from granite and muscle.

Spade smiled at him. Clubs' eyes were wild; his mind tried to figure out where he was and what was happening. Spade waved at Clubs. Spade saw Clubs's eyes relax as they landed on Spade. If Clubs saw Spade, it meant everything was safe. Spade gestured at the pile of clothing next to his coffin. Clubs looked, and then his eyes fell to the clothes that Spade was wearing.

"So, are we feeding tonight?" Clubs asked.

"See, now that's why I like you, man," Spade smiled; it was a smile he knew showed off just the right amount of his incisors, "you've got your priorities right."

Clubs looked around. Bill wasn't there.

"Where's Bill?"

Spade shuffled his feet.

"Well, you know how he was using my computer when I wasn't playing my games?"

Clubs nodded.

"Well, it turns out he was looking into child trafficking."

"And?" Clubs said; Clubs couldn't believe Spade was going soft. Spade sensed it.

"Well, damn it, you ask first before using someone's stuff. Anyways," Spade said, changing the tone, "aren't you hungry?"

Clubs' expression changed; he climbed out of the pod and cracked his neck.

"You know I always wake up hungry. Where's the nearest bar?" Clubs ran his tongue along his teeth.

* * *

"What about her?" Clubs said to Spade. The pair spoke in Russian. It was Spade's suggestion; it made him feel like a spy. Spade looked to where Clubs had pointed with his chin.

"You mean the two blonds standing by the bar?" Spade responded back, but this time in Italian. "I want the one on the right. She has amazing legs."

"Yeah, I'll help you with the one on the left, but then I have to go find myself a meal. I'm starving."

Spade patted Clubs on the back.

"See? That's why I love you, man."

Clubs scoffed. Spade smiled his devilish smile again; the one that he knew would make Clubs know he could never mean it. "Lead the way."

Spade walked up to the two women, slightly passing them and turned to look back over his shoulder.

"Hey girls, I need your opinion on something. My friend and I were arguing about whether you would you rather have a life that was comfortable money-wise but boring every other way, or one that was exciting and reeked of adventure, but you were living paycheck to paycheck?" As Spade said the latter, he looked at the right blond with the amazing legs.

"A stable life," The left blond said.

"An adventurous life," the right blond said, maintaining eye contact with Spade and twirling a strand of her hair around her finger.

"See, you're the cool one," Spade said, putting his arm around the right blond, "but we'd never get along; you're too much like me."

He threw his arm off of her and backed off a little. She moved in closer. Out of the corner of his eye, Spade saw Clubs come in.

"Dude, you are taking forever with those drinks," Clubs said, giving himself a reason to enter into their conversation.

"Dude, Jack, I have to introduce you to these two awesome girls I just met."

"I'm Sasha," the left blond said, "and this is my friend Kirsty."

Clubs showed Sasha a magic trick; he stepped behind Kirsty and Spade; his back cut off himself and Sasha from the group.

"You know, I'm sorry, but my friend can be kind of overzealous. The first thing he does is show people this magic trick. He's a great magician, but meanwhile, I am stuck on the sidelines. Although, this isn't the worst company." He smiled at Kirsty; a glint was in his eye.

"Really?" Kirsty asked. Her eyes showed a playful kind of doubt, before she took another sip from her mojito.

"Of course it isn't. I meant what I said before, about your being adventurous." Spade moved closer to Kirsty. His words seemed innocent enough, but his eyes looked at Kirsty in a way that betrayed his intentions. Kirsty's eyes betrayed her intentions as well, as Spade saw them look him up and down. He played with her fingers, intertwining them in his own. "It's such a shame, you know. I thought you were adventurous, but now I'm starting to doubt it."

"What makes you think that?"

"Well, I'm sitting here, talking to the most beautiful girl in the bar, and all I can think is that it's not enough." He faked a sigh, looked away slightly, but then his eyes met hers again. "I don't want to just talk with you like the same old boys that come to hit on you. You deserve a man; you deserve someone who sees you as more than just a pretty face attached to a remarkably well-toned body."

Kirsty chuckled. "What would a man do?"

Spade's free hand touched her mojito glass. The dewdrops of condensation that had settled on the glass transferred to his fingers. He traced them along Kirsty's arm, sending a tremor down her spine. "A man would tell you that you deserve good conversation. A man would tell you more about yourself. We should start with a palm reading."

His eyes moved to their hands. He rubbed his thumb across her palm, and pulled her close. "There's just one problem: there's not enough light here. Let's go over here where there's more light."

Spade lifted her hand, turned around, and led her away from Sasha and Clubs. There was no resistance from Kirsty.

* * *

Five minutes later, while Spade was sitting there, with Kirsty on his lap, he saw Clubs in his peripheral. Clubs was talking to a different club girl; one that was probably there by herself. Spade looked at Clubs' lips.

"Want to see a magic trick?" Clubs said, grinning.

Spade almost slipped a frown. He felt bad for the poor woman. No, that would've been human.

* * *

Spade opened his eyes. He immediately regretted it. He was met with a strong, annoying florescent-pink wall. It had a poster of the latest boy-man pop star on it. Spade thought for a hard moment… Kirsty, yes that was her name. Kirsty's dorm room was that of a typical college girl. It wasn't just the wall; the entirety of her room was decidedly pink. From the bed sheets Spade had fallen asleep in, to the beanbag chair in the corner. The lamp, the desk, even the mini-fridge every college student should have shouted pink at his poor eyes.

The only things in the room that the color pink had managed not to envelop were the posters of the current pop stars and boy bands. Spade had seen these last night and thought to himself that he was too old for her, but the thought of corrupting another of Europe's youth only served to motivate him even more. Spade rolled away from the light that poured in from the blinds; he rolled towards the wall, where Kirsty was looking at him. The look in her eyes was one that Spade had seen hundreds of times before: it was that of a woman in love.

"I can't believe I found someone like you," Kirsty said, smiling and looking up at Spade shyly, her eyes peeking from the covers.

"Kirsty?" Spade asked as he stroked her finely tapered legs that were halfway out of the covers. He felt the shiver go down her, as she was receptive to it. He knew exactly what to do.

"Yes?" She asked, a smile covered halfway by the bed sheets.

"How do you feel about me?"

"What do you mean, Ray?" Kirsty said. Spade's arm tucked around the small of her back. She snuggled in closer.

"I mean, did you see this as a one night stand?" Spade said, his breath catching, a look of disappointment in his eyes.

"Was a one night stand what you wanted, Ray?"

Spade reached for her hands and kissed the tips of her fingers. "Normally, I don't see women being worth more than one night. They're always too childish or too afraid to admit to someone how they feel. They're too afraid for that kind of emotional commitment."

"Ray," Kirsty said, snuggling even closer towards him; her face was inches from his, "I wouldn't be that way."

"I know," Spade said, his fingers tracing circles on her bare shoulders. "I said normally. We spent hours together last night, Kirsty. Just talking, getting to know each other. You told me about your dreams and your fears; I told you about mine. You're special, Kirsty; you're someone I would want to try to get to know more – someone I already feel I know. I already have feelings for you. So, without any fear of anything, of any judgment or rejection, how do you feel about me?"

"I don't know, Ray. It's not something I say, usually."

"No fear, Kirsty. We talked about it last night. Life is something we don't get second chances at. It's something that we look back on moments, special moments where we wish we would have been brave. If you could be brave, Kirsty, how do you feel about me?" Kirsty looked at him. She started to answer, but Spade kissed her. It was a soft kiss; it was one that made her feel safe. She opened her eyes, and they met his.

"I know it's early, but... I could say I love you, Ray."

Spade leaned his head back onto the pillow. His body began to feel rejuvenated. She rolled halfway on top of him and kissed his chest. He looked her in the eye.

"Then say it."

"I love you, Ray."

An electric shock ran through Spade. Endorphins coursed through his body.

"Thank you, Kirsty. That's exactly what I needed to hear. That love radiating off of you, out of your eyes, it's exactly what I needed."

He climbed out of bed, and pulled his pants on.

"Where are you going?" Kirsty asked, with a shocked look on her face.

"I've got to get back. My job isn't something you want to be late for. My boss is a real vampire. He really sucks the life right out of you."

"I know exactly what you mean," Kirsty laughed.

Inside, Spade scoffed; she had no idea.

"Hey, I'll call you soon," Spade said, looking at her in her eyes. He leaned across the bed; his hand rested on hers. "I promise. After all, I can't forget a woman who loves me, right? A woman who was that brave?" He kissed her again.

He walked out her door, knowing to his core that he wouldn't call her again when he said he loved her. . One tragic part of his life was that he could only feed on her love once. He didn't like what he was, but it was his curse. Now he had the energy he needed for the next mission.

* * *

Spade stepped off the elevator, back at his level of the Fati building. He frowned slightly. The black walls always seemed a little depressing to him. When he went through the door leading to the back, there was a lounge area. Clubs was sitting at a table with a glass of water. There was no sweating on the glass, nor any ice cubes. That was something Spade had never really gotten used to about Clubs. He had asked, and the water wasn't even to drink; it was for show. Clubs used it as a way to appear more human.

"So how was your night, Clubs?" Spade said, throwing an arm around Clubs's shoulder.

Clubs grunted. "Terrible. There really isn't enough meat on these college girls."

"You're a sick bastard."

"I can't help it. The skinny bitches may have the same amount of blood, but once that's gone, their husks are chewy – damn yoga doesn't put any muscle on the bones. That's what pisses me off about this, man: you get a full meal; I get scraps."

"Well, time to wake up Diamonds," Spade said, shrugging it off. He'd rather not think of what he'd lost. He wasn't like Clubs in that way. He always developed feelings for the girls that fell in love with him. He had to love them back, or his ritual wouldn't work. He looked at the dried blood on Clubs's lips. "Dude, you got some of last night on your face," Spade gestured at the corner of his mouth.

"Thanks, man; blondes are messy."

"It's fun to play with your food, but try to be less of a messy eater."

He knew they were evil; he just didn't care. He couldn't let himself.

Chapter 9: A Morning and Scars

Aedon Saint hated the mornings. This wasn't new; he had hated them since before he got out of his cage, but after two weeks, he still wasn't used to the way the sunshine seemed to shake him from his slumber – sunshine was something still new to him.

He sat up in his bed; his bed sheet was wrapped around his waist, but his torso was still showing. Across his chest, stretching across his ribs and his abs, were two long scars that formed an imperfect X. Aedon placed his hand on one of the scars, trying to rub the pain away. The scars ached today; they always did. They were tokens from one of his many fights with the woman that taught him how. The X scars were only two of the many that covered his body. He hadn't had an easy life. He had spent time in NightCard's Gene Coliseum. No one made it out of there without scars as tokens of their ordeal. For a moment, Aedon was 1343 again; his thoughts went back to the Coliseum; they went back to the screams and the pleads of mercy from the countless nameless figures, to those who mercy he had granted none. Then Faceless shook his head again, and his memories went back to the main X scars that refused to be ignored; their dull ache refused to be ignored. His thoughts went back to the woman that had given them to him.

The King of Hearts was unlike any woman he'd ever met. She wasn't kind like Joan, and she certainly wasn't forgiving. The X was a token from his first "training session." It had been less like training, and more like torture. The X wasn't the only scar he'd received from those training sessions. Part of the reason he was such a good fighter now was because he learned, constantly, from those fights. Even in the end, he'd still lose. That was his memory of the time he spent six months outside his room, sadly at the Fati building.

Aedon reached to turn off his cheap, provided for alarm clock. He stood up and looked down; he remembered he was naked. He preferred to sleep that way.

Faceless pulled on the underwear by his bed. Then, dressed in his black boxers, he crossed his makeshift attic room. Surrounding him were the museum's stored-away paintings; they waited there, either taken from the gallery or waiting to replace another painting that called the gallery home. Faceless looked at them; he felt most alive and free when he was looking. Then he noticed there were new arrivals that had escaped his notice. They must have been stored yesterday. There was a sheet over the painting, and it called to him; it begged him to look.

He pulled the sheet back and gasped. He saw himself. The painting had two people that were dancing together. A woman, blond, with long hair in a flowing dress, and a man in a black tuxedo. It was a man whose face wasn't there. It was vacant; it looked like it could be anyone; the way the man without a face reached towards the woman, one could tell he had feelings, like he was aching for her. Faceless felt something in his chest, more than the scars. He felt like he needed that painting; it spoke to him. He knew he would have it, but that he needed to be careful.

The aching in his chest was interrupted by a growl from his stomach. He needed the painting, sure, but right then he needed to leave. Breakfast sounded really good at the moment. He pulled on a pair of dark blue jeans and his lace-up black court shoes, and a black, fitted shirt. Then, for good measure, he ripped his face off. For fun he always changed his appearance before he went out.

He headed down the street, taking in the parts of Paris that he hadn't seen while he was stealing in the dark. Last night he'd ran around, with a misshapen face; he had exercised like he'd done in the training sessions, jumping from roof to roof, swinging on poles in the dark. Feeling freedom in a way to which the constricted walls and objectives of his training could never compare.

His mind went back to what he was doing now. He came back to reality right as he saw her. At first he wasn't sure if he was seeing things.

"Joan?" he gasped.

It wasn't her, of course. There was something different about this girl. She was younger, first of all, and she was more reserved, with an artsy feel to her. Her hair was a stunning blond, a platinum blond that was almost white, to where it looked like snow had captured sunlight. The captured sunlight was straightened; it almost flowed silk-like around her shoulders, stopping midway down her back. She was petite, her skin like porcelain. Freckles decorated the cheeks under her eyes. Her chest was small, but he could still see her curves; it just seemed she was too shy to show them off. Faceless didn't know what was happening. His heart caught in his throat, and he felt light-headed. This was her. Something inside of him just said it; this was the Girl in the

Rain. Those eyes, that hair – it had to be her. He had to find out.

He started walking towards her. He roughly grabbed her by her arm. Not tactful, or delicate, as he was unpracticed in this. The result: she screamed.

"Oh, crap, what?" Faceless said.

She spun around and beat him with her very heavy bag. Faceless had taken beatings from mercenaries, ex-marines, and world championship fighters. He'd been ready for those. With this, he fell flat on his ass.

"Oof," he grunted as he fell. Then the Joan knock-off reached into her purse and pulled out a bag of graphite dust, and threw a handful of it into Faceless's eyes.

"Augh!" Faceless shouted as he fell over in pain.

Mercenaries had never done that to him. He blinked away the graphite, even ripped part of the skin off around his eyes, and forced it out. After he'd uncovered his face, he looked around, and the possible Girl in the Rain was gone.

"Crap," he said flatly.

* * *

Faceless was uncomfortable, his palms were sweaty, and he hadn't been able to figure out what to say to the pretty girl. He wondered if the other men of the world had this problem – surely not.

He looked at the graphite that still stained his hands. Objectively, he felt he had been born with his amazing eyes, which could pick up on the subtlety of the shifting of the body. He knew enough to know when danger was coming, but he knew nothing about how attraction worked. He needed help. He needed to see someone who knew what they were doing, and with his photo-kinetic reflexes, he could learn. So he thought for a second and had to wonder where the best place to see attraction in action was.

"I need to go to a bar," he thought out loud.

He looked down at himself, his clothes were coated, and he still tasted the graphite on his lips. He thought he should shower first. Also, he badly needed a nap.

* * *

Faceless, newly cleaned and dressed, tapped Ricardo on the shoulder.

"Hey," Faceless asked.

"Yes, Aedon?" the pervy director asked. "Have you finally come to your senses?"

"Uh, I don't... I just wanted to know, where is the best bar to meet people?"

"Aedon if you want some company tonight, you just need to ask. There is no need for pretext."

"I'm… good for tonight. I think it's just to help me get acquainted with my new city."

"Still playing hard to get, Aedon? I like that. Here's the address, and I'll give you directions," the director said.

* * *

After Faceless got the directions, he went to the bar, and after paying the cover charge for *Barry's*, he went in.

He saw fog and lights that moved in beams all over the dance floor. He couldn't discern much; all he saw were what looked like women and men grinding on each other. This was not interesting to him; what he was interested in was the bar. One man displaying a lot of dominant body language continued to draw his attention. He approached, trying to observe without looking like he was staring.

* * *

Spade felt himself being watched. He was trained to know; he wouldn't have been a good King if he weren't.

Spade thought to himself that he didn't need to feed tonight. What he needed to do was figure out what the gentleman that was staring at him wanted. He turned and walked straight to the creepy ass man that was staring at him.

"Excuse me, man. I've felt your stare for the last twenty minutes. You're throwing off my groove. What do you want?"

The man that had been staring at him struggled for words. Finally, the words came out in a gush.

"I saw an amazingly beautiful woman today, but when I tried to talk to her, something happened."

"What did?" Spade asked; the man had about ten percent of his curiosity.

"I grabbed her, then she threw graphite powder in my eyes and ran away."

Spade threw his head back and laughed; he had to catch himself on the bar counter to stop from falling over.

"Oh, that's great," he breathed, barely able to get out his words.

"Yeah, that's supportive. Anyway, that's why I'm here," the man said, frowning.

"That's interesting. What led you to think I was the best choice to copy off of?"

"Your body."

"Damn it," Spade shouted, slamming his fist on the bar counter. "I knew this was me being hit on."

"What?"

"Nevermind. What do you mean my body?"

"I read your body language versus everyone else's here. Yours said you knew most what you were doing."

Spade's eyebrows raised. Spade caught his own action and realized that it had been a long time since anyone, male or female, had made him raise his eyebrows out of curiosity.

"Fine, come back here tomorrow night," Spade said.

"All right."

"Do me a favor: wear something more fashionable. Coming here in blue jeans and that ugly-ass shirt was a terrible idea. Put some effort in man."

"That's a little hurtful, but I understand," the man said with a frown.

* * *

Faceless parted from the man. Faceless had to stop by a shop tomorrow. He just hoped he didn't run into the Joan-esque woman before he got his lessons. Even a new face wouldn't hide his embarrassment.

"Hey!" the man shouted from behind him. Aedon turned to see the man that had just offered him help "I'm Ray, by the way!" the man shouted over the bar's music.

"Aedon!" Faceless responded.

That night Faceless went back into the attic. The coolness was refreshing. The artworks that hung on the walls were comforting. They always were. He took off his shirt. The mirror on the wall showed his scars, they cascaded down his back muscles, many of them reaching around to his abs, signs he rolled when he fought, signs of escaping. His body was laced with stem cells, and he could hide them if he wanted, but he preferred to see them. It reminded himself that even he wasn't invincible.

His mind was elsewhere. His mind was on his latest confrontation, which was not nearly as deadly as Hearts, but it hurt even more. He may have lost the first girl that he'd ever felt anything for, but the girl was more than just what looked like a Joan knockoff. She seemed... familiar, like something of a dream he'd once had – a memory. Faceless finished taking off his clothes and slid into bed, his sleep almost immediate.

Thirteen Years Ago

Chapter 10: A Dream and a Memory

The girl sat in the dirt of the playground, a pencil in one hand and a juice box in the other. She wore a bright pink dress, but staring down at the tenth picture she'd drawn today. The other kids would run around and play: jungle gyms, tag, American Football. None of these interested the girl. All she cared about was art. It was more than a passion for her; it was like air, like food, like the juice box in her hand: a necessity to be happy. Her tenth picture was a drawing of a boy and a girl; she was ever the hopeless romantic, and her boy and girl were holding hands. She looked at the boy again; his face was yet to be drawn; she felt that was the hardest part of drawing her male characters. She could not draw her ideal boy if she had no idea what he looked like.

Then a shadow blocked her light. At first she suspected a cloud, but then she noticed it was a shadow with arms and legs. She looked up; since shadows with appendages didn't just appear, it meant that someone stood in her light. She saw a boy about her age; he was around six or seven, and he was watching her draw.

His hair was a shaggy swirl of black and blond. His eyes that shifted from her to her drawing pad were inquisitive. To her surprise, each was a different color. The left one was an almost diamond-like blue, and the other was as green as the sea. He had heterochromia, not that she knew what that was. His smile, his smile was so contagious she found herself joining him. His eyes looked from her to her drawings again. They scanned the drawings.

"You're not drawing faces on your boys," he said. "Why not?"

"Why do you care?" she responded.

"I guess it was just weird to me."

"Faceless boys aren't weird. Once I put a face to him, he's stuck with it," she said; she had never told this to anyone before, and she wondered why she was telling him.

"What's your name?" he asked, holding out his hand, and turning up that smile even more.

"I'm not allowed to give my name to strangers. Right now, you're a stranger," she said between sips of her juice box. She looked from his hand back to his face.

The boy's eyebrows scrunched together. "I'm sorry, I thought that people shook hands," he frowned.

He was about to lower his arm when she reached out and shook his hand. The boy's smile returned fast. There was an awkward quiet, and then he broke their silence.

"What are you going to draw next to them?" he asked her; he had noticed the beginnings of another shape; it was under the boy and girl in her drawing, as though they would be on top of it.

"I'm drawing a pony," she said dismissively, as though it was the only logical thing a seven-year-old girl would draw.

His head tilted to the side. "I'm bored. It's my first time in a city; would you come explore with me?"

The girl looked at him, puzzled. "You mean it's your first time in this city?"

"It is, so I don't know my way around it. What's the best place to go?"

"What?"

"Where's the one place you would go, if you could go anywhere in the city?"

The question took her by surprise. She looked down at her drawings and then at her map colors.

"The art booths in the square. Today's the last day, and I wanted to see the crafts for sale before the fair went away."

The boy's smile got even wider.

"Then let's go," he said.

"We can't go; the gate's locked."

"Trust me."

She squinted her eyes at him, taking another sip of her juice box.

"Will you buy me a juice box?"

"What's a juice box?"

"You aren't from around here." It wasn't a question.

She followed him. When they got to the gate, the boy did some quick motions, and the gates opened.

She led him to the square, and they looked around. There were tons of things there, and they looked for hours.

The girl was looking at a handmade, although poorly so, seashell bracelet, when someone came up behind her. A gentle hand spun her around, and she saw the boy. He smiled at her; his other hand was behind his back.

"I got this for you." With a deft moment, he slid a necklace around her neck. She looked down at it. A thin

silver chain with a hand-bent, intricate heart around it winked back at her in the sunlight.

"Consider it something to remember me by. I can't be around past today," he said. She noticed it was the first time the boy's eyes showed sadness.

"You can't?" she asked.

"Nope, but I wanted you to have something to remember me by." It was a sad smile that lit his face.

Storm clouds were gathering, and there was a crack of thunder. Her's lip trembled. The boy noticed.

"Come with me."

He led her by the hand to an alleyway that was part-way blocking the rain.

"Are you all right?"

"I want to go home," she cried.

"Are you scared?" the boy asked, frowning.

"No, I'm sick. Momma says I have anemia," the girl shuddered, holding him close.

"Well, we'll get you back to the park," the boy said, stroking her hair.

"We shopped too long, the bus went back to the daycare. I don't know how to get there."

The boy frowned and looked down. She looked at his expression; it was like he was thinking something over. He closed his eyes and pulled something out of his pocket. She had seen nothing like it before; it looked like a dog collar, but it had wires sticking out of it. It looked broken open. The boy looked at the girl. With a sigh, the boy reconnected some wires. The device began to glow and beep. The glow of the dog collar sparkled off something else in his hand; it was a blue, crystal dolphin set in silver.

The boy noticed her looking. "It's for my mom. It's an apology; I kind of ran away today. I didn't run from her; I ran away from the monsters that live with her."

"Monsters?" she asked him.

"Well, you'll see your parents soon," the boy said, again with his sad smile.

"What is that?" she asked, this time she pointed at the dog collar.

"Let me ask you," the boy said, side-stepping the question again, "if a boy were different, from any other boy out there, if he looked different, would you hate him?"

"I don't know," she said, becoming unnerved.

"Don't... don't hate me, but I didn't want to go away without showing you," he said. "I'm a Monster too."

"You're a Monster?" the girl said, backing up.

"Not a bad Monster. I don't want to be a Monster. I want to grow up and get away from the Monsters." The boy

looked at her. The girl relaxed her guard a little. "Will you judge me?"

"I won't judge," she said. She was curious as to what it meant to be a Monster.

"Then watch," the boy said, "and remember, not all monsters are bad."

The boy frowned at her one more time. There was a moment where the only thing they heard was the rain. Then, with her breath bated, the boy moved his hands to his cheeks. She saw his fingers dig into his face along his jawline. There was a soft ripping sound, but the girl could not hear it. She could not hear the sound of the rain either. Everything was silent. He peeled back his face, and what lay beneath was a shimmering bed of jelly; it was clear, but it had a sparkle to it. It looked like diamonds to her.

"It's amazing," she said. "May I touch?"

"I... yes."

She caressed his face. While her hand was there she noticed his eyes; they reflected back the wonder shining in hers.

"What's your name?" she asked.

His face hardened back into what it was before. As his skin spread across his True Face, he answered her.

"Faceless," the boy said, winking as the skin formed back around his eyes.

Chapter 11: Inspiration

Victoria opened her eyes, and she sat up in bed. She rubbed her eyes with her palms. It was that dream; that dream was back again. The one with the boy and the monsters. The only good thing was that it served as the inspiration for her artwork. She looked around her studio; she had fallen asleep here last night while painting. The word studio, however, should have been followed by the word apartment. She just neglected to finish the phrase when she spoke to others about it; it wasn't lying, simply not finishing a phrase. Her cheek itched, and she touched it; she pulled away a dark, liquid red. Her eyes widened out of fear. Then she realized it was paint; she had been using red paint last night. That's right. She looked back around where she had been painting; splotches of different colors ran together with tarps and brushes. She really should clean; the rats might come back if she didn't.

She stood up and went to go make some coffee. She stretched and then looked at the walls; the walls were the original, red color they had been when she rented the studio apartment, that dull, neglected red. Her studio had all the harbingers of a cheap rental. It even came complete with a broken toilet. The apartment was inconvenient and it sucked, but it was all she could afford until she became famous.

As the percolator began its steady drumming, and as the smell of cheap, potent coffee began to mix with the ever-present scent of paint, her thoughts went back to her dream. She couldn't believe that the same boy was in her dreams again. They were dreams; that's what she needed to remind herself; she knew it couldn't have been a real memory – only a dream. People didn't just peel off their faces. The kidnapping was real, she was told by the police, and her mind just invented the rest to try and make peace with it. Her psychologist had told her it was a defense mechanism, and that it was one common for children in traumatic experiences.

Still, she'd fought it. She had gone to that psychologist for years. A Swedish company named Fati had offered to pay for her treatments. Between the pills and the looks her parents gave her, eventually she'd just accepted that the psychologist was right. Although a part of her had still hoped, even now, that they were wrong.

She got out of bed and straightened her silver, silk slip-on night gown. She placed her petite, bare feet onto the cold wood floor. After standing up, she went to her easel. It was time for her to get back to work. She popped her first iron pill of the day, having never grown out of her anemia.

She put on music, and the voice of classical music filled the small, quaint apartment as she picked up her pencil. She put the pencil to the canvas and drew out the outline of her newest addition to her *Faceless Collection*. She called it, *The Boy in the Rain.*

Her pencil traced out the face, the jaw, the spots she planned for the light to shine on the boy's face, and then the eyes. Those eyes that looked back at the viewer with a mixture of happiness and a deep sadness. She wondered where the boy was now.

Then she shook herself back to reality. He was a dream, a delusion. She had to keep reminding herself of that. She had to remember the doctor, the meds. Faceless was just a fantasy.

She patted her cheeks with one hand and shook her head awake, then she looked at the canvas so far. The boy was almost fleshed out. All that was missing was his face. There was a knock on the door. Victoria stood up, crossed over to her door, checked the peep hole, and then pulled the door open.

Standing there with coffee and pastries in hand was John. His build was that of gym addict; he was wearing a hat over his usual dirty-blond hair; his chin was sharp, and his eyes were green. The look in them, when paired with his suggestive smile, proved that he didn't just want to be friends with her the way he always said he did.

"What's up, beautiful?" John said while presenting the pastries. "I bought breakfast." He looked down at her pajamas. "I see you put in some effort this morning. When I came over yesterday it was a sweat suit."

"Well, I got paint on that sweat suit. Don't knock it. It's my favorite. I'm going to miss it terribly."

"How bad could it... oh." John looked in the corner and saw the sweat suit. Two giant blobs of paint were splattered where her breasts would be. "Actually," John laughed, "I'd have preferred you worn that."

He reached forward and twirled a piece of Victoria's hair in his hand. From all outward appearances he seemed interested in her. The look in his eyes and the way he smiled all pointed to him wanting to be with her.

Victoria refused to believe it. She was stuck on the notion that he was just a friend. Perhaps a touchy-feely friend, but there were people like that. He didn't attract her; she was just comfortable with him. That didn't stop him from trying like he did now.

He touched her again and this time she knocked his hand away with a nonchalant movement. Her eyes were focused on her painting; it was that and that the Boy in the Rain had been on her mind ever since she'd escaped that one creepy, awkward guy.

She frowned. That was a terrible waste of graphite powder. But her mind kept coming back to that fairly creepy man. But it wasn't the man's creepy factor that was holding her attention; it was his eyes. They were just like the boy's. She shook her head. She was talking about the boy who didn't exist – again. She had to remember that; he didn't exist. She couldn't afford any more happy pills, not on an artist's salary.

"So what are you thinking about, beautiful?" John said, placing his hand on her back a little further down than was friendly.

"I was just thinking about an incident from the other day." She didn't move away. His hand was comforting. After that dream, she felt like cuddling.

John's voice lowered an octave and his eyes sharpened. "What happened?" he said, the sharp tone of protectiveness in his voice automatically.

"Nothing to worry about. Some guy scared me today."

"What guy?" His voice had turned to a growl.

"Nothing. Don't worry about it. I mean; he won't be bothering me again. It's not like he could see me again anyway. I kind of blinded him."

John's aura changed and his eyebrow rose with a curiosity as he bit back a smile. "Blinded him? With what?"

"Graphite powder."

John fell off of the stool from laughing. "Here I was worried."

"Worried about what?" Victoria asked while licking the pastry glaze off her index finger.

She touched her wet finger to the canvas, erasing her line and redrawing it. The eraser that would have done the job was laying two feet away, but she was being a little lazy. She was entitled to be so; she just woke up, and the coffee wasn't finished yet.

John grabbed her, gingerly but assertively, by the elbows and turned her to him. "I was worried that someone was messing with the woman I loved." John pushed a lock of hair from her face.

"That part of us ended a long time ago, John."

John could tell this wasn't working so he drew back. Some part of Victoria missed the contact.

"Let's go," he said suddenly while pulling her towards him. Then he looked down at her.

"Actually, you take a shower and change first." He twirled her and pushed her toward the shower.

"What? Why?"

"Because as soon as you have pants on or a stylish skirt we're going shopping. I think I'd like to buy you more graphite powder."

She dismissed herself; this early in the morning, she didn't feel like arguing; there was also the fact that offering to buy a struggling artist graphite powder was always welcome. As she stood in her shower with the water hitting her face she thought back to that day, that night in the rain, and wondered if the Boy in the Rain had ever thought about her since.

Chapter 12: Science Versus Art

"It's not difficult to romance a woman," Ray said to Aedon.

They were sitting outside a coffee shop. The sun was just about to set, and they were relaxing before going out to the club. Ray had told him this was his first class, so Aedon came prepared.

"Most of how humans interact is body language, tonality, and eye contact. It's not so much what you say Saint, as how you say it."

"All right?" Aedon said, thoughtfully looking at his teacher.

"It's a science versus art, Saint. Body language is a science. I can show you exactly how to position your body, how to look a woman in the eyes, how to stand, how to lean, how to touch. The art of it comes from everything else.

Knowing what to say is part of the art. We're not going to make you into a scientist; screw that idea. We're going to make you into an artist, and very artist needs a canvas. Ours is a club. It's a street, a store, everywhere, but tonight you want the anonymity of a club, because you are going to screw up. That is going to happen. The best way to learn the 90% you need is by observing me, so let's go learn."

They walked down the block and saw a dance club. *Lantern*, the Chinese-themed night club sign showed in gaudy neon lights.

When they walked in, a wall of sound almost seemed to physically hit them. There were dancing lights everywhere, neon and blacklights were the only source of illumination in the place. Smoke machines made low resting fog that settled around their ankles, swirling around them, like a living entity.

"Watch and learn," Ray said with a coy smile across his lips.

He walked up to a brunette woman that could have passed for a model. Her hair was curly and her tight, fitted clothes accentuated her curves. Her friend was average-looking and seemed like she didn't really feel comfortable nor wanted to be there. His look on his face was like he was searching for his friend.

"Hey have you guys seen this really tall guy dressed like a leprechaun? He was meeting me right after work, but he's surprisingly hard to find in this crowd. These blacklights aren't helping."

He wasn't talking to the brunette but instead to the awkward friend. The friend smiled. He talked with her for a while then got the brunette involved. His body language was relaxed, but dominant. His eyes were looking at the brunette with an almost physical lust that rested just under the surface, just barely hidden by his innocent words.

After five minutes of conversation, the woman was leaning on him. Her fingers traced along his forearm. His hand played with her hair as he talked. He twirled a strand of her hair around his fingers. A playful smile lit his face. She returned it. They both know that she was his. Ray took the girl's phone number and returned to Aedon.

"It's that simple. Your turn."

Aedon was trying to psych himself up by humming Beethoven. "What the hell is that?" Ray asked, Aedon's humming ruining his mood.

"What?" Aedon asked defensively.

"That humming."

"Oh. It's my favorite song," Aedon said nervously. "It's a nervous habit."

"Well stop it and go talk to that hot girl over there. Without the song."

Aedon walked up to the pointed-out attractive woman. "Hey, have you seen a tall guy around tonight? He's a leprechaun and he was meeting me here after work." The woman looked at him, cocked her head to the side, then threw her drink in his face, assuming that, even though she couldn't find it, that had to be an innuendo.

Aedon walked back up to Ray.

"Oh shit, have we got some work to do," Ray said, laughing and handing Faceless a cocktail napkin.

"I just thought if I did it exactly as you, it would work."

"Yeah, no. It doesn't work that way. You're counting chickens before they hatch. You have to work to get as good as this." Ray gestured to himself.

Aedon wiped the burning sting of alcohol off his face with the cocktail napkin, really wishing the bartender had mixed the drink a little weaker.

* * *

Aedon trained for two days and nights with Ray. He learned every situation, every word, every contingency. He learned how to read a woman's body language, and how to master his own.

"So that's all I can teach you," Ray said; they were sitting at *Lantern,* and Ray had a red-headed woman to his right.

Aedon was alone. Not because he wasn't able to attract a woman this time, but because his mind was on someone else. Ray looked at Aedon, studying him.

"So what's her name?" he said smiling while he took a sip of his scotch. Aedon looked at him, confused. "Aedon, there are plenty of gorgeous women here, and I can tell you're straight or you'd be eyeballing me, because let's face it: I'm hot. So that means you've got a certain woman on your mind."

Aedon looked down and smiled. "I don't remember her name. I just know what she looks like."

"Tell me about her."

"I saw her; her hair was midway down her back, a type of platinum blond that just looks like it was made of sunlight. Her smoky-blue eyes were like an ocean during a storm. When I looked at her all I could feel-" Ray shoved a fortune cookie in Aedon's mouth and cut Aedon off halfway through his rant.

"Excuse me," Ray said while smiling. "It was just getting too mushy and pathetic for me." He slung his arm around Aedon, almost spilling his scotch. "No, but man, if you found someone you can feel something for, all the more power to you. Me, I can't really feel anything like that."

There was an awkward silence as Aedon felt uncomfortable having Ray's arm on his shoulders while Ray was being quiet and pensive. The redhead, bored, stood up and walked away. "Well, there goes my meal," Ray sighed. "All right, well, let's go see her."

"Of course. But like, tomorrow. Right now it's 3:00 a.m. and I don't think she'll be wanting to see me. Honestly I don't even know where she lives," Aedon said, giving Ray an innocent smile.

"Dude, you're killing my party-buzz. I'm sacrificing a night of feeding – hell I've already sacrificed two – and you're telling me I can't meet her?"

Aedon shrugged.

"Ass," Ray laughed. "All right, let's try that group of two women over there. You won't partake, but you can wing for me."

Aedon shrugged again.

"You're killing me, man. Go start the conversation." Ray gave him a shove and rolled his eyes.

Chapter 13: A Nice Ass

Faceless woke up groggy; he also woke up with a hangover and with a burn in his throat that was due to his shouting over club music until five in the morning – and tequila. A good portion of it was due to the tequila. It had been a good night.

Faceless got off of the air mattress as softly as he could, without waking the woman next to him. It was cool in the living room of the cramped studio apartment. Aedon took everything in; he could defend the place as "eclectic" at best. Pieces of mismatched furniture littered everywhere, stacked on one another and pushed together, waiting for a permanent home in a bigger apartment. Aedon crossed the fuzzy, purple carpet; it felt good against his bare feet. Faceless took a couple of pain meds from the kitchen cabinet, and drank some orange juice from the fridge. As he closed the fridge, he noticed its door; it had a collage of pictures held to the front of it by magnets, all of them different pictures of Grace in America with her family; she was from some small, Texas town. The fridge was Grace's, Spade's date for the night. Faceless downed the orange juice and then slid back into the bed; the woman next to him felt the shift in the mattress and put her hand on his chest.

Allison was waking up and Aedon couldn't help but gaze at her African, mocha skin; it was smooth and she was beautiful, even without the often misleading glamour of the night club lights. He saw her hair was a rich black, with a slightly curly bounce. She was resting on her forearms; her breasts pressed against the bed sheets as she smiled at him.

"Good morning, Aedon," the woman smiled; her eyes were looking at him intently; they had highlights of silver eye shadow and mascara. The eye shadow was slightly smeared from the night before.

"Allison, hey. I was trying not to wake you; you have a shift today at the hospital, right?"

"No, I told you already; I'm just a surgeon; I'm on call today." Then she turned her attention to his biceps. "Your body was surprising, Aedon," Allison said as she rolled around behind him. The next thing he knew he felt her body heat warming his scarred back.

"How so?" He wondered why he felt her body heat so well; he noticed her shirt on the ground next to her bra.

"Well, for starters, it's hard; I mean, look at these muscles." She traced her hands along his biceps as she spoke. "What were most surprising, though, were those scars." She ran a finger down the X-shaped one on his chest.

"I had a hard life," Aedon said, rolling his shoulder away. "I'd rather not go into it."

"I won't pry," Allison's voice changed; it had a little more caution to it. "I enjoyed last night, and I want to see you again."

Aedon smiled; a woman wanted to see him again, and she was an amazing woman. She just wasn't The Girl in the Rain, which is why they hadn't done more than kiss last night. Aedon turned around and held her close, kissing her forehead softly. "I'd like that." He gave her a pained smile.

The sound of breaking glass coming from the other room ruined the moment.

"Get the fuck out, you lying bastard!" a very angry voice said; it was the kind of voice that, in Faceless's experience, often accompanied violence. Grace and Spade were apparently awake. Spade came barreling through, bare-assed with underwear and clothes covering his front as he ran.

"Time to go, Aedon!" a naked Spade shouted as he ran out the front door.

"Well, I still want to see you again," Allison said, ignoring the streaking man and returning her attention to Aedon.

"Well, I do too, but I think Grace has a bat in there and a lot of people want my face not broken so I'll be going now," Aedon laughed.

"Here's my number," Allison gave her one of her business cards. Aedon took it between his teeth as he left with his clothes in his arms. Allison stared at him as he walked toward the door. "Damn, that's a nice ass," he heard her sigh. He felt her gaze, and in a strangely placed vanity's mirror, saw her eyes locked on his hips.

Chapter 14: Art Show

Faceless was standing in front of the painting *Boy in the Rain* by an artist that he didn't know. He was looking around at the wall of the painting, but there was no name tag for the artist. He bit down on the coffee's plastic lid. He wanted it.

A woman walked into his peripheral vision. He turned and there she was: the woman who had thrown powder into his eyes. He almost panicked, but realized that she wouldn't recognize him; it was still a tad unnerving.

He thought about what to say, the right lines, the right movements. Art, Spade had called it. Faceless shook his head. He pushed aside everything he learned from Spade. For some reason, he didn't want, if things worked out with her, to have it be built on something fake. So he just went for it.

"This piece is interesting, isn't it? It's kind of cheesy though, don't you think? The love of your life is just out of reach. Kinda a played out premise," he said, looking at her.

"I drew this," the girl said, raising her eyebrow at him.

"Uh, then you should know what I mean," Faceless smiled. Mace Girl's mouth dropped open. "I guess it's just that I've seen this sort of thing in my life before. Having kissed a girl in the rain, all I ever found was that I got cold and wet, but I get the idea; there's someone out there you can have a moment like that with, and not care that you're freezing your ass off." He looked at her with the same sly smile he had been. "I'm sorry; it must be the Texan in me. We're pretty cool though. We don't all ride horses to work; that's a regional thing."

"But surely you've got one of those glittery belt buckles," she chuckled.

"Excuse me, they're called rhinestone. They're the man's version of glitter," Faceless said. Then he noticed her smile. "You know, as beautiful as you are and as reserved as you are, I bet a lot of people think you're cold and distant. But I think you're just really paying attention. You're the observing type that really thinks before she responds. I like that."

The girl's smile got bigger; she touched her hair, unconsciously. Faceless couldn't help but notice that she hadn't reached for the graphite.

"What's your name?" the girl asked.

"Aedon Saint. You?"

"I'm Victoria Hosk," she smiled, extending her hand.

"Hosk? See, I knew I was right. I was sitting here thinking you were Swedish. High five." Aedon held his hand up and Victoria touched her hand to his; her smile wasn't fading anymore.

"So what are you doing here, Miss Hosk? You're not just getting an ego boost by admiring your work, right?" Aedon smiled and winked as he said this.

Victoria laughed. "No, we're getting ready to display all my artwork. This just happens to be my favorite piece. It's the one that inspired them all, even if kissing in the rain is uncomfortable." She was joking back with him.

"So what else do you do besides paint?"

"Not a whole lot," Victoria said. "I mean, I have a cat."

"Oh, wow," Aedon said, "Victoria, how did I guess you were a cat lady?"

"Shut up." Victoria pushed him in the chest playfully. The first thing she noticed was that it was pure muscle underneath that shirt.

"All right, all right. So you like to travel?" Aedon smiled.

"Actually yes, I used to travel around Europe during my university summers."

"That's great. I love traveling; my mom and I used to visit France especially for the art shows. I loved looking at the paintings and thinking about how I could do that for a living. Just sit at a canvas and paint. Total freedom. Freedom is something I've grown to treasure lately."

"Freedom is nice," Victoria thought aloud. Ever since she'd been preaching about the Boy in the Rain, her parents had been shuffling her from psychiatrist to counselor to witch doctor to exorcist. She didn't have a lot of freedom. She took comfort knowing there was only one exorcism attempt.

"I know this sounds crazy, since we just met, but you seem fun and like someone I want to get to know better. What are you doing this Friday?"

Victoria thought for a second. Nothing really. "Nothing really."

"Then let's go out. I know a great diner, and then we'll have some ice cream," he smiled. "They even have gummy bears. I know you were wondering. I could see it in your eyes."

Victoria laughed. "All right," she said, before she realized it.

"All right, Friday at 7:00 PM, meet me here as the museum is about to close."

Aedon handed Victoria a piece of paper, and she scribbled her cell phone number on it.

"All right, I'll meet you here tomorrow."

Aedon looked at her hand, which she'd extended out to shake his. He took her right hand in his left and pulled her in for a hug.

One of the things he did remember from Spade was the importance of physical contact early on. He recalled what Spade had said two days ago in the club.

"Physical contact is the defining line between friend and lover," Spade shouted above the pulsing bass. "Think about all your female friends you were interested in."

Faceless's first thought was that he didn't have any. "Okay."

"Even though you liked her, or wanted to do dirty, dirty things to her, she could never think of you as more than a friend. What stopped her from thinking of you as someone she could do dirty, dirty things back with, was physical touch – or the lack thereof." He paused to take a sip of his scotch. "If a woman isn't used to your touch early on in the

conversation, whatever passion she feels for you will die out and turn into the dreaded friend's zone. After which, you will never get to see any of her naughty bits – and trust me: the naughty bits are the fun part."

"That kinda sucks," Aedon said, not entirely sure what naughty bits translated to, but he wanted them.

"Yes it does. So remember, whenever appropriate and not socially inept, initiate physical contact."

He playfully pushed Victoria off him; he remembered Spades other lessons and kept smiling. "That's all you get for now," he smiled and stuck his tongue out playfully.

They kept eye contact until he had turned around. Then, his back facing her, a childlike, ecstatic smile spread across his face.

Chapter 15: A Celebration and an Alley Fight

"Congrats man! I was worried," Spade shouted, well on his way to being drunk and still drinking.

"Worried? I listened to your advice, ass," Aedon laughed.

"No, dick," Spade laughed, "I was worried you actually were looking at me back in the bar. Like, you actually did want my naughty bits."

Aedon's face scrunched up in primal disgust. He did not want to think of Spade's naughty bits. They were bits he couldn't help thinking could use a good bleaching.

"Nice," he said aloud.

"I'll be honest, I was there," Spade loudly whispered in Aedon's ear.

Faceless knew this, of course; he was trained to before he ever met Spade, but showing that would seem abnormal.

"What do you mean you were there?"

"I was at the art museum."

"You bastard!" Aedon laughed, punching Spade in the arm.

"Seriously man, she was hot. Like, maybe even a two-nighter," Spade said. A two-nighter was incredibly high praise. "So help me wing tonight, before I lose you forever to platinum blond, artistic, flat-chested Barbie." Aedon shrugged. He figured he owed his guru that much. "Bar wench! One more round, for me and my pupil!" Spade shouted, and Aedon caught the wafting scent of alcohol like an overpowering force.

Spade was drinking a lot, and the artfully stacked pyramid of empty shot glasses was growing, becoming a rather impressive display.

"Who do you want?" Aedon asked.

"That sexy beast in front of me," Spade said, looking forward.

"That's your reflection."

"Ah, I knew I saw pure, unbridled sex appeal," Spade said, pushing together his lips and sending his reflection a kiss.

"See? He thinks I'm sexy too."

"Wow. Well, I can't help you bed yourself. You can do that any night anyways."

Aedon thought for a second.

"Hell, I bet he'd give you a hand job."

"Oh, hah. A masturbation joke."

"Come on man, do you see anyone there? Besides yourself?" Aedon added, turning Spade in his bar stool as he began to turn back towards the mirror.

"That tall girl, I think, the sexy black-haired girl with the nice ass."

Aedon smiled. He looked over, and the sexy black-haired girl seemed to have hardly any breasts. That was a man.

This was going to be fun. "All right, let's go," Aedon barely held back a chuckle.

"Well all right, bitch; I been here waitin' for you," Spade said, stumbling out of his chair. Spade shuffled over to the "girl" and put his hand on "her" shoulder. "Damn, bitch, you's got the shit. I'm-a take you home and show you my naughty bits."

Aedon slapped his face with his hand. This was going to end badly.

"Thank you," the man blushed.

The man held eye contact and blushed as he moved his hand into Spade's. This just got back to being fun.

"Are you hitting on my boyfriend?" a gruff voice called from behind Aedon.

Aedon turned and saw a 6'5", 300lbs giant. His eyes widened.

"I don't know, does this look like I am?" Spade grabbed the she-man by the ass and squeezed. It just got back to being bad.

"Well, I'm glad we got a playmate," the giant said, giving his boyfriend and Spade an unnervingly lustful smile.

"You jerk!" An angry male voice came from behind again.

"What now?" Aedon said, turning. He saw Grace, and about five or six men. Beefy men. Steroid-laden men. "Crap."

"You messed around with my girl? My girl?" The angry man wasn't addressing Aedon; he was addressing the drunken Spade.

"Hey! Not tonigh'; tonigh' I messin' around with this girl," Spade said, pointing to the petite, blushing man. Spade looked at the giant bearded boyfriend, "and maybe that hairy girl, I have extra energy," Spade said. "Hell, if you talk to my secretary there and leave her name, address, and number, I'll see if I can fit her in," Spade nudged Aedon, the secretary, in the ribs playfully with his elbow, "or see if I can fit myself in her."

Everyone stood there, soaking up everything that had been laid out in that last rant.

"Bring him," Grace's boyfriend said.

"Screw him over, baby," Grace said.

"Shut up, whore," the boyfriend said.

The group of men picked up Spade and carried him toward the door.

"Hey!" The rambling Spade said, "Don't call her a whore. She's a lady; she's a lady with a very nice reverse cowgirl."

"Well I guess I'd better go. He's likely to get killed," Aedon said out loud.

He excused himself from the adventurous gay couple and followed. When he caught up, the group had just thrown Spade onto the wet sidewalk.

"Guys," Aedon began, "I know we all have feelings about shit here, and people not crossing their legs to certain people's naughty bits. But I can't let you hurt him."

"Oh yeah?" The angry boyfriend growled. "And what will you do to—"

That was as much as he got out before Faceless cracked him across the jaw with an elbow strike so hard, the rest of the group heard the jaw crack and fracture.

"Crap," Faceless looked around. "Can we just excuse that as him being all up in my grill?" The group attacked in unison.

Faceless easily dodged the punch coming at him from the first attacker. Although to be honest, the man wasn't entirely sober.

Faceless spared a glance at Spade. He was looking at a trash can with his naughty glance. He had to protect his friend; screw his secret. Then he raised his eyebrows in surprise. He had a friend.

"Guys," Faceless said, his voice deep and booming. There was a dangerous glare in his newly red eyes. The semi-drunk men stilled. The more sober of them even felt fear. "Leave us alone. If you charge me, I will break you. I'm having a good night, honestly the best night of my life. Don't make me ruin it because of you."

There was a sharp edge to his voice that sent a chill down their collective, inebriated spines.

One of them approached, too far gone to care, and threw a punch at Faceless.

Faceless wasn't taught the gentler martial arts like judo. The only martial arts he knew, that he was told were worth any value, were the ones that maimed and killed.

Faceless intercepted the fist by catching it. He delivered a sharp blow to the man's elbow. There was a loud snap and the man crumpled to the ground, screaming. The man, while his attack failed, managed to set the wheels in motion.

They charged Faceless from his front. He punched the first in the throat, choking him and making him drop. Faceless turned just quick enough to dodge the worst of a knife aimed at his head. The knife cut into his face, enough to ruin his mask.

"Ouch, dick," Faceless shot his hand out, breaking the man's grip on his knife, then grabbed his wrist, and twisted it sharply inward. The man screamed as his whole arm and every bone in it were spiral-fractured.

Faceless's face was beginning to fall off. He put his right hand to his cheek, keeping it still as he picked up the knife. He twirled the knife, holing it by the blade and used it as a billy club, smacking the rest of the gentlemen in various parts of their heads.

Finally, as the bodies lay heaped around him, he checked to make sure most were unconscious or at least the more sober ones were.

Then, he felt the slice on his face and winced. He put his fingers on either side of the cut and pulled it apart. He pulled the mask off his face. His True Face felt cold, but he basked for a second in the cool night air, then allowed the face to harden back into Aedon Saint.

He heard the loud clang of a trash can tipping over and turned.

"Well, that's interesting," Spade said, swaying, propped up on his elbow, then Spade collapsed; Faceless went to his unconscious friend.

Chapter 16: Confession

Aedon hefted Spade up and carried him back to his loft above the museum.

He threw him down on the bed and then fell back into a seating position on the floor.

"There you go buddy," Aedon sighed. "Sleep it off."

He threw himself backwards and passed out.

* * *

"What's this?" a loud, shrill voice shouted.

Aedon woke up and got ready to attack. It was the museum director.

"I thought I made it clear, boy," she said, "If you wanted sex, I was right here. How much less subtle do I have to be?"

Aedon didn't really have time for this. He rubbed the sleep from his eyes.

"He was just crashing here because he's drunk."

"Oh," the director said, "then carry on. I just came here to tell you that it's 2:00 pm and you wanted me to wake you up. Something about a date?" the director said, but she did so in a huff.

"Don't worry," Aedon said, sensing the director's jealousy, "it's nothing serious yet."

"Ah," the director said. "Well, go have your fun, but remember, sweetheart, I'm here when you're done playing."

The skin began to crawl on Aedon's back. His sphincter instinctively tightened. "Will do." The director left.

"So," Spade's voice came from behind Aedon. "You want to explain how you can take a knife to the face and not have a cut?"

Aedon looked at him innocently. "My face was too pretty to stay cut." Spade looked at him. "All right," Aedon laughed. "What I'm about to tell you is going to sound crazy, and ridiculous, but you want the truth."

* * *

"I know it seems ridiculous, and I wouldn't believe me either, but you're my friend, and I wanted you to know."

"You could have just left me there."

"They would have killed you."

"So?"

"So you're my friend, my best friend, my only friend. I couldn't let that happen."

Spade's expression softened. "Shit. You're the good guy."

Spade thought about his video games, and it just fit. Faceless was the naïve hero. The bumbling good guy that couldn't stop himself from helping people.

"What?"

"Nothing. So why'd you pick here? So close to NightCard?"

Aedon looked out the window. "When I was a kid, there was a woman I met here once. That girl, the one that you saw me get a date with, I think was her: the Girl in the Rain."

"Cool." Spade didn't know anything else to say.

"You know, most people would give off some sign of surprise."

"I've done stupid shit for women before."

"Not that, jackass, my being able to rip my face off would surprise most people."

"Eh, I've seen some shit," Spade laughed. It seemed hollow and fake to him, but Aedon seemed to accept it. No, Faceless accepted it.

Spade was at a loss. He knew he had to report this. He had to give them the lead they needed so Clubs could come over here and turn Faceless's bones into putty. Actually,

Spade should just kill Faceless now and be done with it. The power in Spade's hands was charging up, letting off a slight crackling in his hands; it sounded like knuckles' cracking.

Faceless was right there in front of him. Maybe two arms' lengths away, but something was stopping him. The thought of killing Faceless was something that filled Spade with an almost sick joy, but the thought of killing Aedon Saint made Ray's chest hurt.

After ten minutes of thinking, Spade stood up. The sound of knuckles popping, he extended his hand to Faceless.

"I'm glad you're my friend," he said. "Let's shake on it."

Chapter 17: Memories of Scars

The King of Diamonds walked up to the King of Clubs, who was in the living room of the studio apartment they'd broken into; he was playing on the new V-Jet gaming console. The smell brought her attention to the corner of the apartment; its former owners were crumpled, broken in a heap they were waiting to be Clubs's next meal. They hadn't wanted to let the Kings in; the Kings had insisted.

"Don't you think we should be doing something – anything?" she asked, her attention moving away from the bodies.

"No, we'll do something when we need to. Otherwise, try not to move around too much or draw too much attention to yourself. People tend to die when you move too much."

"Fine, I'm going to take a bath," Diamonds pouted.

* * *

"Screw that," Diamonds muttered to herself as she pulled on her black trench coat over her bodysuit.

She climbed out of the window of the studio apartment, then headed for the roof.

She didn't trust Spade. She couldn't allow herself to trust him – never again. As she leaped from roof to roof, following the collar on Spade, those memories crossed her mind. Those memories of back then.

* * *

"So you really think we'd work?" Diamonds said, her long black hair was down and over her naked, almond-colored shoulders. The bed covers were draped on top of her in a way that showed off her perfectly tapered legs. Candlelight bounced off them, casting dancing shadows on the walls behind the two lovers.

On her bed with her was Spade, his hips covered by the bed sheet. What had started as a night of his being denied a trip into town had turned into something wonderful. Their clothes laid on the floor next to the bed, discarded in a drunken, heated night of passion. Spade looked at Diamonds. She had admitted to herself a long time ago that hers were lost in his. His that told her that he loved her – only her. She looked back at him with her sharp, Filipino eyes; they were eyes that he constantly reminded her he fell in love with.

"Of course I do. You're the only one that I could ever truly feel something for. You're the only girl in the world that could ever really understand me," Spade said, kissing her shoulder. On her shoulder was her namesake, a red Diamonds tattoo; its colors were still bold, even in candlelight.

"I'm afraid," Diamonds said.

"Why?" Spade kissed her softly.

"Because I want to say 'I love you.'"

"Why would you be afraid of that?" Spade said, brushing the hair off her shoulder. She trembled at the stroke of his fingertips.

"Because then it's said, and then I can't unsay it." Her words were distant – as though she were lost in a trance.

"Don't be afraid to say it," he chuckled. She felt Spade move aside the dog collar she wore. It was the same kind as he did. She felt him place a gentle kiss on her neck. "Because I love you," Spade whispered, his breath on the nape of her neck. His lips caressed her collarbone.

On her neck was an old scar that reached from her clavicle to across her chest to the bottom of her stomach. Diamonds was secretly ashamed of her scar. The one time she screwed up due to pride. She thought it was like an ugly trophy of war, and one she despised. Spade kissed it, tracing his lips down the length of it slowly. She loved it but couldn't show it.

"I won't say it," she said, stubbornly.

"Say it," he said; his hands traced along her body.

"No," she panted; her defenses began to fail.

He kissed her again and ran his hand through her hair. "Say it."

"No." Her voice was barely a whisper.

"Fine," he said; he backed away.

She whined; in an almost panic, she reached behind her, and she pulled him in close. She turned to face him. "I... I love you," she said, looking him in his eyes.

Diamonds stared into his eyes. She loved their color, their shape, and their intensity; what she loved most was the look in them that said she could let her guard down; they said he meant that love – they said she was special, and she believed them. She was completely happy and completely in love. Both of them were eager for morning to come, but as she found out, they were eager for different reasons. For her, it was finally finding love. For him, he had fed for another night.

They both fell asleep with smiles on their faces.

Chapter 18: A Secret

Faceless shook Spade's hand. Spade winced. His fingers had just popped beforehand. He couldn't kill Faceless. No, he couldn't kill Aedon. "We're friends now, you creepy, face-peeling bastard."

"Sweet," Aedon said, "Well, I'm going to go pass out."

When Aedon had just laid down, a beeping noise started going on near Spade's head. The dog collar was beeping.

"Shit," Spade said, running out of the apartment.

The beeping meant his tracker was active. Someone was trying to find him. The light on the collar was green. It was one of the kings looking for him. He climbed to a rooftop.

"Who was that?" Diamonds asked.

"Aw, little girl, you came looking for me," Spade said.

"Shut up man-whore. Who was that?"

"That was my lover. Certain women in my past failed to satisfy me."

Diamonds threw a ninja star at his face; Spade threw a knife from his hip, cowboy style. The two collided, crashing to the floor. The technique was one he was famous for.

"So demanding," Spade said with a mock sigh.

"Tell me who that was, Spade, or I'll just kill him."

Spade had no choice.

"That may be Faceless."

"May be?"

"All right, it's him."

"Cool, I'll be right back," she said, unsheathing her sword as she walked forward.

"No…" Spade said, slowly grabbing her arm and turning her back around. "We wait."

"What? Why?"

"First, we would save NightCard a lot of money if we convinced Faceless to come back, which they could then spend in part, on us; I want more romance video games."

"Perv."

"Bitch," Spade retorted offhandedly. "Two, if we can't convince him, I still want to know his limits, and his weaknesses, and who he's contacted on the outside."

He could see the doubt in her eyes, but it was only there for a second. "Well, I know you wouldn't be feeling anything for him. You're not capable of that emotion." The last bit was said with an almost palpable disdain. "There are others out here. He might know where Fractal and the Living are. You've got a little bit of time, Spade. Don't be fucking with me again."

"I wouldn't fuck with you ever again." The subtext to his words was hardly subtle.

"Later, little dick." As silently as she'd arrived, the King of Diamonds disappeared.

"Shit."

* * *

Spade went back to Aedon's room. As he approached the bed, he stood still and looked down at the passed out face-ripper. He thought about waking him up, but changed his mind.

"I'll let you have one last peaceful sleep, you bastard. When you wake up, we have work to do." Almost in retort, Aedon snorted in his sleep. "I'll take that as a yes."

He turned and sat down, his back against the bed, his head resting over it.

"It'll be the last night of sleep I get at all," Spade said, closing his eyes. He was scared he had grown a conscience. Maybe it was just the liquor.

* * *

Ray was making breakfast. He had never tried to make microwaveable pancakes before. He looked at the old, stained microwave that Aedon had. It had to be easy enough. Aedon was able to do it, after all. He looked into the trashcan, where the first three, burned attempts sat discarded. He heard a groaning; it was Aedon. He was groaning, moaning the sounds of the morning after drinking.

"It feels like life pimp-slapped me," Aedon said in a very quiet voice.

"That's called a 'hangover,' and drinking causes that," Ray laughed. "You've never had that, have you?

"I've never really drank, man," Aedon said, palms to his eyes, "and I'm not keen on it again."

"Wimp," Spade said at regular voice level.

"Stop yelling," Aedon said, rubbing his temples and striking out at the air. "I need to think. It feels like I'm forgetting something."

"Hey man, didn't you have to go to work today?" Ray asked, swearing as he burned his hand on a pancake.

"Oh, crap!" Aedon gathered all of his clothes, and fell on his face in his rush to pull up his pants. He groaned facedown on the carpet. Still laying down, he wriggled his pants up.

Spade looked down at him and laughed. His friend was klutzy. Spade's eyebrows raised. His *friend.* "Aedon, how hard is it to do your job?"

Aedon gave Spade an offended look.

"What's that supposed to mean?"

"I was thinking while you were unconscious and drooling on yourself; you should take that girl out on a date today. Strike before you regret it." After which, you're dead. Spade brushed aside his thoughts.

Aedon looked down at his nametag, like he was pondering it. "Victoria said she had some time off."

"Then do it; don't wait."

"Screw it," Faceless said. "Why not?"

"Good. Now give me that nametag, call up that girl, and take her out on a date."

"All right, Ray. I have a call to make," Aedon smiled.

Spade watched his friend leave the room to make the call. He watched him go and something happened in the corner of his eye. He lifted his hand and pulled away something watery.

"I'm sweating out of my eyes," Spade thought out loud.

He reached over and turned down the burner on the stove.

It had to be sweat. Nothing else made sense.

Chapter 19: French Ruffles

Faceless was walking up the stairs of Victoria's rundown apartment place. He looked at the cracking walls and listened to the neighbors' shouting in various languages that he both could understand and speak fluently; they didn't sound like they had a good marriage.

He had no experience in this. That thought was echoing through Aedon's mind as he walked up to room 4B and knocked.

"Who is it?" Victoria's voice came from the other side of the door.

"It's Aedon," Faceless said, "I'm here. You know, for our date?"

There was a shuffling sound, then a thump, a swear word in French, and the sound of someone rushing to clean up.

Two minutes later, the door opened. Victoria's long, almost-white blonde hair had been hastily put up, with a few strands having been missed. Her glasses had flecks of paint on their lenses.

"Did I come too early?" Aedon asked, wondering if this was a typical guy problem.

"Most guys do here. I don't think that will become a recurring problem with you." Victoria looked at a plastic, waterproof watch; it was stained with paint. "I just lost track of time. That's why I wear this thing; I guess that only helps if you look at it."

"I don't mind waiting, if you want to change; hell, we can go like this," Aedon offered, smiling.

"No, I refuse to be seen in public like this," Victoria said, "nor so by most people, either." Victoria looked at him, and Aedon Saint returned a hopeful smile. "Just give me ten minutes and I'll be ready for our date; I'll have a lot less paint on me."

"Good," Aedon said, winking. "I don't like too much makeup."

Victoria felt herself go a little red, before excusing herself to the bathroom.

Aedon noticed the painting she was doing; he walked up to it and smiled. It was funny: everything but the face of the man was drawn. It felt familiar to him. She may very well be the Girl in the Rain. Out of the corner of his eye he saw more colors: deep blues and blacks. He turned to it; there were dozens of paintings hanging on her walls. They hung haphazardly from nails that hung from awkward angles, as though someone in a hurry just to get them up and out of the way. But then he noticed the floor, littered with others. Then he noticed what shapes the blues and the blacks were making, and he gasped.

Each one of them was a scene with a faceless boy and a little blonde girl. There were scenes of them in a market, scenes of them in alleyways, playgrounds, together. Then there was one more that he noticed; it was the one that cemented his belief: there was one portrait of the boy looking at the girl, but his face was Aedon's, translucent like water with lights behind it, and the eyes: those were his eyes. This was her: he had found the Girl in the Rain; there was no doubt anymore.

* * *

"Sorry!" Victoria shouted while in the bathroom. She waited for a second to see if Aedon had heard. There was nothing but silence for a moment.

"For what?" came the reply. It came rushed, as though something had shocked him. She chose to ignore it.

"For falling behind! I just want you to know; I'm not usually this distracted! It's just been a little bit stressed, I guess." She put a bobby pin in her mouth and her voice sounded clenched. "I've finished up this series of paintings, I think. I'm thinking about what else to do, but I'm getting stuck."

"Stuck?"

Victoria pulled up her sundress and made sure the girls were sitting properly, or as properly as they could; she hated her small frame. She always looked like she was delicate, like she was about to break. She gazed at the pink and white sundress with the French ruffles. "I mean; it's just like I can't find anymore inspiration. I feel like there's one more piece left."

"That's a typical hurdle for artists to get over though; I'm sure it's fine."

Victoria pulled on her flats and opened the door. Aedon was waiting for her in the living room/bedroom/kitchen/studio. She needed a bigger place. Aedon looked like he wanted to say something, but couldn't. "Are you okay?" she asked.

It took a moment, but Aedon recovered. "I'm fine; it's just, well I guess for a moment there, you were literally breathtaking."

Victoria felt her cheeks get hot.

"Thanks," she said, then she tried to change the subject. "You still haven't told me where we're going."

"I was thinking we should go get you some inspiration," Aedon smiled.

For the first time in years, Beethoven popped into Victoria's head, as Aedon took her hand and led her down the rickety stairs and the paint-cracked walls.

Chapter 20: Don't Tell Me I'm Pretty

Aedon and Victoria walked side by side down the city of Paris; the sky was overcast and cloudy, but the weather was just warm enough to keep it comfortable. Victoria could feel Aedon's nervousness. He kept his hands in his pockets, a slight shrug in his shoulders as they walked.

"So, was there a plan," Victoria asked; she felt comfortable enough with him for some light teasing, "or were you just going to wing it?"

"Hey, don't hate on 'winging it,'" Aedon said to her. His eyes held that playfulness to it that she couldn't place, but it somehow seemed familiar. "A lot of cool things come from winging it."

"Oh, really? Maybe in Texas," Victoria scoffed.

"I mean, sometimes great things come out of just winging it. You know, I moved out of my parent's house recently. I just kind of decided I wanted to be my own man. Plus, my dad was kind of a dick. He liked to take me shooting, but it wasn't really my thing." Aedon gave a sad smile.

"Your dad took you shooting?"

"Yep; it's a commonplace thing in Texas. We've been open carry for the last decade." Aedon gave her a wink. "Plus, I'm actually not a bad shot."

"Oh, you're not? You're not just trying to make yourself sound good in front of your date?" Victoria asked, a playful tone to her voice; she had learned that banter is just a healthy part of a date.

"Sure," Aedon said. "In fact, I don't need to make myself sound good; I can do that by making myself look good." He looked around them. He saw a small water fountain that had a small, stone boy holding up a jar that was pouring water out. His attention shifted back to Victoria. She saw his smile take on an even more playful look than was usual. "Do you have a coin?"

Victoria looked in her purse and pulled out an One Cent coin. It was old and tarnished, but Victoria only had that and Euros in her purse. She held it out. He stepped close to her, that same smile on his face. She handed the One Cent to him, and he took it gently; for the briefest moment she felt their fingers touch. His were so warm. He looked at the stone boy again.

"How about a bet, then?" Aedon asked.

"Oh?" Victoria said, shaking away the recent feel of their fingers touching. "What did you have in mind?"

He held up the coin for her to see, as though it held the secrets of the universe. "You see the boy over there?" he said. She nodded. "You see how he is just wasting water from his jar? If I can get this to land on that jar, then you owe me a kiss."

Victoria looked at the distance; it was way too far, and some part of her wanted to put a hole in all his self-confidence. She returned his smile, but a more excited look in her eyes coupled it this time around. "Sure, that sounds fine, and if you can't?"

Aedon considered it. "Then I owe you one."

"I don't see how you would consider that losing."

"Someone is full of self-confidence, but yes, I thought that might have been a bit reaching. All right, then I will find you a man that's even better-looking than me," Aedon chuckled, "I promise that I know a lot of different faces; I'm sure I can find a face you'll like."

Victoria thought the way he worded that was weird, but she wouldn't hold him to that; she just wanted to embarrass him.

"Sure, player. You go for it." She beamed at him; the shot was way too far away.

He walked up to the stone fountain boy and gingerly dropped the One Cent directly over the jar. It landed perfectly, stopping the fountain's stream.

He walked back towards her, and it was only then that she realized her mouth was hanging open. He walked by her, leaning in as he did so. "I'll collect later," he chuckled. He reached back and took her hand gently. As he led her towards the market, her eyes met the One Cent piece and met the stone boy's mocking, chiseled smile. Then she turned towards Aedon and felt a gentle squeeze of his hand on hers. She squeezed back.

* * *

Aedon took her hand to lead her through the crowd. They approached a mask vendor, and Aedon stopped. The old, oak cart sold masquerade masks, clown masks, and masks with sticks. The vendor with a deep-set frown on his face was reading a paper. Thinking about the man's job, and looking at all the other people running around and having fun, Aedon couldn't blame the man.

Aedon suddenly had an idea. He grabbed one of the pure white masquerade half-masks and held it to his face. He turned to Victoria.

"Would you still like me, if this were all you saw?"

"What do you mean?" Victoria asked. The combination of the cute knitting of her eyebrows and their slanted, quizzical look drew Aedon's attention.

"I mean if I didn't look like I do now, would you still like me?"

Victoria looked at him. Her attention was drawn to the odd expression in his eyes through the eyeholes. It was an expression she couldn't quite place. One that she felt she had seen somewhere before.

"I don't know. Why?" she asked.

"Because I look at you, and I think you're pretty but—"

"Stop," Victoria interrupted, physically raising her hand in front of her face; it had been the hand holding Aedon's. It was as though she was trying to wave the thought away. "Don't tell me I'm pretty."

Aedon cocked his head to the side. "Why not?"

"Because what does that really matter? What does that really mean?" she asked. She looked over to the card and grabbed a full facemask. She held it against her face like

Aedon held his. "Does this mask change who I am as a person?"

"Well, no," Aedon said; his grin noticeable under the edges of the paper Mache mask.

"Beauty, and how we look, is only surface. It's not what we see that matters, but what we experience with a person," Victoria said, touching his arm.

"Who taught you that?" Aedon asked, taking off the mask. He rubbed the satin lining to comfort himself.

"A boy from my past," Victoria said.

"Well, I agree with that boy. In fact..." Aedon's voice trailed off as he looked at the mask in his hand. He put on the white masquerade mask in his hand, and slipped Victoria's over her face. He paid the vendor and focused his attention on her. "I have an idea. I want to test this theory of yours."

"What?" Victoria asked from behind the mask.

"We'll play a game. First one to take of a mask off loses."

Victoria laughed. "All right, but you're going to lose," she said, refitting hers snugly on. Her eyes shone through the holes with a playful twinkle.

"I doubt that," Aedon chuckled; he had a lifetime's worth of experience.

He led her down the stairs to the beach. This beach was special; it had been there since World War II, when the landscape had actually changed. Due to the failure of the storming of Normandy, the war had lasted even longer. The war had altered the very landscape, giving Paris the prestige of being shoreline.

"So, tell me more about you," he asked her as they walked along the beach. They walked closely together. There was the moment of tension where they were unaware if they wanted to hold hands or not; both wanted to, but neither wanted to make the move. The sun was beginning to set and was shining its last pleas of life; its cadence of striking red and soft oranges danced onto Aedon and Victoria's white masks.

"What's there to tell? I was told as a kid that I was crazy from an early age," she said, scoffing.

"Do you mean, like in a homicidal way?" Aedon faked shifting away from her slightly. She laughed. She pulled him back to her. He came back to her, following her footsteps in the sand as they led closer the waves.

"What? No. As a kid, I swore this event, this thing had happened, but apparently it was just something I made up."

"I'm sorry." Faceless knew what she was talking about.

"Not your fault, I was simply a weird kid. I apparently got kidnapped as a child, and my head invented a story to deal with it."

"Do you ever believe the story?"

"That I got kidnapped?"

"No, I'm talking about the fantasy you invented. Do you ever stop to think that it was real?"

"Do I ever believe it was real? Like some kid with a removable face came and whisked me away for the day? No, I don't. It was just a fantasy." She looked out at sunset as it continued its cadenza. "It was a fantasy that was amazing, though," she smiled, remembering what her mind thought were fantasies.

* * *

They walked back to the square. There were bands beginning to play for the festival. A waltz began to play. Victoria looked on at the dancers that were there. It wasn't something she normally saw. She tended to stay cooped up in her apartment.

"Do you know how to waltz?" he asked.

"No," Victoria said. She didn't, but her eyes followed the people as they danced around.

"Well, then now's as good a time as any to learn." He held his hand out to her; she was unsure for a few moments, but then she grasped it.

He led her to the dance floor, and took her right hand in his left. He lifted it to his left and took her left hand and placed it on his shoulder. His right hand found the middle of her back.

"Its easy, all right? We'll do a simple box first. Go back on your right foot." He went forward on his left as she went back on her right. "Good. Now go left. Move your left foot to the side and then collect your right foot to your left."

He mirrored her movements. "Now go forward on your left as I go back on my right. Then move sideways on your right then collect with your left. Good, that was a basic. Move like this."

He counted off the waltz count as they began to move to the music. "One, two, three. One, two, three. Good," he said as he led her. "Now we'll turn."

It was somewhere in the turning boxes that she looked into his eyes. It was somewhere after the first song that she began to fall for him.

"Victoria?"

"Yes?" she said. Aedon thought she was enthralled still in the music, but the way she moved – it was something else.

"You can stop dancing. The song ended," he said.

"Oh."

He led her back to the beach. Music from the dancing square carried over to them; the songs themselves danced on the breeze to them as they sat on rocks close to the shore and watched the final whispers of the sunset to the sky.

"I like you," Aedon said to her.

"What?"

"I like you. You're different from other girls. I feel like I don't need to wear this around you." He tugged on the corner of his mask.

"Ah, so you're admitting defeat?" she asked with a smile; she touched her own mask absently making sure it was still in place.

"Come here," he touched both of her hands and pulled her closer to him. There was a soft knock as the two masks bumped against each other. He was close, and she reached toward the edges of his mask. Then the objecting sounds of thunder interrupted, and rain drops began to fall lightly.

"Crap," Aedon said.

* * *

Aedon and Victoria huddled close together as they made their way under the pier. The sun had finally set, and the sky, having said goodbye to her lover, had the bright beams of her nightly mistress dance across her; clouds covered part of the sky, but the stars and the moon offered enough light to see the soft movement of the ocean. Aedon and Victoria huddled close, searching for each other's body warmth to combat the soft, ocean breeze; it was an excuse, of course, but they didn't call each other on it.

Aedon stood up and pulled her to him. He took one of her hands and twirled her into his arms: a final bit of dance. His hands caressed her shoulders and their eyes locked.

"I can't believe this," Aedon chuckled.

"I know, going under a bridge in the rain is so cliché," Victoria said playfully.

"I didn't mean that. Okay, well I did, but I can't believe that I of all people would lose." He pulled her mask up over her face; he watched her blonde hair flow around it as it came off. He threw it down into the sand nearby; his mask landed next to hers, the sides of them barely touching each other.

* * *

Victoria felt Aedon run his fingers through her hair, trying to fix what she assumed had to be a disheveled, frizzy look; his fingers twirled her soft hair, playing with it. He looked at her; she could feel his gaze; it was looking for permission. She felt his fingers followed her blonde locks down her shoulder; she felt his fingertips move to her back, and the tips of his fingers pulled her toward him. It was a soft pull, looking for permission, as though he expected resistance. There was none. He kissed her. It was passionate, but not aggressive. It was a strong kiss, but Victoria felt a vulnerability in it. It was as though this kiss was all that he had wanted in the world, as if it had been for a lifetime.

She smiled at him and he smiled back.

"Now close your eyes," Aedon said. She did. "Did who I am change?"

"Not at all." Her smile spread to her closed eyes.

"Open them." She did. "Now watch closely and remember what you said."

Aedon's fingertips moved from her back, to along her arms, and withdrew to his face. He gave her a look, that for the briefest moment showed fear, but then she saw his smile. His fingertips pinched the sides of his jaw; it looked as though he were having some struggle with it, but then the sides of his face began to come off. A soft layer of skin separated itself from a clear-white, glistening surface. It shone in the moonlight with the slightest sparkle.

Victoria was quiet. Her eyes soaked in everything that stood before her. They studied every part of his face, lost in wonder.

For a moment, time froze to Victoria. She needed assurance this wasn't another fantasy. She needed to know. She reached out her fingers and the lightest brush of her fingertips ran across the slick, soft surface of Aedon's... Faceless's real face.

"You're real."

Chapter 21: Asshole

Faceless looked in Victoria's eyes. This was the girl he'd been waiting for years to touch, to kiss, to hold.

"You fucking asshole!" Victoria said. She shoved him away; her face was contorted into a mixed, confused expression between righteous fury and pain – the kind of agony that comes from knowing you were right, but never believed.

"What?" Faceless's eyes widened. She pushed him again and again until he was backed up against one of the pier's support beams.

"I knew you were real! I knew, no matter what they said, that you were real! I knew that what actually happened was amazing."

"I'm glad."

"No! You're an asshole. I'd finally forgotten you. I'd finally accepted that you were just a dream. I'd finally moved on, Aedon," her voice cracked on the last part. Tears welled up in her eyes. She slammed her fists on his chest and began to cry.

Aedon kissed her head. He smelled the soft, vanilla scent of her hair as he held her close. "It wasn't my fault. I didn't choose to leave. I never meant to hurt you."

Victoria looked up at him and saw that the Boy in the Rain, all grown up, was crying. Tears were falling down his non-face. She looked in his clear eyes, and she thought about her paintings hanging up in the museum. "You didn't."

"I won't ever again."

She watched his face harden into skin around his lips, and then the newly formed lips turned into a smile. "Damn, that's cool." He leaned in and they kissed again, but this time it felt more real. This time she kissed the Boy in the Rain. As they kissed, the skin around his lips spread and hardened into Aedon's face again.

"It's time for me to tell you everything," Aedon said, looking at her with eyes that stayed clear.

* * *

"This is my friend, Ray," Aedon gestured to Spade, who was playing with his collar, hidden under what he thought was a rather masculine scarf. His mind was preoccupied. He had a meeting with Diamonds and Clubs that night. Apparently Hearts was coming into town.

The very thought of that sent a chill down his spine. He couldn't stand her. She was the only woman, ever, that scared him. He thought about it. He looked back at Aedon and Victoria. No, he looked at Faceless and Victoria. Faceless, one of the few experiments to come out of NightCard's twisted assembly line to find happiness. Some part of him thought that was worth preserving – a new part of him he didn't remember being there.

The director walked in. "Aedon, I need you," he said, looking at him.

"For what?" Aedon asked.

"We got in a shipment of paintings, and I believe you still work here." He looked at Victoria with distaste; Spade snorted a stifled laugh.

"All right, Ray, can you hang out with Victoria for a second?" Aedon asked.

"Not a problem, man."

Aedon walked out. Ray looked at Victoria. There was a moment of awkward silence before Ray spoke. "So, it's none of my business, but has Aedon gotten laid yet?"

"You're right. It isn't your business," Victoria said, flustered.

"That's fair enough, but you are treating him right, aren't you?" Spade's eyes softened.

"Yes. Yes, I am."

Spade looked at her. She was special to Aedon. He thought about how highly Aedon talked of her. There didn't seem to be anything interesting about her. "You need to be good to him," Spade said. "He's a very special man."

Victoria's gaze at him was guarded. "Yes. He is very special to me."

"Not just to you. He's special to everyone."

"I know."

"Do you know?" Spade asked.

Victoria looked at him; this time she was more focused. "Yes."

Spade's eyes widened slightly, and he smiled. She must be very special.

"If you know, then what is it?"

"He's a super-soldier built by a company called NightCard that creates soulless mercenaries that whore themselves out for profit."

"Well, I mean… yeah. That's a pretty good summary," Ray said. The "whore" and "soulless" comments stung

Spade a bit. The soulless not as much; he accepted that about himself. It was the whore comment. He didn't get paid. "Aedon is being hunted. The fact that you know this means that he trusts you."

Victoria smiled. "I know."

"Then know that no matter what he says, there are still people looking for him. He is still being hunted. You need to keep his identity a secret – for his sake and for yours." Ray's eyes squinted a bit, and his voice got deeper, turning into a slight growl towards the end.

"Was that a threat?"

"No," Spade said, shaking his head. "That was a statement. You're involved now too, whether you want to be or not."

"I want to be," Victoria stared him in the eyes. The expression on her said said she did. It was like she had for years.

Aedon walked back into the room. He gazed from Spade to Victoria and back. "Did I miss something important?"

"Aedon, can I talk to you for a second?" Spade said, his demeanor changing suddenly.

"All right," Aedon said, his tone slightly confused.

They stood up and walked off outside. Spade looked and didn't sense Clubs or Diamonds.

"Aedon, I'm Spade," Ray said flatly.

There was a very long pause while the information sunk in.

"Are you going to kill me? Was this all an act?" Faceless narrowed his eyes. His hands reached around for something – a rock, a stone, a brick, something to use in defense.

"Well, hold on now," Spade said. "You came to me, and I didn't even know you were Faceless until it was already too late."

"Too late?" Faceless asked, still on guard.

Spade grimaced as though what he was about to say was going to be painful. "You're my friend now. Sure I have Clubs, but he's a dick, and he was only there out of necessity – out of convenience, but Aedon... Faceless, you're my friend."

Faceless sat in stunned silence.

"As my friend I need you to listen to my advice," Spade continued. "Take this girl out on the town. Show her a good time. Make her happy. Make love to her. Don't do it tomorrow; do it tonight. I can only hold off Diamonds and Clubs for one more night. Diamonds almost came after you the other day. I told her I was going to try and convert you."

"Are you still?" Faceless asked.

"No," Spade said. "I know better than that. Just take her and flee, but know that starting tomorrow night, you're going to be hunted. Its not fair, and it's not ideal, but you'll be alive. Victoria will be alive. That's the important part right? She's the one, right? The Girl in the Rain?"

Faceless's jaw dropped.

"I read your file," Spade said. "So did everyone else. They know about her. That's why we chased you to this city. We knew where she lived. We just weren't allowed to do anything. One of the other Kings wouldn't let us, but now we are so you should follow my advice. Tomorrow night we hunt you, and I'll have to do it too."

Faceless nodded. "I understand. Thanks, Ray."

"You can call me Spade."

"I will call you Ray. Spade didn't save my life tonight; he hasn't been looking out for me. Ray has."

Ray smiled. "Thanks, man. Now go take your woman for a night on the town, and do some horizontal tangoing." Aedon turned and walked back in. A drop of liquid rolled down Spade's cheek. He smeared it along his face as he tried to wipe it off. "Must be the rain."

There wasn't a single cloud in the sky.

Chapter 22: Linger

Aedon held Victoria's hand as he led her to her doorstep. "Remember, tomorrow night you're mine too," Aedon said.

"Yeah, and you remember it's *tomorrow*. You better not wait another decade," Victoria said, nudging him.

"Are you kidding?" Aedon said, gently placing his hands on her triceps as he stepped in closer. "I don't know if I can wait until tomorrow," he placed a gentle kiss on Victoria's lips, "but I will." He sighed and looked a way with a soft chuckle.

As he turned, his hand found hers and he squeezed it softly. Her fingertips curled, catching his hand. "Then don't," she said.

"What?" Aedon asked.

"Linger," she said, her eyes softening.

She pulled him through the door, and closed it gently behind.

* * *

The couple laid in her room; the soft sounds of crackling wood came from her small, quaint little fireplace as it tried its best to shower the couple with warmth. The two looked at each other while dramatic shadows were cast along the walls. Strewn about the room were easels and paint supplies. There was a bottle of wine laying next to them on the floor. It lay on its side already finished, next to two glasses with remnants of red at the bottom. They lay in the middle of the floor, the bed too messy, stockpiled with art supplies and still-sacked groceries.

She felt things all over his chest. They felt like, scars? She pulled his shirt off and gasped. They were everywhere. Long, short, fresh, and old. She traced her fingers over the oldest-looking, the X-shaped one across his chest. The intersection of which was directly over his heart.

"Do they disgust you?" he asked timidly; it was almost as though he was afraid of the answer.

"No," she said, the proof of his dangerous life excited her. They kissed again, and then she slipped his shirt off.

The moonlight shined through the window, as the two lovers discovered each other.

* * *

Time passed and then they cuddled next to each other on the canvas tarps that had fashioned as a makeshift bed. Their breathing had finally settled, and Victoria looked at Aedon as she realized something.

"Aedon, am I your first?" Victoria asked.

"No," Aedon laughed. "First implies that there will be a second. You, my love, are my only." She was happy, and she looked at her man in the eyes. He was finally hers. "Am I your first?" Aedon asked her. The fear was back in his voice.

"No," she admitted, "but you're my last."

Aedon kissed her and then reclined. She moved her head to his chest, hearing his heartbeat under his old scar.

The couple, after making their promises, laid together, looking out her window at the stars in the French sky.

Chapter 23: Among the Paintings

They were laying on her bed, basking in the afterglow. Her room still had the easels and the paintings she was working on. The room was messy and haphazard. Aedon smiled. He was happy. He looked at Victoria resting on his chest and he felt her heartbeat on his ribs.

"Your hair has changed," Faceless said, touching a strand. "It used to be short, but you're still you. You're still painting, just as I remembered. When I saw your artwork, when I saw you, I had this feeling that you were still that girl I carried out of the rain. You haven't changed at all."

"Well, that's not true," she said.

"Really? How is that?"

"I'm hotter now," she joked, kissing his nose.

"Oh, I definitely noticed," he laughed.

She tilted her head up at him, still resting it on his chest.

"I like your heartbeat," she said; Aedon felt her snuggle closer. "It's comforting."

"I was just thinking the same thing," Aedon laughed.

"Was it hard?"

"It certainly felt hard. I mean, you seemed to like it," Aedon chuckled.

"What? No. I mean, yes it was, but I was talking about growing up in NightCard."

Aedon looked wistful. "It was, but someone I cared about got me through a good portion of it, someone that actually loved me. She was the closest thing to a mother I ever had."

"Who was it?"

Aedon smiled, remembering his first Keeper.

"Her name was Joan Saint," Aedon reminisced fondly, "and she was one of the most amazing women I have ever met, one of the few that cared about me."

"I had a sister named Joan," Victoria said sleepily, nuzzling into him. "She was going to college in Sweden. She got a degree as a pharmaceutical technician and she got an internship straight out of college; we kind of lost touch. I still miss her though."

"Well, she's probably kicking herself," Aedon said. "Because she's missed out on spending time with the most beautiful woman in the world."

Victoria smiled and kissed Aedon's chest; she kissed the corner of the X scar running across his heart. The raindrops came down and made noise on the metal roof above. The collective sound drowned out the rest of the world. The only two she had, the only two who mattered, were herself and Aedon. All that mattered were the heartbeats. The two beat pleasantly side by side, singing soft, rhythmic love songs to each other as lullabies.

Chapter 24: A Timely Distraction

Spade was lying, which he didn't particularly mind, but he was lying for another person. That was almost unheard of. He realized that there was something about Aedon that made Spade almost feel... human.

"I told you: we need one more day," Spade sighed as he repeated it for the eighth time to Diamonds.

"Yeah, dipshit, but once again, you have yet to tell us why," Diamonds said sharply.

"I'm thinking; give me a second," Spade said.

"What?"

"Well, I mean, I'm hungry," Spade said.

"Then order a pizza and let's go kill this bastard."

"I don't mean the pizza kind of hungry," Spade thought for a second then looked Diamonds up and down. "I'm in the mood for Asian, actually."

"Fuck you," Diamonds said.

"Not Filipino, I was thinking Japanese."

"I could go for some Filipino," Clubs said, not looking away from his video game.

"Yeah, but do you really want my leftovers?" Spade asked.

"Nah, I prefer a little more meat with my meal."

"Fuck you both. I want to get this mission over with and go home," Diamonds shouted, punching a hole in the wall.

"Look, there's another perfectly good reason for me waiting," Spade said, thinking quickly.

"Oh yeah? What's that?"

Spade reached. "I think we should wait for Hearts. Remember, if we can bring him in alive we score bonus points. Hearts is the one that could do that best."

"Hearts would kill him," Diamonds argued.

"Hearts does tend to kill people," Clubs said, monotone.

"Thanks for the add-in there, Clubs," Spade said flatly.

"No prob. But, seriously, he does have a point, Diamonds. Besides, we both know that Hearts has the most claim to this one. If one of us killed him, there's a fair chance she'd kill us too."

Diamonds opened her mouth to argue, then she shut it. That did sound like Hearts. "Fuck it," Diamonds said. She nudged Clubs. "That a two player game?" she asked.

"Yep."

"Hand me a remote."

"I call next," Spade chimed in.

Chapter 25: The Last Date of Your Life

Aedon woke up next to Victoria. She opened her eyes, and then covered them. "Oh, crap!" she said, standing up and rushing to the bathroom.

"I didn't think I was that ugly in the sunlight!" Aedon called, smiling.

"It's not that," a voice called from the other side of the bathroom door. "I slept with my contacts in." She emerged two minutes later, wearing a black slip-over nightgown and large black-rimmed nerd-chic glasses.

"Aw now that's just not fair," Aedon said. "How are you going to get even more cute?"

She crossed the room and kissed him. His lower body was still covered by the blanket, only his chest showing – his chest of chiseled muscle and scars. She kissed his lips and pushed him onto the bed. "You are so freaking sexy," she said, teasing him.

"You are so adorable I can't stand it," Aedon said as he looked at his love.

"Sweetheart, you had no problem standing last night," she rubbed her nose against his.

"Sweetheart, is it?"

"I gave you a pet name; sue me."

"There are a lot of things I would do to you; suing you isn't one of them," Aedon smiled, placing a quick peck on her lips.

"So what do you have planned for us today?" Victoria asked, resting her hands on his pectorals. Her chin rested on her hands.

"Well, I was thinking we hadn't done the traditional mall date yet, and I know that may seem cliché to you, but I absolutely have to live it."

"Sigh, I am dating such a child," Victoria smiled, kissing his nose. "I'll get dressed." Victoria sat back up and turned to walk to her dresser.

Aedon slapped her butt as she went and she laughed. When she had finished pulling her dress over her head Aedon had stood up and was walking over to the corner of the room to which Victoria had thrown his pants. Victoria was fixing her hair in the mirror.

"Damn, that's a nice ass," Victoria said. Aedon saw her observing him in the mirror as he pulled up his pants. After they were both wearing clothes, Aedon grabbed Victoria's hand and ran out of the door with her.

* * *

As they entered the mall, Aedon looked around, almost searching for something.

"What are you looking for, Aedon?"

A broad smile spread across his face. "That," he pointed.

It was an old-fashioned photo booth. The kind that gave the photos back in a strip. Victoria rolled her eyes.

"I am dating such a child."

"You bet you are. Now live with it," he laughed.

They sat in the photo booth. Afterward, Aedon printed two copies. Giving one to Victoria, they began to look at the shops. They browsed for hours. Then, as they took a break for lunch, Victoria had to ask.

"Aedon, are you in trouble?"

Aedon choked on his Chinese food. "Why do you ask?"

"I ask because you're a runaway experiment. I would think that they'd be after you by this point."

"Well, they were. As soon as I left they sent some people named the Tens after me. It didn't work out too well for them. So I guess they decided it was better to leave me alone after that."

Victoria frowned. "I just would have figured they'd have sent someone by this point. You are kinda important aren't you?"

"I'm expensive," Aedon laughed, "but you know what I have always wanted to do?"

"What?" she asked with a twinkle in her eye.

Aedon leaned forward onto the food court table. "I've always wanted to see a movie. I never have before."

Victoria laughed. It was a typical date. Walking around the mall, going to a movie, taking the cheesy photo strip, but with Aedon it felt different. The sheer wonder in his eyes, like everything was special, made it feel special to her as well.

"I don't think there's anything good out right now."

"Let's go anyways."

Victoria smiled. "All right."

They went to the movie theater inside the mall, catching the first showing. It was a movie called *The Rain Falls on the Green Man*. It was nonsensical, impressionist garbage — low budget and terrible, but they weren't really paying attention to it anyways. Another thing Faceless wanted to experience was the simple joy of making out during the movie.

After the movie they made their way back to Victoria's room.

Chapter 26: Another Love Scene

Aedon kissed Victoria. There was a different tone to his kiss this time, Victoria noticed. Almost a rushed passion, like he was trying to soak up as much of her as he could.

"Sorry. I'm kinda in a rush," Aedon said.

"Why's that?"

"Sweetheart, we got pretty physical last night. I liked it."

"Haha, it's just sex."

"No it isn't. It was making love, to the woman I love."

Victoria pushed him away slightly and looked in his eyes. "That you love?" she asked in disbelief, searching his eyes for a sign of doubt.

Aedon smiled. "That I love. That I had thought I loved since I carried her out of the rain. But no, I love you now. I didn't really know this is how love felt until I met you again. Everything from before was this idealistic fantasy. But you, with me now, proves to me that maybe we aren't as far from that fantasy as I thought."

Victoria smiled. She chose to believe that. And she chose to believe that for a very important reason.

"I love you too," She said; she was able to without any hesitation. She should have felt some, simply because it was so soon. She should have felt like it was overbearing; she should have been uncomfortable with the love that was in his look, but she didn't. She could only feel safe with him; she could only feel love; it was like she'd never felt in her whole life. She had dreamed about him since she had met him. She had obsessed over him, hated him; he had consumed her. This was a man that she had obsessed over. Loving him felt like the next natural step.

She kissed him; they had strayed near her bed. Victoria looked at the bed and saw that there wasn't anything valuable laying on it.

"The bed," she said; she was on the precipice of losing herself in ecstasy. She wanted to with the one she loved and to prove to herself that it wasn't just sex; it could be making love. It had never been making love.

Aedon tore himself away from her lips. He looked at the bed and relented. With a passionate sweep of his arm, he flung the miscellaneous items and paint brushes off the bed, save for a few, which stubbornly rolled to the corner of the bed.

"I think that's good enough," he growled with a smile. She giggled as he threw her onto the bed.

* * *

He closed his eyes as his hands ran along her; he tried to remember how her body felt. He wanted to memorize every curve of her body, every soft inch of her skin, and her warmth. He knew there was a good chance he wasn't coming back, and he wanted every bit of who she was burned into his mind.

The window of her room slowly began to fog from the heat of their bodies.

* * *

After an impressive amount of time, Victoria repositioned herself next to him; as their breathing began to level out again, Victoria kissed him, planting a soft peck on his cheek.

"I do love you," she said. She looked at him, streaks of paint on her cheeks.

"I love you too," he smiled. She felt the slight tug of the paint handprints drying along her body. Aedon reached over, knocking aside already-spilled paint buckets and pushing brushes that betrayed her ticklish side off the bed; he turned off the light and the couple lay together in the darkness. Victoria laid her head onto Aedon's chest, and after a his heart had sung its soft lullaby under her ear, Victoria fell asleep.

* * *

Aedon closed his eyes, pretending to sleep. He felt the gentle breeze of her breath on his chest; eventually it slowed, and Aedon knew she was asleep.

Aedon slid out from under her, careful not to wake her. He grabbed a pen and some paper and wrote her a letter, explaining that he had to go and that there was something of which he needed to take care. He wrote about the Kings, and what he was about to do. He promised he would return. He placed the letter down next to her on her nightstand. He grabbed his pants, resolving that he would need to go by his hidden stash of weapons. He would need his sword and his gun if he were to take on the Kings. He pulled on his shirt and it slowly slid over the scars on his abs; he wondered how many more would join them. He tied his boots with a quiet resolve. As he stood up and prepared to leave, he spared a moment to kiss the forehead of his Girl in the Rain, of the woman he loved.

Before he walked out the door, he rested his hand on the door-jam and gazed at her nightstand. There was a picture, one of Victoria next to her sister. The sister had signed the picture. *Love you, V,* it said. Next to the letter something caught his eye. It was the necklace he gave her all those years ago. The necklace was on top of Victoria's copy of the photo booth's film strip. For a moment, Faceless thought it was strange that her copy had one less than his. He brushed aside these thoughts as a glint of moonlight caught his attention.

The moonlight glinted off the hand-bent, intricate heart necklace. The one he'd given her all those years ago. The one she'd still kept. His eyes drifted from the strip to the necklace to her.

He had to come back.

Chapter 27: Not a Life

Faceless waited for Spade on the roof of Pierre's, a restaurant a half a block down from the gallery he called home. It was fancy, French cooking; although when in France, that wasn't so special. Faceless was wearing a tan trench-coat. It was stolen, but such offenses seemed inconsequential to a man who thought he was about to die.

Faceless was humming Beethoven again. It was his nervous habit, and he had every reason to be nervous, considering what he was up against. Faceless heard a sound and looked up. Off the roof of the next building, Spade jumped down. His black sweeper jacket bellowed out behind him like a cape. There were two slit holes down the back. He wore a black Henley shirt, and his pants matched. It was his war gear. His landing was effortless.

"Why didn't you run?" Spade asked.

Faceless took out his copy of the photo strip he had of the woman he loved. He looked from it to Spade and then shrugged. "Where would I have run? The Kings would have followed me everywhere I went. Victoria and I would have ran forever, constantly looking over our shoulders, and waited for the day you and they would come. Ray, that's no way to live."

Spade beat his fist on his chest; his face contorted as it expressed the deepest mixes of rage and caring.

"It would have been a life!" he shouted, furious at Faceless. "You idiot! You walked into this! There's no way you can escape. Now I have to kill you." His voice petered out and became a whisper.

Faceless's face showed how sad he was. "You were the best friend I've ever had Spade. Hell, you were the only friend."

Faceless pulled off his trench-coat. He was wearing the body armor he had taken from the Ten. Strapped to his back was the samurai sword and on his hip the gun. Around his belt were multiple spare clips.

Spade's collar beeped. His voice echoed, hollow. "They're here."

Without a sound, Clubs and Diamonds landed on either side of Spade.

"Finally!" Diamonds said. "You have no idea how long I've been wanting to kill you."

"I know, and I'm going to try my hardest to stop you. I don't really have any malice against you. I just want my happiness," Aedon looked at Spade with a sad smile. "She's my happiness, Ray; I have to protect my happiness."

"Shit," Spade said.

He drew his arms across his chest and curled his back. Metallic wings shot out of his jacket. Each feather was its own razor sharp blade. They were attached to him with a harness. Either side of the harness had five rings on it; he slid his fingers into the rings and unlocked them. He spread his arms wide and attached to each ring was a razor wire leading to the bladed feathers. With these, control was second nature.

"Shit. Shit! SHIT!" Spade said, striking out with anger.

* * *

With a few expert movements of his fingers, Spade struck with his razor wings. They pierced into the chest of his victim like a spear. Faceless's eyes widened as he saw the blood dripping. Clubs fell to his knees. He felt shock and disbelief as he clutched the metal wings sticking out of his chest.

The wings were cutting into his lungs; he could feel it. Clubs gurgled and spat up blood. Clubs reached his hand to the wing and gripped the feather-like blade as he looked Spade in the eyes. Clubs's existence had been a horrible nightmare, even to himself. He lived off the blood and body of others, and he didn't know how many nights he'd laid awake, unable to shake the terrible memories of what he'd done. It had simply been easier to accept that he was a monster. It made him feel less like everything was his fault.

Clubs smiled at Spade and a single tear fell down the monster's cheek as he slid off of Spade's wing. He crumpled to the ground, dead before he hit it, smiling.

* * *

Diamonds was shocked. She was afraid for her life; because while she was fairly certain she could take Spade by himself, or Faceless by himself for that matter, she doubted she could take both. Luckily she wouldn't have to. The collars that Spade, Diamonds, and the dead Clubs wore started to glow red and beep.

"She's here," Spade said, turning pale. Diamonds recognized the fear in Spade's voice. It mirrored her own; they both feared what the collar meant, but for the first time Diamonds's fear of the red glow and beep was accompanied by a fearful laugh.

"Who's here?" Faceless asked.

"Hearts," Diamonds said, throwing a dagger at Faceless.

Faceless reacted just fast enough. He drew his sword, and with that drawing motion he knocked away the dagger. With another swift movement he locked blades with Diamonds. A loud clang echoed throughout the night air. He blocked her perfectly.

"You know my moves?" Diamonds asked in disbelief. The little bastard was blocking her perfectly.

"Of course I do. I was NightCard's contingency plan against the Kings. Why do you think they sent four of you after me?"

Their blades separate; they jumped apart from each other.

"All right. You copy my moves, but how about my speed?"

* * *

Faceless's eyes widened as Diamonds shouted her battle cry. She dove at him, drawing her other sword from behind her back. She slashed at him with a speed that shamed lightning. Faceless barrel-rolled as the sword made impact, but he felt it: he was cut, and part of his face fell off. His eyes widened. She was fast.

Fighting Diamonds and watching her moves on a hologram were two very different things. In the hologram he was objective, studious. In real life, when her blades were pointed at his head, everything changed. She was unbelievably fast – faster than the video. It was then that Faceless made a horrifying realization: NightCard had slowed the video down.

Faceless spared a moment to look for Spade, wondering where he went.

Chapter 28: Spade Versus Hearts

Spade went to the Eiffel Tower. He was on the viewing deck, waiting. He looked over the city. He thought about what he'd done, the man he'd just killed, and thinking about his newest and only friend.

He finally heard what he'd been waiting for. "Hello, Hearts," Spade said; he was still looking at the Paris skyline.

A woman dressed in black landed behind him. She wore a slim biker's helmet and a skintight suit; she had a sword on her back and was wearing a gun belt that hung loosely on her hips.

"Hello, Spade." The voice chilled Spade; he blamed it on the wind at the top of the Tower. He turned to face her.

Her sheer presence was incredible. There was a tremendous pressure about her. It was a pressure that made his core tell him to run. Spade knew he was going to die that night.

"So here's the deal, I have to protect Faceless," Spade said, trying his best to appear brave.

"I think we both know, Spade, that you'll fail on that, and that after I kill you, I'm going after Faceless and that little bitch of his."

"So I can't convince you to walk away?"

"It's not looking likely," she scoffed.

"Well, then I guess I should just walk away, lay down, and make this easy on myself right?"

"Probably a good idea."

There was a moment of silence.

"You know I can't do that," Spade said, reaching behind his back and grabbing the rings for the wing blades.

"Yeah, you're a stubborn ass."

"No," Spade smiled. "I'm just tired of being the bad guy. I want to be one of the heroes. No good story only has one."

Hearts threw a knife at Spade, who reacted and blocked it with a metal wing. The blade would have struck between his eyes. Spade knew that, and it terrified him.

Hearts was in front of him in the span of the time it took to blink an eye. He barely parried her attack and jumped away.

"Wow, Spade, I remember you being a little better at this."

Spade slid his fingers into the other rings and spread both of his wings. He rushed at Hearts and attacked her. He missed, his wing slicing into one of the support beams of the tower. "Damn it!" Spade knew he couldn't let her see that he was flustered. He attacked her again, and once more, she dodged easily. Again, his wings only met the cold steel of the tower.

"Please, Spade, make this a challenge." Hearts rushed at him, she feigned an attack to his face and struck his ACL with her heel. The sheer force of the blow tore into it, and Spade crumpled backwards. He threw his wings in front of him; it was the only thing that forced Hearts to back off.

He tried to stand. He couldn't place any weight on his left leg. She was toying with him. He still had one good leg. He used one of his wings as a crutch, making it hold his weight. She had simultaneously cut his maneuverability and his attack in half. At the same time, she had created a blind side in his defenses.

He rushed her again, propelling himself with his right leg and his left wing, catapulting himself at her. She was surprised, but she dodged him. To his surprise though, he was able to cut into her shoulder.

The blow was a glancing one, and his wing buried itself into another support beam. With the other hand, he was able to knock off her helmet. The face that met him was covered with a cloth mask. The mask was black and had a blood-red heart drawn across it. The visible lips and the chin provided proof of an amazingly beautiful woman hiding under it, a beautiful woman who showed a stunned expression on her face. Spade could only see a flash of platinum blond hair before Hearts jumped around behind him.

For a moment of time, Spade thought that he might win; he thought that he could go back to Faceless; he could escape NightCard; he could finally be happy.

His thoughts distracted him just long enough for Hearts to find an opening. Spade looked down, and saw Hearts's sword pushing further into his left lung. "Damn it," Spade wheezed, coughing blood. "I was counting chickens."

"What?" Hearts asked.

"Nothing, it's just something I learned in a bar."

He coughed blood into his mouth, collecting it and grabbed the sword with the other. He ran himself through with the sword and pulled Hearts closer to him. He spat the blood from his mouth into her eyes. Hearts was momentarily blinded.

He reached her belt and felt for her BloodVial, crushing it in his hand. She may have won, but she wouldn't be getting his powers. He folded his wings around her.

He kissed her. Hearts pushed him off her. "You're a player to the very end," she grinned, his blood on the corner of her lips.

Spade pushed himself onto her and leaned into her ear. "He'll beat you, you know." His voice was soft; his whisper was wet and thick from the blood in his mouth.

"1343? We'll see about that."

"But the secondary hero can't go out without a grand exit." He reached into his pocket and pushed a button.

The explosives that he had set on different levels of the Eiffel Tower began to explode in sequence. The cuts he'd made to the tower were causing it to fall down around them, cutting off Hearts' escape.

"You'd die to save 1343?" Hearts asked as the floor beneath them began to rumble.

"His name is Aedon Saint," Spade said, the metal sinking on one side.

"There are no more Saints," Hearts said. "I killed the last one."

Spade didn't hear her. As the light left his eyes Spade, all Spade thought about was Aedon and Victoria; he hoped they'd have their happy ending. He smiled as the Eiffel Tower fell apart around them.

Chapter 29: Evenly Matched and a Fast Learner

Faceless was staring at Diamonds. The woman was a King, and he was winded; then again, so was she. They looked at each other, glaring. The cool, Paris breeze was cutting through the alley.

"So this is kinda sad," Faceless said.

"How's that?"

"Even if I beat you, I still have to go find Spade."

There was an explosion sound, and they both looked. The Eiffel Tower was falling to the ground. It was just then that Diamonds' collar beeped, blinked red and blue then went back to green. Diamonds smiled. "I don't think you'll have to worry about that."

"What?" Faceless asked, his stomach tightening.

"That red-blue sequence means Spade just died." She pointed to her collar.

The color drained from Faceless's face. "No."

"Yep, so I'm going to kill you then go after that bitch of yours." Faceless loosed a shot at Diamonds. The edge of her sword, the incline of the blade tip, redirected the bullet harmlessly away. "Temper."

Diamonds shot back, but Faceless did the same deflection, only he did so as he charged. He spun and the sword came around, but Diamonds blocked the sword with her gun barrel. With her sword she jolted forward; Faceless barely saw it in time to move.

He didn't quite make it. Instead he chose to move enough to where it wouldn't kill him. The blade punctured his body, but avoided any vital organs. Faceless loosed a shot at her head and then quickly slid the blade out at the exact angle of penetration, avoiding any more damage.

He was bleeding, and it was bad. His hand pressed to the wound, blood flowing out of it. "Well, that hurts," Faceless said, forcing a chuckle.

"You're buddies with Spade, aren't you? I figured you're used to being stuck by this point."

Faceless avoided another slash aimed at his face. "That's just rude. Can't we just have a nice, civil death fight?" Diamonds' response was another, faster attempt to lop off his head. "I suppose not then."

Faceless back-spun and kicked at Diamonds who jolted back and swatted away Faceless's blow.

"We've both been trained by Hearts, haven't we? I recognize these moves," Faceless said.

"Yes, that's true, and I was the only one to ever cut her during training. That's why I've got this scar," Diamonds said, pointing to the tears in her suit. Faceless could see a continuous scar that ran along the tears. "Hearts hit me because she was happy."

Faceless cringed. That sounded like Hearts, and this is the same Hearts who was coming to kill him; that's what he had to remember. Hearts was coming, and Diamonds wasn't the end boss. She was just a mid-level – a mid-level with a very sharp sword.

Faceless's only thought at that moment was that this was going to suck. As the blade came at him again, he took it under his arm, trapping it in his armpit, getting cut by the blade with a shallow, long cut. He took the opportunity to slice into her leg. All he could manage was a minor slice. It wasn't really worth the surprisingly large amount of blood coming out of his armpit. He retreated.

"Come on now, I'm a King. Did you really think that a stupid-ass stunt like that would stop me?"

Faceless was beginning to get woozy from the loss of blood. "I was hoping so," he chuckled. "I don't think I'll win if we drag this out."

"See? Who tells someone that, especially when they're trying to kill you?" Diamonds chuckled.

"It is if it's a guy that is trying to relax your guard. You see this massive bleeding? That's just a diversion."

"Really?"

"No, I'm pretty screwed here."

They laughed and rushed at each other again. Aedon could tell she was learning. Every move he used was becoming less and less effective. She was his match, and she was getting better. Soon Faceless would run out of tricks. The blades kept colliding; the bullets kept either being blocked by gun barrels or redirected by the blade edges. Faceless would have to finish this soon. He still needed to put as much distance between himself and Hearts as he could; he couldn't let this lesser fight slow him down.

A particularly strong swing from Diamonds knocked him out of his thoughts. He fell, rolling backwards and sliding on the scabbard on his back. By the time he got to his feet, Diamonds was already sprinting towards him. Faceless could feel that this might well be it.

At least he wouldn't die in that damn cage. His thoughts went back to Victoria. "Fuck dying," he said to psyche himself up. "I just found her."

He looked and saw a puddle of alley muck to his left. He threw his sword at the approaching Diamonds, and she knocked it to one side.

* * *

As Diamonds prepared for the swing, she saw 1343 pick up a handful of street sewage. He threw it at her eyes. She reacted impulsively and flung her hand in front of her eyes to block the mud. The next thing she heard was a gunshot. She bucked back and hit the ground with a thud. She had been shot in the throat, and she pressed her hand to the left side of her neck. She could feel every pump bringing her closer. She looked at 1343; he had his hand on his hip; her mind went to Spade.

Diamonds collapsed backward against one of the buildings in the alley. As the light faded from her eyes, her final thoughts were that if it weren't for Spade showing that move, she'd still be alive. Spade, not 1343, had messed with her again.

The blood trickled from her head, beginning to touch the scar she had on her chest; it moved gently like a kiss. Its warmth reminded her of a kiss from a man she once loved.

"I don't want to say it back," she said without thinking. Her eyes closed, and her thoughts went back to his eyes.

Chapter 30: Unearthed Graves

The wreckage of the Eiffel Tower was twisted and sharp – and loud. It was really, really loud; there were clanging sounds of metal pieces hitting each other and police sirens on their way.

One particularly heavy piece was still moving. It finally lifted, amazingly by one hand, torn and bloody. The steel girder fell to the side harmlessly, and out slumped Hearts.

"Damn it," she thought aloud. She hadn't expected Spade to tear down a national monument. She had to smile. Her student was still surprising her. Well, not anymore – now he was dead. "He did make a nice shield though," she continued aloud, wiping Spade's blood off her body. She was herself unhurt.

Hearts looked at the broken BloodVial stain on her hip. The only good thing about Spade had died with him – not that she needed his ability. What she needed was to try and find Faceless. That stupid bastard; he had such potential – if only he hadn't run away, if only he hadn't tried for the illusion of freedom.

She tried to remember when she was childish like that. When she thought that things like "freedom" were important. She thought about the word for a second – what a joke. She remembered Joan Saint, and her thoughts went back to the Black Joker's Playroom.

* * *

"With freedom comes worry, and with worry there is hesitation. Hesitation, in the field of battle, will kill you," the Black Joker said, throwing a woman on the floor.

NightCard's torture expert wore a black jester suit and a white jester mask. The mask was splotched with black paint. Black paint, as well as the gore of his previous patients. He was often a fan of fixing his "patients" with his "toys," found in his Joker's Playroom, where they found themselves.

The Playroom of NightCard was square and white from top to bottom. Hearts looked on from the corner of the room, as Joan Saint was disciplined.

"There is nothing wrong with wanting to be free," Joan said, blood tainting the corner of her mouth.

"So you keep telling 1343. You let him get away, Joan. You let him escape. We finally caught him, but for every second you let him escape, you are going to be punished. Each second you let him escape is going to be one more hour I spend teaching you. You need to learn, Miss Saint, that 'freedom' is a bad, bad thing."

"Why's that?" Joan spat in rebellion; she incited another blow from the Black Joker.

"Because, you stupid bitch, freedom is separation from the group – separation from the family, and family keeps us alive." He knelt down beside Joan Saint. "Our family isn't very forgiving, and leaving our family? Well, that's not an option."

A NightCard agent walked in with a silver briefcase. Underneath the jester mask that Black Joker wore, Hearts knew a demented smile was spreading. "Oh they brought me my fun toys, Joan. Now we get to fix you."

"Fix me?" she asked, her eyes wide.

"Yes, sweet, ignorant Joan – you're broken. You've got ideas in your head, that are so bad for you – so terrible. I am going to help you get them out; I'm going to rescue you."

Joan Saint's eyes widened as the Black Joker pulled a particularly nasty looking "toy" from the case.

* * *

Hearts made it back to Diamonds and Clubs. The bodies were burnt. That meant Faceless knew about BloodWine. Hearts had half-hoped Diamonds would have killed the bastard; she had more important shit to do. She hated seeing Faceless. She hated seeing that innocent look in his eyes, and that playful smile – it sickened her. No one had the right to be innocent, not when they were born as an experiment.

Hearts kicked the deceased Diamonds' head off its charred body. "Stupid bitch. Completely worthless."

Hearts would have to find Faceless again. She wondered what Faceless was doing with his last few breaths.

Chapter 31: Plastic Smiles

Jenny, the receptionist for the Descartes Plaza Hotel, was busying herself with her nails when an average looking red-headed man with freckles all over his body walked hand-in-hand with a petite woman. She had long eyelashes with shoulder length straight, black hair and gaudy ruby red lipstick. Jenny just hoped they didn't come to her. They walked up to the desk.

"My name is Gerald Truman," Gerald said, his girlfriend smiled past her black-rimmed nerd chic glasses, "and this is my hot girlfriend Lindsey. She's totally out of my league, but I have an amazing personality, so it worked."

Lindsey chuckled. Jenny smiled a fake, plastic smile. She dealt with amateur comedians all day. Gerald smiled back with the same one.

"We don't have a reservation. Do you have anything?"

"We have a room in the west wing. You'll like it. Plus it's far, far away from the lobby," Jenny said.

"Well, I hate the atmosphere of the lobby anyways, so we'll take it."

Chapter 32: A Moment's Peace

Lindsey and Gerald got to their room and closed the door behind them. They kissed each other softly, slowly treasuring what time they had and enjoying a moment's peace. "Hold on, let me get this stupid wig off," she said. Victoria took off the wig, and carefully peeled off one of her fake eyelashes. "You know," she said slowly, pausing to take off the other eyelash, "if I had your abilities, doing my makeup in the morning would go so much faster."

Gerald peeled off his face. After a few moments it hardened back into Aedon Saint.

"Victoria, I think we both know you don't wear makeup." He leaned close to her and kissed her neck. "I would have tasted it," he said with a gentle growl.

"Shut up," she said playfully, and threw him gently onto the bed. He pulled her by her hips as he fell. She landed on top of him gently.

"I want to enjoy tonight," she said, her face inches from his.

He placed a gentle kiss on her lips. He pulled a strand of her platinum blond hair out of her face.

"I'm simply happy I'm spending another night with the woman I love."

She smiled. "I love you too," she said.

Faceless kissed her softly; he gently ran his hands over her body – as though it was their first time exploring her body.

He couldn't believe she was his, but more important, he couldn't believe he was hers.

* * *

A half hour later they were holding each other, content.

Faceless nuzzled her with a playful growl. Her mood had shifted though. Now she seemed disconcerted. "What's wrong?"

"I just don't know how we're going to run," Victoria said. "We're just… I don't see it."

Faceless rolled over. He was now taking a long look in her eyes, trying to guess her mood. "We've made it so far.

We just need to get enough money to America. I just need some time to heal. I'm not quite done yet. Diamonds got me pretty good, but, when I'm full-strength, everything should be fine. We just need to get away from here."

Chapter 33: Underground Fights and an Old Friend

A red-headed woman in a skimpy black dress walked into a seedy biker bar. She was wearing the kind of dress that attracted attention. Everything about this woman seemed to radiate the urge for attention, and to demand that she be noticed; that was the kind of woman she needed to be right now.

A rough meat-head walked up to her as she approached the bar.

"Buy you a drink?" he growled; his eyes were already undressing.

"I'm waiting for my boyfriend, thanks," she said, ignoring him. "Plus that was hardly even a sentence."

"Come on, whatever he's got's nothing. I'm known as Donkey in some circles. Some very tight circles." He laid his hand on the woman's arm.

She looked down at the hand. "Shouldn't have done that," she said with an over-exaggerated sigh.

Into the woman's view, a biker with an iron grip grabbed the meat-head between his thumb and the outside of his hand. The new man squeezed, quickly breaking the knuckles and twisted, spiral fracturing the asshole's arm. The muscle-head yelled for a second, then another arm slammed his face into the bar, knocking him unconscious. The man who broke his arm stood there; his hair was long and his eyes were blue, radiating a cold indifference and dressed in biker leather.

* * *

"Ah, so you're here for the fights, then?" the bartender asked the man, pushing the unconscious asshole off his bar and onto the floor. The arm-breaking man nodded. "Sign up's over there," the bartender said, gesturing with his eyes as he wiped off the blood from his counter.

The man looked at his woman and grimaced. It was part of the plan, to have her be that enticing. That way someone would make a move. He needed the cred. The man with the iron grip and the skimpy red-head went to the designated corner for sign up. As they filled out the paperwork, the bar staff were moving tables and placing mats on the floor.

"All right guys, today's challenger – who's obviously never seen one of the defender's fights – is Robert Long. His prize, one thousand dollars, which he can use as a deposit on his hospital bills."

Faceless took his position on one corner of the mat; he gave Victoria one more look, still upset by her outfit, then turned for the biggest surprise so far.

"You ready? Don't go easy on me because I'm an old man now – or do; I'll still hurt you just as bad."

Faceless's stood for a second in amazement; Patterson stood before him. "No way."

This time he wasn't tied to a wall.

* * *

"What are you mumbling to yourself?" Patterson asked.

"It's nothing; I just wasn't expecting to hit a brittle old man today," the boy said to Patterson with a mocking tone. Patterson's mouth pursed into a line. He didn't know why, but this kind of insolence seemed familiar.

"Begin!" the announcer said from his safe spot outside of the ring. Patterson rushed his opponent, thinking it a typical bout and he wanted to end it fast.

With a speed he wasn't expecting, the boy blocked Patterson, and kicked him. The man grabbed the biker's leg and flung him away; the biker rolled and was back on his feet. Patterson smiled. "All right, maybe this will be more fun than I thought."

"I know I'm enjoying myself," the biker said.

Within a few seconds, Patterson's opponent charged at him, going into a classic boxer's stance and punching Patterson with a straight right.

Patterson blocked and delivered his own straight right. With as much force as he could. He felt he could let himself go a little more with this opponent.

* * *

The punch caught Faceless off guard, but not because he wasn't expecting it. So he took the punch. What he wasn't expecting was the sheer force of it. He'd forgotten what one of Patterson's punches felt like. He went flying. Apparently Patterson had been holding back when he would occasionally hit Faceless.

"Hrgk," Faceless grunted. He staggered up. Patterson gave him a look of disbelieving shock. "Let's try that again," Faceless said, returning to his boxer's stance.

He went in close to Patterson, this time switching to a southpaw's stance halfway through. He delivered the force of a right hand's straight with a jab and then followed through with his own southpaw left. The blow connected to the tip of Patterson's jaw; the man stayed on his feet, but Faceless could tell he was dazed.

Faceless shifted his weight down and delivered a strong left hook to Patterson's body. Patterson buckled, and Faceless caught him in the temple with an elbow.

Patterson slumped down, and Faceless watched him fall. Patterson didn't move. He was knocked out.

"I owed you that one, dick," Faceless said, walking away.

He walked to the announcer, who handed him the thousand dollars fearfully. Faceless smiled at him.

"Don't worry man, you didn't shoot my ass full of Happy Juice." Faceless took the money and walked away. "Come on, sexy," Faceless said in his biker voice; he grabbed Victoria around the waist and strutted out. They left a crowd of astonished, semi-sober patrons in their wake; only half of them were sober enough to remember the details of it in the morning.

Chapter 34: What's in a Reflection

Faceless was in the bathroom of their hotel room. He'd taken a couple of shots to the face, and he was carefully peeling off the remains of his biker persona. "Damn it; that hurts." He looked at his reflection. He looked at his True Face harden back into Aedon Saint. A man like Faceless was never sure what his real face was. His True Face needed to harden quickly, never exposed for long. It could get damaged.

If he had to constantly be wearing another face, who was he really? He touched Aedon Saint in the mirror. Aedon was just pieces of others, thrown together. Victoria walked in and held him. "Who am I?" he asked her. Victoria's frown in the mirror's reflection asked for clarification. "I created this face from different pieces of men in a magazine. Except the eyes. I used a woman's eyes."

"That explains why they made me jealous," she chuckled. He turned to her, to show her he was really hurting, deeper than physically. "Aedon," she started, reaching out to touch his hand on his face, "so what?"

"What?" His face betrayed his surprise.

"So what if you're a collection of pieces of people? So am I. You think that every piece of me is totally original? No, most of what I am are pieces of family. My eyes are the same as my mother's. My father gave me my ears. My teeth I got from my grandma; I'm just a bunch of good chromosomes and bad chromosomes. That's all anyone is, just a collection of others, of our family."

He smiled; he thought for a second and closed his eyes. When he opened them, they were the same color as hers. "There," he said. "Now you're a part of my family too."

She smiled and looked into her own eyes. "We were family before that. Genes aren't the only things that make us family, my love. Feelings are. Family loves, and family is who we choose to be with, not who we have to be with. I choose to be with you."

Faceless pulled her close. "I choose to be with you, too," he said.

"I wouldn't have it any other way."

They took a moment's peace together. They had a big day tomorrow.

Chapter 35: Plane Tickets and Security Checks

An Emo girl with cropped-short black hair and scene glasses walked down the airport walkway. She and her boyfriend, an equally Emo boy with a fauxhawk and eye shadow, were standing in an airport. They were waiting in line to buy airline tickets.

"You said Ray gave you these passports before he died?" the scene girl asked.

"Yep," Fauxhawk answered.

"It's that easy?"

"Yep. Let's move on."

"Sure, sweetheart; we're next anyways."

"Hey there, sweetlips," Fauxhawk said to the ticket counter lady.

"Wrong dialect, sweetheart," Scene-glasses girl leaned to her boyfriend.

"Hey, we'd like two tickets to England, please."

"Sure, why not," the ticket lady said; she seemed to ignore the sweetlips comment.

They handed over their money and went through security. Faceless waited for Victoria on the other side. As Victoria was walking towards him, a security guard stopped her. She looked confused, and the security guard grabbed her arm.

Faceless was powerless. If he moved, if he came to her aid, his cover was blown. So he waited. Hours passed; people passed. As he continuously changed from spot to spot in the airport, he began to worry. He had missed his plane, and he was getting anxious.

The airport had all-seeing fisheye lenses. What they saw, NightCard saw, and NightCard was looking very carefully. Faceless was able to escape the facial recognition that was constantly running, but he feared that Victoria hadn't; there was only so much that makeup and wigs could do. Faceless began to intertwine his fingers; his leg was bouncing. Finally, Faceless decided to go to Victoria's apartment.

* * *

When Aedon reached Victoria's apartment, there was a note held it place by a piece of tape. The image itself, looked gentle, taunting. Aedon picked up the note. Aedon's face paled. He dropped the paper. He turned and ran.

The abandoned factory on 8th, Experiment to Experiment, or she dies.

Chapter 36: A Special Kind of Fucked Up

Faceless showed up wearing the same uniform from his bout with the other Kings. He looked up at the abandoned factory; it was rotting. The smell of mold was in the wind. It was dark inside the building, and the sun was beginning to set. He would have an hour, maybe two, before he would be fighting blind. He breathed in one more breath of moldy air and walked in the front door.

"Hello there, Faceless," Hearts said. Faceless drew his sword in response to the voice coming from his right. He spun around to find himself facing a speaker box. "We haven't talked since you were a child. I am planning on killing you in the very near future. I've got a couple of surprises in store for you, between this bottom floor and me. So please, try your best to enjoy them, and remember,

Victoria is waiting for you. In case you're questioning it, yes, she's very much in danger."

Faceless stabbed the speaker with his sword. He looked up and noticed a camera staring back at him. He flipped it off and walked up the first flight of stairs.

* * *

On the tenth floor, Victoria sat, helplessly tied by rope that constricted her breathing. She was bitterly watching Hearts stare at a computer monitor. "Well, now that's just in bad taste," Hearts sighed, looking at Victoria and shaking her head. She walked away from the monitors, each looking at the floors between Aedon and herself. Victoria watched her approach, and she had the full view of the monitors between them.

Victoria looked at her. "You're a special kind of fucked up."

"You're damn right I am," Hearts smiled wickedly.

It was then that Victoria finally placed the voice. It took her forever. Victoria could hardly recognize it,; it had been lost in all that anger and madness. "Joan?" Victoria asked hesitantly. Victoria watched as Hearts pulled off her mask. "Oh, my god," Victoria gasped. It took her a second to recognize the remnants of her sister in Hearts. Victoria could finally see the ghost of her sister that was left in Hearts' eyes.

It was Joan, just with an older face; it was a face that had an evil smile perverting it.

"Hey, sis. It's been a while," Joan said, laughing. "Sorry, I'm going to kill your boyfriend." Hearts cracked Victoria on the side of the head and everything went black.

Chapter 37: Every Book Needs Zombies

Faceless hated stairs. "God, I hate stairs," he said.

It wasn't that he was out of shape, far from it; he simply hated the monotony of them. He turned a corner and saw darkness. There were no sources of light in this room, save for the one that was blinking overhead, and that was about to fizzle out.

He looked left to see if there were any of the surprises Hearts promised on this level. He looked right, back towards the stairs for this level, and came face to face with the reanimated flesh of a human. It wore the helmet of one of NightCard's guards.

Faceless jumped back, swinging. The head of the would-be zombie came off in a clean, smooth – albeit panicked – stroke. He watched the head as it rolled on the floor and stopped, facing him. The jaw of it snapped at him in vain; its eyes were lifeless. They weren't looking at him as a person; they only looked at him with a hollow hunger.

He recognized this thing. Joan had shown him this one time to prove a point.

"This is our Reanimation Project," he remembered her saying.

"That's pretty gruesome," a young Faceless had said.

"I know it is, but why do you think I am showing you this?"

"You want to traumatize me?"

"No, it's because this is a project NightCard is doing to save lives. Instead of sending in more soldiers that could die, NightCard has decided that it would be better and more economic to reanimate the dead. They don't want to use them in anything that requires a brain, but for raw killing; they reanimate just the animalistic, primitive parts of the brain to do the job. I want you to see them."

"Why?"

"Because you aren't them, Young One. You have a soul; you have free will. You're not just a tool for killing, and I want you to know that, even if I have to leave."

"Why would you leave?" Faceless shifted forward on his bed.

Joan smiled. "Sometimes things happen we can't always control. The Black Joker wants to have a talk with me. It's something about your getting away from us during our little field trip." Joan kissed his forehead and smiled, mussing his hair. "Just remember, Young One: you're more than that," she said, *gesturing at the pictures on the table.*

Another growl brought him back to the present. He then began to notice that more of them were coming down the stairs.

"Of course, it would be zombies."

Chapter 38: Cutting Through

Faceless held his katana in both hands, centering his weight. He looked at the horde amassing in front of him. The solitary florescent light overhead flickered for a second and came back to life.

He didn't want to kill them, but if it was between them and Victoria, then they didn't even merit a second thought.

They attacked; the light began to flicker again. Faceless raised his sword as the light began its strobe effect again. Each movement he had was like a slow shutter-speed camera, and in his mind, each time he sliced the head off one of the Reanimated, he felt more and more like the cold monster that had placed the poor things in his way.

They were collecting behind him, too many to fight off. One took a bite out of his shoulder. "Ow! Motherfu—" Faceless managed to get out, before the Reanimated clenched its bite harder. "Screw you, too!" Faceless said, ripping the Animated off him and biting its shoulder.

"AUGHH!" it growled.

"Hurts, right?" Faceless said, his teeth still clenched on its shoulder. He managed to wrench free his arm, and then he slid the katana between the bite victim's ribs.

He slid it out, taking the entrails with him. He spit out the chunk of zombie he had in his mouth, hoping that zombie wasn't communicable. He began to just swing wildly, and by the time he was finished, the walls were painted with splotches of gore and red.

He was exhausted. He looked at the staircase of which the Reanimated had walked out. He had to climb it.

"I really hate stairs," he groaned.

Chapter 39: Level 2

The second level of the factory was worse than the first. At least the first had a light source. It took a couple of minutes for Faceless's eyes to adjust. He didn't move until then. The only faint light that was coming into the room was from the stairs he just came from. The creature that was in front of him he was hardly able to make out.

"Any chance you're friendly?" Faceless asked. It growled at him. "That's a no?"

Then the black mass charged at him. The creature was almost up on him when Faceless's hyper-reflexes allowed him to slide the katana in between the thing's teeth. The force of it still knocked him onto his back.

He crashed through a rotted drywall. Using his feet he catapulted the beast over him and scrambled to stand. As quickly as it had come, the beast disappeared.

He calmed; he was too tired to panic. Faceless looked up, his eyes barely made out the lights; they didn't work, but still had bulbs in them. He smiled in the dark. With one quick motion, he slashed the katana against the bulbs and closed his eyes. The shards fell everywhere; some landed on him – and on the floor. He listened.

For a moment there was nothing. Then, as he readied himself again, he heard the cracking sound of bulb pieces crunching under the weight of the beast. He quickly drew his gun and shot the beast.

He heard the beast's dying cry and it landed on him. He felt warm blood fall on him. It took him a moment, but he realized it belonged to the creature.

With an almighty wrench he threw the beast off of him. He wasn't about to take any chances, and he cut the beast's head off.

He stood, weakened, and made his way to the next set of stairs.

* * *

Hearts watched Faceless as he made his way up the stairs. She had given him a few floors for a breather; it wouldn't have been any fun if he were completely exhausted.

She grabbed the still-unconscious Victoria, and dragged her to the ninth floor. Hearts remembered there was one more surprise; she smiled under her mask.

Chapter 40: Ninja

Faceless entered the seventh floor. There were no lights, and the eerie dark simply returned him a silent gaze. It took Faceless's superior eyes a moment to adjust to the dark. A small, dark figure walked out and looked at Faceless. In the dark only the silhouette of its head could be seen, but it visibly tilted its head to the side.

A narrow beam of light lit up Faceless. "Hello, 1343," a child's voice broke the darkness. The voice was young, but it distinctly lacked emotion.

"And you are?" Faceless asked.

"I am the Queen of Hearts," the boy's voice said.

"The Queen of Hearts?" Faceless asked. The boy simply stood there, and shrugged. "Well, you're kinda in the way between me and my woman. Could you move?"

"Yeah... no, that's not an option," the Queen of Hearts said. Then he chuckled again and pulled out two small knives.

"Are you sure you're old enough for the big boy knives?" Faceless asked, trying to provoke a reaction.

"You see, that would be funny if I wasn't about to kill you with them." The boy looked at Faceless. Then Faceless noticed that the air was becoming more humid. The air got more opaque, and then a fog seemed to radiate from around the Queen of Hearts.

"My body is able to create an aerosol that forces a chemical reaction with the air. The chemical gas is hydrogen sulfide." Faceless frowned and covered his mouth. Hydrogen sulfide was very dangerous, and he believed the Queen of Hearts; the smell of rotten eggs filled the air. He needed to find a way out of this before the classic effects of the gas killed him. "You really shouldn't have underestimated me," the Queen of Hearts said, his voice coming from somewhere in the fog.

Faceless looked around him. The room was now completely full of the gas. The boy was well hidden from him. There was a slash to his back. Faceless turned just in time to see the boy disappear back into the fog.

"This could be bad," Faceless said frowning.

* * *

Faceless wasn't doing so well. His body was beginning to ache, a side effect of the gas; the boy Queen was adding more and more new cuts as he struck from the swirling cloud of gas.

"This isn't exactly fair," Faceless choked out.

"It's not exactly supposed to be," the Queen said.

Faceless heard the misstep of the Queen. Faceless reached out quickly through the fog and grabbed the boy by his throat. He flung him down on the ground in front of him with all of his strength, which had become greatly diminished. Still, a less-than-prime Faceless was still a more-than-average human. The boy landed and his breath escaped from his chest. Then Faceless picked him up again and looked at him. He grabbed the boy's right hand and broke it.

"Ahh!" the boy cried.

Faceless stared at him. "Leave me alone," Faceless coughed. "Stop with the gas. I really don't want to hurt you. I like kids and you remind me of a younger me, except more gassy."

"Go to hell," the boy gasped. The boy smiled and chuckled slightly. He opened his mouth and Faceless was caught off guard as the boy sprayed hydrogen sulfide in his face.

"Damn it!" Faceless choked as he dropped the kid. Faceless looked around and pulled his sword out and swung it around in circles. It was wild and it was desperate, but Faceless could feel himself circling the drain.

Then he noticed the window. He ran to it and busted out. He swung around and used the sword to stab into the building. Then he threw another flash grenade into the room. One of the things Faceless knew of hydrogen sulfide was its tendency to explode.

The flash grenade rolled over in front of the Queen. "What's that? Oh, fuck."

The flash grenade exploded and the vapors ignited. The whole floor set on fire for fifteen seconds. When Faceless crawled back up, the stench of burnt hair hung in the oxygen-depleted air. On the ground lay the Queen of Hearts – or what was left of him.

"This didn't need to be this way," Faceless coughed. He struggled up the first steps to the vacant eighth floor.

Chapter 41: Young One

Faceless entered the ninth floor; he saw the woman that had scared him, scarred him, terrified him, and torn him: Hearts. Her face was masked behind a pure black, form-fitting mask and across the center was a blood-red heart. She wore a flack-jacket that covered hidden weapons strapped to her side; one of the weapons was in her hand. She was across the room, starring at him. Victoria was being choked, held at tonfa-point. Hearts's gun was in her other hand, aimed at Faceless. "I will kill her," Hearts said coldly.

"Hey, Hearts," Faceless said, sliding his sword back into its scabbard. "It's been a while."

Hearts began to walk right, keeping Victoria between Faceless and herself. Faceless moved parallel to her, keeping Hearts in the center of his vision.

Hearts stopped walking; she was in the center of the room, and Faceless was standing by the window. His shadow cast a silhouette on Hearts and Victoria. Using a move he'd learned from Spade, Faceless drew his gun. He was about to fire it when Hearts moved Victoria in front of the barrel, in an instant. Faceless froze right before he pulled the trigger.

"Come now; be smarter than that, Young One," Hearts condescended to him. Faceless frowned. Only one woman had ever called him Young One. Hearts pulled off her mask; Faceless saw Joan Saint's face staring back at him. "It really has been a while, Young One."

Faceless steadied his gun. "Bullshit; this is a trick."

Joan Saint snarled. "Believe it or not, I really don't give a shit. I'm going to kill you, then this little bitch."

Faceless wanted to doubt it, but he knew it was true. It was the way she said Young One. In that moment, he knew beyond a doubt this was the woman who had taken care of him all those years ago.

"Joan, I thought you had died," he said, lowering his gun.

"I did," Joan said, raising her gun and shooting at Faceless's chest. Faceless barely deflected the bullet from piercing his heart; he used the gun barrel to deflect the bullet away harmlessly; while he was distracted, Hearts appeared in front of him.

Faceless didn't make a move to stop her. He couldn't; she was his first Keeper. The first person he ever loved, his only family. She slammed her tonfa at him. He used his hand to protect himself. The force of the blow knocked him out the window. He grabbed at the tonfa to keep him from falling. Hearts held him up for a few moments; with a smile, she let go.

* * *

Black Joker looked at Joan Saint. Hearts was in the corner, where she never seemed to move, staring at Joan and the Black Joker. The Black Joker had a patch over his eye; it was a trophy from the one time he did mess up. His good eye looked at the severed head in front of him. Then he looked back at Joan. Her hand still had blood dripping from it. The kill was fresh.

"Well now, dear, it seems you have outdone yourself," he cackled.

"I just did as you requested," Joan said.

"You did more so," he said, nudging the head with his foot. His attention turned to Joan, and he stepped over the head. "You've grown my dear. You've come to accept the reality: family is all that we live for; it's all that you can allow yourself to care about. Family keeps you safe; family keeps you fed; family keeps you alive." It's even more

valuable than your best friend." He kicked the head again. It slammed into the wall with a wet thud; it left a blotch of red.

"I know, sir," Joan said. It wasn't acceptance; it wasn't belief. It was desire to make the pain stop. All that mattered was stopping that pain.

Black Joker got closer to her, his mouth inches from her ear. "I got you a present," he said, his voice a whisper dripping with excitement and venom.

"You didn't have to," Joan said humbly.

"Oh, but I did, my dear," Black Joker said, jumping up and moving to his case. Joan winced; her body had come to assume anything coming out of that case was horrible. The Black Joker pulled out a needle the length of Joan's hand. "This is something I really shouldn't give you," Black Joker debated with himself, "but I really can't think of a better way to celebrate your victory."

He looked at her. She was trembling. "Bend over," he said; his voice lost its usual playfulness. All that was left was the authority and the venom. She did. He grabbed her by her hair and threw her onto the chair. Shoving her head into the chair and with a mad laughter he stabbed the needle into the base of her brain. "You'll thank me for this!"

The BloodWine coursed through her body, and the Black Joker whispered in her ear, "This BloodWine is special my dear. It's the BloodWine of that boy you let get away for an afternoon; this is the BloodWine of Project Morph. Soon you will be faster, stronger, and more powerful than the best experiment we have. Consider it a gift. How do you repay my kindness, you ask? You participate in the Gene Coliseum."

Joan felt the burning sensation in every piece of her body. She looked around at everything – anything in the room that might have been able to save her. She saw Hearts in the corner; Hearts was the last thing she saw before her eyes rolled into the back of her head. She lost consciousness; Hearts looked on – always smiling.

* * *

Faceless was embarrassed. If he had cheeks, they would be burning red right now, but he didn't. The window had cut his face, and it hung off, tattered. His arm was dislocated, but more than that, his pride was even more in tatters. That woman, his mentor – who had always preached to him about peace and love and forgiveness – she had kicked his ass more thoroughly and completely than the other Kings combined. No one moved as fast as he did. More than that, she was faster; he didn't know how, but she was stronger than he was.

The first thing he did was pop his shoulder back into place. He decided to slam it into a wall. He stood there for a second, leaning against the wall. He couldn't believe this was really happening. She was Joan; she was the only one who had ever cared for him. She fed him and loved him; she put bandages on his wounds. Now she was trying to kill him. It wasn't he that mattered in his logic.

She was trying to kill Victoria. That was the only thing worth thinking about; he couldn't allow that.

He picked up the tonfa she had used and splinted it around the broken hand. It shouldn't take long to rejuvenate, but until it did, it was going to hurt like hell, and all the hand was good for was a club.

He got up and stumbled after Hearts, hoping it wasn't too late to save Victoria. Before that, he put his hand in his pocket and pulled something out. Faceless smiled and his face cracked even more.

"It's time for round two, bitch," Faceless said as he limped back into the building; he hoped the zombies were still dead.

Chapter 42: I Hope That Hurt

Faceless shuffled in just as Hearts held the gun to a still unconscious Victoria's head. She saw Faceless and instantly reacted by pulling Victoria in front of her. Joan or not, she was holding Victoria hostage.

He holstered his gun and pulled out his sword. "I won't shoot. Face me, experiment to experiment," Faceless said.

"Why would I do that? I have the advantage here," Hearts said.

"Because this whole thing was about you proving you are better than I am," Faceless said.

"I am better than you; I have the family," Joan said.

"Bullshit. You don't have a family. You have a group of homicidal psychopaths with really good genetics."

"You ran away from the family! You *never* run from the family!" Joan shouted; her spittle flew from her mouth.

That lesson was ingrained into her body a long time ago. She had the scars to prove it.

"Talk about that all you want, you're still using a gun and a hostage to beat me," Faceless said.

Joan's mouth snarled. "I can kill you regardless," she said, loosing a shot at him.

Faceless saw the bullet and deflected it with the sword. The bullet went harmlessly through the walls of the condemned building. "You can do better," Faceless said.

"Yeah I can," Hearts said. The room was big, the size of most houses. It was an abandoned factory, after all, and this was one of the sweatshop floors. There were tables, abandoned and strewn to the sides. "All right, Young One, let's see if you can kill me if I do this."

Faceless watched as Hearts reached for the corner of her face. She gave it a tug; it didn't come off; Faceless said nothing.

Faceless's sword glinted in the moonlight as Hearts pulled out her sword. Both of them were left handed, and they were both skilled; she was slightly faster. He pointed his left foot at her and slid the rest of his body away from her, minimizing the areas she could hit. It was a classic fencing pose.

"I won't underestimate you again," he said.

"You can't play it safe when you fight me," she said, charging and swinging down. He parried the blow, and she swung the gun around and loosed a shot at him. He immediately pulled his splinted hand around and parried the bullet with the tonfa's edge.

The bullet went towards her leg; Faceless moved his foot behind hers, and he trapped her leg in place. The bullet went into her thigh. It was a shallow wound, but it slowed her down and brought her attention to her leg. Faceless gave her a head-butt.

She fell back, and when Faceless looked at her again, part of his face had come off on hers.

"Damn," Hearts said as she shook her head.

"I hope that fucking hurt," Faceless said, smiling as his face cracked.

Hearts staggered backward and Faceless took this as an opportunity to try to get behind her. She recovered enough to parry the oncoming slash and even enough to attack back. She fired her gun and he blocked it with the tonfa.

Hearts noticed Faceless wince in pain. Although the tonfa held, the bullet was close range and had shocked the broken arm. She spun around and slammed the sword into his braced arm. Faceless caught the blade on the tonfa edge.

The force threw Faceless back against the wall and shattered the bones in his arm and wrenched his shoulder.

"Damn it," Faceless said as he cradled his arm. He stood up just as Hearts struck again. The force made him crash out the window. Faceless grabbed the ledge and flipped backwards. He crashed into the floor below him. "Hggk," Faceless sputtered. Broken glass cut into his face. Faceless ripped his face off. He pulled the glass out, and the stem cells began to heal. Faceless pulled some of the stem cells and rubbed them on his arm. The hyper-growth stem cells repaired the damage to the bones.

Soon the arm wasn't perfect, but it was manageable. Faceless pulled a sword off of one of the dead Reanimated. Then he checked his gun. Nine bullets left. "It's time for this bitch to die," Faceless spat, blood dripping from his mouth.

He concentrated hard and his body began to harden. It wasn't anything drastic, just slightly tougher than normal. His eyes began to almost glow a bright red. He twirled the sword around. It was time to be serious.

Chapter 43: A Death in the Family

Faceless decided that he should leave the tonfa on. It would make Hearts think his arm was still broken, and he could use every advantage. He ran up the stairs one more time.

"Damn it," he said, looking at her. "You made me climb those fucking stairs – again." Victoria was stumbling up in the corner. "Run!" Faceless told her; he ran between Victoria and Hearts, taking a knife in the stomach that was meant for Victoria.

"You are a stupid bitch," Hearts said to Faceless. "I guess I'll just have to pick a higher window."

Faceless looked at her, trying to force a smile, even though he was cradling his arm. Hearts noticed. She charged, aiming specifically at his broken arm. He ducked down, catching her left arm in his left, trapping it. He aimed for another head-butt, but she was ready, rocking her head back, and that's when she made her first mistake. She rocked backwards; she lost her sight line with Faceless. He took the opportunity to slam his tonfa-laden hand into her kidney.

"Hrrk," she choked, looking back just in time to catch the tonfa in her eye.

"Fuck you!" she shouted angrily, throwing a wild punch as Faceless jumped away.

Faceless drew his sword and sliced at her newly blinded spot. She was trained enough to know that was where he would aim, and she bucked back, drawing her sword and knocking it against his, parrying it away.

He looked surprised, unable to believe she was still able to think straight with a blinded eye. Faceless threw down his weapon. It was heavy and he was tired. He was bleeding out. He had to finish this quickly, or risk not finishing it at all.

He could see Hearts was breathing heavy as well.

"I want to kill you with my hands; I need to know you're gone," Faceless said, panting.

Hearts smiled, trying to cover her exhaustion. "Well, if you're tired, Young One, I suppose we can do it your way."

They walked towards each other, exhaustion apparent in both their eyes. They traded hits like heavyweight boxers. Any thoughts about guarding were gone. Finally, Faceless caught a right hook to the jaw. He went stumbling backwards. He grabbed at Hearts, grabbing her flack jacket. He regained his balance and with all his strength rocked forward, slamming his forehead into her nose. He broke it; blood and tears filled Hearts's eyes.

Hearts fell, stunned; blood gushed from her nose and her eye. Faceless slammed his heel on her kneecap, shattering it. She growled and tried to dodge, but his fist slammed her other kneecap; it snapped backwards, and with a shriek she collapsed.

Faceless slumped to where the sword had fallen. He practically had to drag it to Hearts, who was dragging her legs, crawling away on the floor. She was trying desperately to get away. With an almighty downward thrust he slammed his sword into the heart of the woman he'd once loved more than anyone in the world.

Hearts touched the katana blade sticking out of her chest. Her eyes were unfocused, as if she wasn't there, really she wasn't. Her mind flashed back to Patterson.

* * *

"You let your little pet project get away," Patterson said, throwing Joan Saint down on the ground.

"I did," Joan said. "It was all my fault and I take responsibility; leave Faceless out of this."

Patterson growled, pulling out a cigarette. "Here's the thing. If you don't take the blame for this, I leave you alone. Instead I'll hand Faceless over to the Black Joker." The blood drained from Joan's face. "Or," he said, "you take the blame and Faceless gets a new Keeper, and I leave this alone, but you never get to see him again. Ever."

Joan smiled. She had on the necklace Faceless had given her from his trip to the city. He had told her part of why he escaped was to get her the necklace. It was silver and a blue dolphin that was inlaid in silver.

"But then I take you to the Black Joker."

Joan's body began to shake, and she bit her tongue. She thought hard. She ran her thumb over the dolphin. "It was my fault," she said.

Joan Saint looked at Patterson with an adamant look in her eyes, as though she dared him to question her resolve. That look surprised Patterson.

"You're only twenty-two. Are you sure you want to waste your life?" Patton said. Joan Saint looked at him and smiled. Patterson nodded his head, solemnly. "Let's go then."

Patterson led her by the elbow to the Black Joker.

* * *

Hearts was looking up at Faceless with her one good eye. Through her tear-filled eye, she could only see his blurry shape. Her mind went back to the boy she protected, the one that played with the train sets she allowed him, and ate the candy she snuck in.

"I'm sorry, Joan," Faceless said, his voice fragile and childlike.

"It's all right, Young One," Joan Saint whispered, then her eye shut.

Faceless looked at the hole in her suit, the one Faceless's sword had made. Something glistened from the suit's tear. Reflecting moonlight, stained with Joan Saint's blood, was the dolphin necklace. Faceless picked it up. He shook with a cry he would never let out.

Chapter 44: Woozy

Faceless had finally descended the stairs. His body was feeling weak, and he was still bleeding.

He held his side; it hurt. He had to get to Victoria.

He stumbled to one knee. The alley was dirty; it smelled of sewage and rotting food. He collapsed facedown on the alleyway's dirt and grime. His face was half in a puddle as he looked down the alley, towards the direction of where she should have been.

"This… is a terrible place to die," he chuckled to himself – with that, everything went black.

Chapter 45: Family Ties

Faceless woke up in a room surrounded by people dressed in matte black, each of them with a different patch on the shoulder of their uniforms.

"This is the guy?" asked a man whose black hair reached the flame patch on his upper arm.

"This is him. The one we've been looking for since we got the intelligence. Faceless," a slender and full-chested, beautiful half-Indian and half-Black girl said. Her raven hair was dyed with pink stripes. Her shoulder patch was a blue heart.

"Where is Victoria?" Faceless asked. He tried against his restraints and held back hiss panic.

"Whoa, man, it's all right. Those shackles were more for *our* protection. We didn't exactly know how you were going to react," a blue-eyed, sandy-haired teen said while smiling. His patch was a silver circle. "I'm Crux. You're safe here."

"I'm only going to repeat it one more time: where is Victoria?" There was a sharp tone in Faceless's voice that made them collectively uneasy.

"There's not even a bit of worry about your own safety. I like that. She's in the next room, champ. She'll be happy to know you're awake." A man in a black, three-piece suit came around from behind Faceless. His posture was dominant and his steps soundless. Faceless knew this guy could only be the boss. His hair was oak brown with white streaks in it. His face had two-day-old gray-and-brown scruff. The man had a scar down the length of his face just outside of his left eye.

Faceless recognized this man. Faceless had fought this man; only back then, he didn't have that scar.

"Fractal?" Faceless asked, disbelieving.

The man smiled. "Let's get these restraints off him. I think we should all be a little more sensitive about that kind of thing. We've all felt it."

The blue heart girl moved to help him. "No need," Faceless said. He handed her the restraints.

"Showoff," Blue Heart crinkled her nose.

"I figured they wouldn't hold you," Fractal said, "but I needed you to at least see me before you were able to beat my men senseless."

"*Men* maybe," Blue Heart said, popping a blue gum bubble and putting her hand on her hip, "and you mean he would try."

"My apologies, Linger: Men and women," Fractal said, rolling his eyes. "Remember, though, he *tried* to kill the Kings, and he did that."

"He only killed two. Spade killed Clubs," Linger pouted.

"Linger?" Faceless asked, curious about the moniker.

"It's a codename, stupid," Linger said.

"Codename?"

"Wow, boss. This is the guy that's supposed to help us take down NightCard?" She rolled her eyes.

"You see, we're special, Faceless. Just like you," Fractal said.

Faceless looked up at the ceiling. It was black, just like everything else this group seemed to possess.

"I doubt that," Faceless said, scoffing.

"Really?" Fractal said with a smile. Faceless turned to face him. Fractal held his hands together, intertwining his fingers, and closed his eyes. A haze began to form around Fractal. It was like Faceless's eyes were crossed, as a secondary hazy double began to emerge from him. The haze began to solidify next to Fractal. Then the haze began again. Within seconds, there were sixteen Fractals standing around Faceless.

They became disfigured. Stretched, and then they sucked back into the original. Faceless caught a glimpse of the black-haired flame symbol guy. He had a green flame engulfing his hand. He was giving Faceless the middle finger. A blond, long-haired girl had her finger up and was tossing coins. Each landed one atop the other, each stacked piece barely looking like it was holding. Impossibly slim odds, but she was doing it.

Two twin Korean girls dressed in frilly black-lace dresses stood side by side. One had hair of jet black, the other of snow white. The white-haired girl looked directly into Faceless's eyes.

Try not to faint, she thought into Faceless's head. *The last guy fainted.*

"I'd say we're pretty damn special," Fractal smiled, "and we need your help."

Faceless fainted.

~Arc II: The Gene Coliseum~

Chapter 46: Fractal

The man that called himself Fractal was looking at the Black Joker. This was a person the Black Joker had to see with his own eyes. He was there, staring at Fractal. His face was sharp, with black hair and red eyes. The soulless, red eyes had black eye shadow around them. He looked at Fractal. Fractal was young; he didn't seem to be capable of killing, much less leading the Carnival. Black Joker referenced his file; it said Fractal was twenty-eight, but he was aging well. But the Black Joker reminded himself that he had seen stranger things; much many stranger things had been seen in the Joker's Playroom.

Fractal had his hands bound together behind his back and was unable to intertwine his fingers. Fractal had been beaten; one of his eyes was black and blue; the other was staring at the Black Joker defiantly.

"Well now Mr. Fractal, we have taken a special interest in your case," Black Joker said, slapping Fractal on the head with his folder.

"My case?" Fractal scoffed. "Why, whatever do you mean?"

The Black Joker laughed. "I mean your ability to split yourself into multiple people."

"You mean my carnival act? I'm just a simple carny. It's nothing but smoke and mirrors."

The Black Joker had a smile cross his lips. "Come now... neither one of us believe that." The Black Joker slapped Fractal's face. The blow cracked his jaw and would have left a weaker man knocked out. Fractal just stared at him, amused, with a blood-soaked smile of innocence.

"I'm not," Fractal smiled. "There really isn't anything special about me."

"Oh, I think we both know that's not true. You've killed for us before. I think you've got more talent than just good marksmanship."

Fractal looked at the Black Joker. Fractal's face scrunched hard, like he was searching for a memory his mind couldn't quite reach. Then Fractal shrugged. "You really want to see my ability? Untie my hands."

The Black Joker laughed again.

"Why not?" he said, pulling out the key from his pocket. He unlocked the handcuffs.

"You might want to stand back," Fractal said.

The Black Joker stepped back five feet. Fractal intertwined his fingers; he pressed together his forefingers and middle fingers. He closed his eyes, then he opened them; he stared the Black Joker in the eyes.

The Black Joker watched, as the man in front of him began to haze and get blurry. The man split in to two, then four, then eight. Each time, the clones began to walk around the Black Joker.

The clones' mouths opened in unison. "You really want to see what I can do?" they said. "Watch."

The clones charged at the Black Joker, who stood there, smiling. The first punched him. It was a solid hit, and the Black Joker faltered for a second before throwing a punch that would have killed a regular human, but the Black Joker's fist went through Fractal like he wasn't there.

"Wrong Fractal," the one behind him said, and with a fast stroke, he stabbed out one of the Black Joker's eyes.

The Black Joker howled in pain. Swinging wildly, he couldn't even hit the Fractal that was in front of him. The Fractals stood back, and they smiled.

When the Black Joker would look at the film later, he wouldn't see what he saw then; all he would see was one man, moving around like a ninja, who reached in and pulled out the eye of the Black Joker.

The Black Joker stumbled to his feet, laughing like a madman. "Hahahaha! HAHAHAHAHA! That was impressive! It was a hypnosis trick, right?"

Fractal frowned. No one had ever guessed.

A tranquilizer dart came from out of the wall and hit the real Fractal in the neck.

The others disappeared and Fractal fell to his knees. He gave the Black Joker one more satisfied smile before he slipped into unconsciousness.

The Black Joker looked at him from his one good eye. "I like him," Black Joker said to a nurse that was rushing in to take care of his eye. Black Joker looked straight into the camera. He was smiling as the blood dripped into his mouth, reddening his teeth. "He goes in the Gene Coliseum."

Chapter 47: The Gene Coliseum

When Fractal awoke this time, he found himself laying on a stone floor. The stone was rough, and iron traced along the wall. This was a prison. He was sure of that. The only lighting was by torches, and surrounding him were other people. They were scarred and bandaged, with rough-hewn clothes Fractal found himself wearing. On it, written in red spray paint was the simple moniker, FRACTAL. He felt something clinging to his throat. It was a collar.

"Is it true?" one of the less scarred asked him, a young Indian-and-Black woman with jet black hair.

"Is what true?" Fractal said, finally finding his voice.

"That you plucked out the eyes of the Black Joker," she asked.

Fractal stood up, again finding his hands bound – at least in front of him this time. "No," he sighed, "I only managed to pluck out one."

He looked at her and laughed. She returned it.

"I'm Linger, by the way," she said, extending her hand.

Fractal reached up his shackled hands and shook hers. Her exotic looks were appealing; his attraction to her was instant, the second he looked into those rich, honey-colored eyes. His eyes looked up and down her curvaceous, top-heavy Indian body. Her long, black hair made her seem wild and dangerous.

"Fractal," he said.

"Yeah, you're saying that like we don't all already know that."

"I'll take that as a compliment I guess. Where are we?" he asked her.

The hints of smile that had been on Linger's face dissipated like smoke. "We're in the Gene Coliseum." Fractal looked at her his expression proved to her that he was lost. "Oh, right. Well the Gene Coliseum is kinda like a Roman one." She gestured at the giant doors in the corner of the room. "See those doors?"

"Yes."

"Those lead to this giant arena, where NightCard allows the rich and powerful to come and watch us fight. Those of us that die, they consider that our lives and our powers weren't worth keeping in the first place. Those of us that live more than twelve fights, we win our freedom. In the form of them allowing us the 'privilege' of becoming a full time member of NightCard, as one of their Suits."

Fractal didn't understand the word suits. "What's a suit?"

"Suits are members of their elite. They classify them, from Two to Ten being regular members. The Royalty Cards, Jack, Queen, King, Ace are special. They are treated like royalty. If we win, we earn ourselves the chance to either challenge a regular member, or challenge one of the royalty. If we win, we take their spot."

Fractal tried standing, but the tranquilizer wasn't completely out of his system. "Well, isn't that nice. I'd rather the opportunity to leave."

Linger laughed. "That opportunity doesn't exist." A bell chimed three times.

Linger looked up and left. To Fractal's right there was a LCD board inlaid in the rock. It began to scroll words across it.

Joan Saint vs Origin Sakura.

"That poor new girl, she's like you," Linger said, looking at the new girl in the corner. She was platinum blond, and built delicately, with a small bust and gorgeous, vibrant blue eyes, and she looked afraid. "She's up against Sakura. She was the one who had the best skills using a sword out of all of us. She was the Origin they used to give Project Morph part of his power."

"You know I followed none of that right?"

"You should've; you're an Origin."

"How do you mean?"

"Origins are the first people to have an ability. NightCard farms them and gives their powers to other people, called Knockoffs. I'm an Origin too," she said, "and that poor girl over there has to fight the fastest and strongest out of all of us." Linger looked out the window. "I wonder who she pissed off in NightCard to make her be the first to fight Sakura."

Fractal got up and walked to the window. Guards opened the big doors leading to the arena and were holding rifles. "Joan Saint, come on."

Fractal followed their eyes to a petite blonde in the corner. She got up and crossed the room, her head down. As she walked through the door, she turned, making eye contact with Fractal for a second. She gave him a sad look, and then she disappeared behind the door and out of sight.

Fractal watched as she went to the center of the ring, with Sakura.

Linger looked at him. "She might make it," Linger said, looking at the concern on Fractal's face. "There's a fifteen-minute time limit. If she can survive that long, then the match is over."

Fractal thought for a moment. "This is her first fight?"

"Yes."

"Then she should be fine."

"How do you know?"

"Because," he said. "NightCard wouldn't have given her this fight unless they already knew what her powers were. The Black Joker likes torture, but he likes making profits too – and testing abilities. It wouldn't be a very good test if he knew it was going to be the only one. It wouldn't give him the data he needed. The only logical conclusion is that he already had the data. Besides, he'd make sure she suffered a few fights before trying to kill her."

There was the sound of cheesy fanfare, like this was sport, and then the two charged each other. Sakura had her katana, and one had been given to Joan.

They clashed swords with a clang that echoed in the coliseum. Fractal looked on in wonder; Sakura was faster than Joan, but Joan was still able to block, though she was being pushed back slowly.

Fractal saw the sad look on Sakura's face; it was as though she hated the thought of fighting Joan; still, she struck with a sad determination.

Joan made a stabbing movement, pushing all of her body weight behind it. Sakura turned, allowing Joan to pass. Sakura made a slash at Joan, who was barely able to block with her sword. The blow caused her to lose her balance. Sakura turned slowly, pressing her blade to Joan's throat.

Fractal was clenching his hands to the stone window sill. He looked at the wall, checking the time. Forty-five seconds left. He looked slightly above the clock, and the light from his shackles was reflecting onto the stone. He quickly got an idea. He turned his shackles, moving the reflection.

Sakura raised her blade, poised for a downward strike. The light from the shackles glared into her eyes, blinding her. She closed her eyes and tilted her head away instinctively.

Within a second, Joan shoved her katana straight through Sakura's heart.

With a gurgle, and blood spilling from her mouth, Sakura looked from the blade to the window, where a horrified Fractal was looking back. They made eye contact and Sakura's eyes looked at him; her eyes were accusing, but they weren't accusing Joan.

She fell over, dead. Joan stood up and her hands were trembling. Fractal looked at the clock: five seconds left. She could have just ran. They could both be coming back.

Joan was escorted, wiping Sakura's blood off her hands onto her canvas, potato-sack-inspired shirt.

Joan Saint walked back into the doors. As the guards shut them, Fractal crossed to where she was and pushed her to the wall with a growl.

"I didn't save you so you could kill her!" Fractal said, slamming Joan into the rock wall again.

Joan gave him a sad smile. "I didn't want to," she said, almost to the point of tears, "but if I hadn't, she would have had to fight someone else. If that happened, then she would have done the same to them."

Fractal looked at her in the eyes. He hated this, but he knew the truth behind what she said. "All right," he relented.

He let go of her and she dropped to the floor. He turned, and without emotion went back to his corner and pressed his back against the wall. He looked up and slid down the wall, resting in a seated position.

"Thank you," he heard Joan say; he turned to the cold metal wall.

Night set in the French sky, but none of the captives of the Coliseum could see it.

Fractal missed the stars.

Chapter 48: Operator Versus King Clubs

Fractal awoke to the dings. It had been a week. He was used to it by now. He rolled over and looked at the board.

Operator vs King Clubs

Fractal looked at the new girl: Taiwanese, small build, but quiet and reserved. He hadn't ever heard her talk. It was almost like she was lost in her own head. She was lucky, all of her fights had been easy, and she'd evaded the enemy. She was able to throw her thoughts into others' heads. Everything she had ever experienced, beamed into her enemy. Every second. It drove them mad for the entirety of the fifteen minutes, but now she was up against King Clubs.

* * *

Clubs was standing in the middle of the arena. His weapon of choice ready; his preferred weapons were always ready. They were his hands. Fractal had seen one of Clubs's fights before, and he knew why. Clubs ate people. Not just in a figurative sense. His hands decayed them, sucking out their life force, leaving a rotting corpse. A corpse he had a tendency to eat.

Now his attention was focused on Operator.

The petite Taiwanese 18 year old looked at him, horrified. She was preparing, getting ready to push all of her thoughts into his head.

Clubs's hands began to glow black, and with a locked eye contact, she began; she pumped all of her memories into his head.

"That won't work for me, Sushi," Clubs said.

"My name is Operator, and I'm Taiwanese, not Japanese. Don't be racist," she said, the first time her voice was heard.

"You're Sushi, and I will really enjoy eating you," Clubs smiled, licking his lips. "Now you really want to get to know each other? Why don't you let me open up too?"

Clubs thought really hard at Operator. He thought of every evil thing he'd ever done, every man he'd ever eaten, and every horrible desire. Operator shouted, and pitched herself away. She stopped looking the monster in the eyes.

Clubs was on her in a second, he touched her under the chin, and she felt the energy wither from her. A black mark began to grow under her chin. It spider-webbed along her jaw. He removed his finger. The spider-web faded into her skin.

"I took away a year of your life," Clubs said. "Now stay still, and I promise I'll kill you off quickly."

Fractal was burning with anger. Operator was barely more than a child and Clubs was toying with her.

"CLUBS!" Fractal shouted, entwining his fingers. Clubs looked at him. "Fuck you!" Fractal shouted, locking eyes.

Clubs's head rocked back. When he opened his eyes he saw Operator, but then he looked around the ring and saw a hundred more.

"Now see that's interesting," Clubs smiled. His glowing black hand slammed into the nearest Operator. It went right through. He pulled his hand back and examined his fingers. "No problem; I'll just kill them all."

For thirteen minutes Clubs jumped, trying to shove his hands at every Operator. For thirteen minutes, the crowd looked on at Clubs jumping around and stabbing the air like an idiot. Finally, the chimes rang again and the match was over. The Operators disappeared, leaving the real one that was running back to Fractal.

* * *

Fractal was glad; he was exhausted. Clubs got up, and followed Operator in. Fractal got up and stood between them.

"It's over, Clubs. Let it go," Fractal looked at him, naturally defending Operator.

"That's some venomous look in your eyes," Clubs said smiling. "But if you ever fuck with one of my meals again, I'll kill you." He grabbed Fractal's right hand and squeezed, breaking his fingers. Clubs could control his ability, and while he wanted to hurt Fractal, he didn't want to kill him without an audience.

"Fuck!" Fractal shouted, collapsing to the ground.

"I can't wait until we meet in the ring. I'll have an answer to that trick of yours by then." Clubs walked out, smiling coldly.

"You didn't need to do that," Operator said, kneeling down and looking at Fractal.

"No, I suppose I didn't. But you would've gotten killed. And believe it or not, I used to be a newbie too," Fractal smiled. "I know how it feels."

Operator smiled. "Thank you," she said.

"Hey," Fractal asked, "is it true that you really have the ability to read people's minds? And to send your thoughts to them?"

"No," Operator said, "I can communicate people between each other like, well, an Operator."

"Cool," Fractal said smiling. "That'll be good to know. In that case, let's test this."

I've got a plan, Fractal said. *I want to get out of here.*

A plan? Operator said, smiling. *I like the sound of that.* Fractal told her his plan. *I really like the sound of that,* Operator said, looking at the twin Korean girls in the corner.

Fractal looked at the twins again; they were nothing special in terms of raw survival ability. They were called Reader and Writer. Reader was black-haired, and similar to Operator in some ways; she could read a person's memories. Everything, every thought a person ever had. The white-haired twin was Writer. She had the ability to implant thoughts, to override a person's memories and desires with whatever she wanted.

Tell them I want to talk to them, Fractal said, *and that they need to not draw attention to themselves.*

Operator looked at the twins. Operator was able to spread her brainwave spectrum, matching other peoples'.

The twins shared a brainwave. As soon as Operator connected to Writer, Reader sensed it.

Who's in our head? Reader asked.

That skinny, Taiwanese woman Fractal saved, Writer said. *What do you want, Operator?*

Fractal has a plan, Operator said. *Listen to him, and the Taiwanese woman.* She thought the last part with sarcasm.

Girls, I want to get out, and for that I need Writer's help, Fractal said. He smiled. To an outsider it looked like he'd thought of a funny memory.

I don't like it, Reader said. *It puts Writer at risk.*

If we stay here we're all at risk, Fractal commented quickly.

There was a pause.

He's right, Writer said. *And I know that it's plausible. There's the one investor that's crazy about me.*

Are you sure? We have the same face and he didn't bat an eyelash at me, Reader frowned.

Your hair isn't white. It's boring black, Writer said. *White's the new blond.*

Bitch, Reader thought, laughing.

How long would it take to make this happen? Fractal asked.

When can you send a guard in to come look me in the eyes? Writer laughed.

I'll work on that. It's almost feeding time, Fractal smiled.

The guard came and brought them the cart. Each of their names was marked on a dog bowl. *I just love the gourmet cooking here,* Reader thought.

They snickered.

"Hey guard man," Fractal said. "I'm kinda nursing a broken hand here. I could really use your help."

The guard grumbled, thinking to himself that this wasn't his job, and he approached.

Writer crossed the floor and tapped the guard on the shoulder. The guard turned and Writer locked eyes with him. "Hey guard, you remember how you've always had a terrible crush on me?" Writer said.

The guard's eyes were as big as saucer plates. "I seem to recall that." He looked at her. "Sexy." He added the last as an afterthought.

"Good, well I need you to deliver a message for me," Writer said, "since you love me so much."

"Since I love you so very much," the guard corrected.

"Right, so very much," Writer said, rolling her eyes.

Chapter 49: Redux

Fractal was about to eat his dinner when a slender blond came up to him. She seemed fragile, like the slightest wind would blow her over. She was out of place in that environment. Her clothes seemed to swallow her up; her top looked more like a poncho than a shirt.

"Can I help you?" Fractal said.

"Yes," Redux said, presenting him with her food rations. "How about a gamble?" In her other hand she held up a handful of rocks. Fractal's interest was piqued. "If I can bounce all of these off the wall, making them land and balance on top of each other, then you give me your rations. If I miss even one, I give you mine."

Fractal smiled. "All right," he said.

She took the first of the five and bounced it against the wall. It landed predictably. Then she smiled; the second one bounced off the wall a little higher and landed perfectly on the second. Fractal raised his eyebrow.

"Okay," he said, choosing to reserve judgment. She threw two and they bounced; one landed right, and the other landed on the ground. "Seems you missed."

"I've got one more," she said, holding up the last one. She threw the other one at the one on the ground, it bounced the one on the ground onto the wall and the one that was thrown bounced onto the stack. The one that had been on the ground bounced off the wall and landed on top. "I win," she said.

Fractal's lips turned into a line and he handed over his bowl. "It was worth it, I suppose."

She gathered the food and walked away. Then Linger walked up snickering.

"She did that to me when I was new, too."

"You couldn't have warned me?"

"Where's the fun in that?" Linger smiled and gave Fractal a piece of food.

Chapter 50: Ash

Ash was cradling a broken arm. Fractal had told him earlier that day that they were just supposed to act their fight; they were to make it look good, but hurt no one. Of course Ash had been sure it was a trick. He fought to kill; everybody else fought to kill; why should Fractal be any different?

The man was somehow able to talk inside his head; he was able to try and get him to see reason. When that failed, Fractal used a rock to break the fire thrower's arm.

Ash had thought for sure he was going to die. He was sure his dominant arm had been broken in three pieces. It felt worse than broken; it wouldn't even move.

Then Fractal sat down six feet from him and waited out the clock. He stared at Ash the whole time with a look that said 'you're an idiot.'

Ash had been wrong. He poked at his food rations. To add insult to injury, Fractal had given his own rations to Ash. Said it was an apology.

A petite, blonde girl with a mischievous smile walked up.

"Hey," the blond, skinny girl said. "How about a gamble?"

Redux explained the rules. Ash agreed. Thirty-two seconds later, there were four rocks in a row stacked one atop the other.

Redux was holding the last rock in her hands, smiling.

"I'm sure I'm just lucky," Redux said, portraying bashful and innocent perfectly.

"I'm sure."

She threw the last one and Ash watched it bounce off the wall. With a lightning-fast movement, he caught it in the air and smiled at her. He threw it away from the others. "Look at that, you missed," he said, sending her bashful and innocent look back at her.

Redux just looked at him. She had lost. This was a first. She looked him up and down, impressed. "Keep your rations," he said, as she was presenting him with hers. "I was just bored. I thought this would be interesting. It was."

"Well," Redux said hesitantly, surprised at his generosity. "I suppose I owe you one." She looked at his broken arm.

"Maybe I can set that for you."

He looked at the arm. "Can you do that?"

"Who knows?" she said with a coy smile. "Maybe I'll get lucky."

Ash smiled. He had a feeling she would.

"Go ahead," he said, presenting it.

Redux, who had been a nurse in a previous life, gave it a look over, feeling on it.

"I can't," she said, frowning.

"Why not?"

"It's not broken."

"What?"

"He didn't break it," Redux said, familiar with the fight. She ran her fingers over it, searching. She smiled. "He just hit a nerve bundle." She looked up at him. "Your arm will be better by tomorrow."

"So the bastard missed."

"No," she said, shaking her head. "If he'd been off by even a centimeter either side of this, he would have broken it. He chose to just immobilize you." Ash looked at her in disbelief. "You owe him a big thank you."

She stood up and, her food in hand, walked away. She left Ash with a lot to consider. Then he looked at his bowl. "The bitch took my food." he realized.

Chapter 51: Faceless Versus Fractal

The next morning, Fractal woke up. His broken fingers were still swollen. He obviously wouldn't be using his skills for a while.

There was a chime. Fractal looked up at the board.

"Oh, crap," he said.

Fractal vs. Special Guest 1343

"You gonna be okay?" Linger asked.

"Yeah, I'm used to it by this point. I'll make do."

"I doubt it," Linger said. "I couldn't scratch him. All I did was sit in a force field and panic."

"I didn't know you had that ability," Fractal said, dismissing her.

"That's not the point. Your hand is broke. You can't use your ability."

"My ability isn't the only dangerous thing about me," Fractal said smiling. "I didn't need my ability to save Joan, just a well placed light ray and a reflective handcuff." He raised his cuffed hands as proof.

"Just, you're a really nice guy, Fractal. I've seen nice guys come through here. They don't make it here for very long."

"No, I suppose they don't."

"Fractal!" the guard shouted. "It's time! Get your ass over here."

"All right," Fractal said, raising to a full standing posture. Linger raised with him.

"For luck," she said, extending her hand.

"For luck," he said, taking it.

In one quick movement, she drew him in closer and kissed him.

"See? You already let your guard down," she said, smiling.

Fractal kissed her forehead and then walked toward the gate. The guard gave him a brotherly wink then led him to the middle of the arena.

The guard un-cuffed Fractal and looked wary, but the guard wasn't wary of Fractal. He was staring at the man across from him, who couldn't really be called a man at all. He wasn't much more than a boy.

"This is who I'm fighting?" Fractal asked, scoffing.

"Well, if you don't feel like hitting a child, old man, just stay still while I punch you," Experiment 1343 laughed.

"Come on now, I'm old school," Fractal said, "I believe when a child is misbehaving, he needs a spanking."

Fractal tried desperately to intertwine his fingers. It wasn't working.

"See, now that makes you sound like a pedophile," 1343 said, shaking his head.

1343 charged a grimacing Fractal. Fractal turned, avoiding a punch meant for his jaw and used his elbow to strike Faceless in the back of the head.

The child went sprawling. When he shook his head and got up Fractal was looking at him, his hands in fists, like a boxer.

"You're the first person to land a hit on me," 1343 said.

He charged Fractal again, desperate to make that the last time. Fractal's left hand switched from a fist to a grappling hand and he snatched the incoming fist, flipping 1343 over his head. The prepubescent experiment hit the ground hard.

"Oh, bitch move," the boy groaned. Fractal was smiling. Maybe he could do this after all.

1343 kicked out with his leg, knocking Fractal on the ground. Fractal protected his hand as he fell, landing on his elbow and knocking the wind out of him. He walked up and kicked Fractal hard. Fractal was amazed; the little boy hit so much harder than anyone had before. He felt a rib crack.

Fractal rolled away from another blow. He got to his feet and was blown back by another stomach punch. He flew back and hit the wall of the arena. The stone granite was unforgiving as he slammed into it.

1343 was looking strangely at the man. Aside from a couple of blows, his opponent hadn't really done much to fight him.

"You don't want to hurt me, do you?" the child asked, cocking his head to the side; he found it curious.

"Not particularly, no. Just wanted to defend myself. Looks like I'm not doing too good a job at that."

"It's nothing personal you know," 1343 said.

"You don't think that maybe there's more to life than this?"

"It's all I know."

"Then maybe I can help you see more."

Operator, Fractal said. *Show him.* Operator smiled. He was resourceful.

Faceless's body rocked backward. Filling his head was every treasured memory of the world that Fractal had ever known. They were every place he had ever seen that had a pleasant memory attached to it.

"There's so much?" 1343 began to cry. "So much I haven't seen?" He fell to his knees. "It's so beautiful." A tear rolled down his cheek.

Yeah, it is, and I'm going back to it. I challenge you: get out of here and see it all for yourself. I'll see you on the other side. Fractal drove his knee into 1343's head, knocking him unconscious.

Fractal waited out the rest of the time. Waiting for the chimes. They finally came.

The Black Joker was looking at Fractal through the window of the sky box at the top of the Coliseum.

"I love this guy," Black Joker laughed, pitching his head backwards. He slapped his hand to his forehead, slightly shifting his newly-fitted blood-red eye patch.

Chapter 52: Linger with Me

Linger rushed Fractal after his fight. "Ow, sore," Fractal groaned. She kissed him; Fractal returned it. It was a soft, loving kiss; it was one that seemed out of place in such a contrasting environment. Her full lips tasted amazing, and he could feel the passion from her side of the kiss.

"I think I feel better now," Fractal chuckled. "Well, at least a little."

Linger smiled. "Well, maybe I can help get your mind off it?" she said, nuzzling his neck. Her hand reached up his shirt, feeling his chest.

"Not a lot of privacy here," he said, not really an exhibitionist.

"There is when you can construct opaque force fields," she winked.

Fractal smiled. "I think that would make me feel a lot better," Fractal said, "but let's wait until night."

* * *

The air around them was humid, but cool. The soft sounds of light breathing that echoed around their little cage ensured everyone was asleep. Linger came up to a snoring Fractal, and she nudged him. Fractal was only half asleep when Linger kissed him.

"I think it's time to make you feel better," Linger said.

She led him by the hand to their most isolated corner.

Linger touched her fingertips together, and then drew a circle with them. The circle was real; it was drawn out of bio-electrical energy and static from the air; it condensed the molecules and pulled molecules from the rock and thinned them; it made a force field of constantly moving molecules; it was one of pure energy.

"I think we have privacy now," Linger said, and with that she threw him on the ground with a playful growl.

* * *

Thirty minutes later they were laying next to each other, basking in the ambiance of their lovemaking. Fractal was still amazed by her shields; he looked up at it, and wondered how much damage it could actually take.

"I'm happy," Linger said in his arms. She was wearing his shirt and her pants. "It's nice to find happiness in a place like this." She spoke with a sleepy tone; Fractal knew she was close to falling asleep.

"Well, then we should hold onto whatever happiness we can find."

"Exactly, old man." Then she rolled over and with a final nuzzle, she was asleep. Fractal was surprised; the shield around them dropped, leaving him stark naked with the young Linger around him. Luckily they were mostly asleep. Fractal heard movement further down the corridor. It was Joan Saint.

"Oh, that's not cool," Fractal groaned.

Joan Saint raised an eyebrow casually, as though impressed.

Chapter 53: A Heated, Lucky Love Scene

Ash was seated in his corner. Everyone else in the Coliseum knew it was his. They tended to give Ash space. He wasn't exactly known as having a nice reputation. He hadn't outright threatened anyone, but no one was to mess with him – Fractal's orders.

He was lost in thought when he heard a movement. He quickly readied a fireball. Then he noticed who it was; Redux was looking at him.

"What do you want?" he asked, keeping the fireball ready.

Redux looked at him. She walked up to him and knelt down, her knees between his open legs. She kissed him. The fireball went out, and he embraced her.

"No one else has ever outsmarted me," she said, pulling her lips away and making eye contact. "No one else has ever been that lucky."

"Is it better to be smart or lucky?" Ash said, chuckling.

"In my experience, it's better to be lucky," Redux said.

"How lucky are you?"

"I'm lucky enough that if we do what I think we will, no one is going to find us."

"I think we should test that," Ash laughed.

He leaned forward and kissed her, wrapping his arms around her and drawing his legs close to hers, entrapping her.

She lifted her shirt up, throwing it away. It landed on the only camera in the area, blocking the view. It was better to be lucky.

* * *

"You're warm," she chuckled as they held each other afterwards.

"You have your superpowers; I have mine." Then a thought crossed his mind. "You're not going to get pregnant are you?"

She looked up at him with a mischievous smile. The one she always used with him. "Don't worry," she said. "I'm very lucky."

Chapter 54: A Mistake Swept Under

A week passed. Linger and Fractal were still together, still happy. Joan looked at him across the rock cavern. Something about him continued to tantalize her.

Joan saw from their relationship, at least in her mind, that it was off and on with Linger. They looked happy, but if they really were, then Fractal wouldn't be looking at her like that.

"Joan," Fractal said, coming over to him.

"Yes?" Joan said, reading his body language.

She could tell what he wanted, and it excited her, because she wanted it too. She had, for a long time; she had since he had saved her.

"I need your help," he said innocently.

She read his body. She knew exactly how he needed her help. "My help with what?"

"It is kind of embarrassing, especially me being an old-fashioned kind of guy and all, but I need your help learning how to fight. I can't, and I'm tired of depending on others. I want to go into the arena and rely on my own strength." Joan relaxed. Of course this is what it was; it was stupid to think anything else. Fractal was one of the worst hand to hand fighters; he relied on his wit, but that could only last for so long. "I want… to be able to protect you – all of you."

Joan Saint smiled. "I think I can help. I'll show you some moves."

* * *

Fractal found himself looking at Joan Saint; both of them awkwardly standing there. They were stuck in a prison of rock, and they had found a little corner, hardly ever used. Finally it was Joan who broke the silence.

"What would you like to know? Distance fighting or close combat?"

Fractal shifted around uncomfortably. "Well, I feel like if it's distance, others could deal with that. I want to learn how to fight someone up close."

"Then charge at me," Joan said, without hesitation.

Fractal did hesitate, however. He knew Joan; she was still getting used to her powers. Still, she was the teacher. So he charged at her, and she grabbed the potato-sack that he called his clothing. She slid down on her back and then kicked him over over her shoulder; he landed hard.

"Bitch-crap," he groaned. He was looking up at the cavern roof. Joan looked down at him.

"You're too predictable. Everything you do is a straight line. Mix it up."

"All right," Fractal said, still laying on the ground. "Let's try that one again."

Fractal got back up, this time he aimed to her left, then spun right and was blocked. She slammed her elbow into his bicep and rendered his arm numb for a second. He couldn't move it; the nerves were shocked. Then she grabbed him by his neck and between his leg, then flipped him over her.

"Mother-bastard," Fractal said.

They continued in this fashion for twenty minutes. Finally, as Fractal charged he dove down, getting out of her eyesight. She couldn't see as he hit her in the back of the head.

She lost her balance and again, from her blind spot, he kicked her. She flew backwards into rock.

"That won't happen again," Joan said.

"Wanna bet?" Fractal laughed, crossing his fingers. He bit back the pain and concentrated.

For another twenty minutes he fought with her. She was just dodging, but he was keeping up surprisingly well. Finally she waited for his fist to connect with her, then she grabbed it and pulled him in. She kissed him; the 63 others disappeared. With another flip, he was on his ass.

"That was… actually a very effective strategy," Fractal said.

"Sweetie you haven't seen anything yet," Joan said, then she joined him on the ground.

"Really?" Fractal said.

"No, but you're about to," she laughed, and pulled off her clothes.

* * *

"I wasn't expecting that," Fractal said, after they finished and were holding each other.

"How do you think I feel?" Joan laughed.

Fractal held Joan in his arms; only two thoughts rang in his head: his first that this was a mistake and the second thought was that it was a mistake he would be making a lot.

Chapter 55: A Few Months Later

Fractal's hand was finally healed. It was six months later and he was able to create doppelgangers again. Linger was happy he was able to use both hands; she was very vocal about that. Fractal flexed his right hand and smiled. There was no more need to have Operator save his ass.

It's time, he said. *We can move forward.*

I'll tell the guard, Operator said. *Or rather, we'll have Writer tell the guard.*

Tell Ash, that guy that can light himself on fire, that we'll need his help, Fractal said.

Writer closed her eyes and thought to the guard. *We're good to go,* Writer thought to Operator and Fractal, *but it'll have to be tomorrow.*

That's good; nothing too pressing, Fractal said.

Chapter 56: Something Pressing

The Black Joker held Joan Saint in his Playroom. This time however, Joan wasn't tethered to the table.

"Ms. Saint, we have a problem," Black Joker said. "Fractal keeps winning. And now you tell me, his hand is healed."

"He's been using it anyways. I've seen it. He's actually getting better. We've been... practicing."

"I've seen your practicing. We have mini cameras installed. I have to say, I admire your teaching... technique. Especially when you have the luxury of a man that can become two men," he smiled. Joan Saint's jaw dropped. She flushed red. "But that is neither here nor there," Joker said. "You've been practicing fighting him, too; haven't you?"

"You know that's true," Joan said.

"Can you beat him?"

"I don't know," Joan answered. It was the truth.

"Is it your skills?"

"No. It's a... it's kinda emotional."

"Emotion!" he spat. The Black Joker grabbed Joan's throat. Joan couldn't believe his strength. Even with her powers, as she clawed at his hand, she couldn't break the grip. "Emotion is the enemy! Loyalty, that's what I've taught you, loyalty to the family! You need to be retaught that lesson."

The blood drained from Joan's face. The Black Joker turned to his tool set. He picked out a particularly nasty one. "After a night of this, you'll be begging to kill him in the arena – and you'll get that wish."

He brought the tool to her eye and laughed. Hearts watched in the corner, emotionless.

Chapter 57: Hearts Broken, Hearts Born

Fractal was getting worried; Joan Saint hadn't come back. Even as Linger held him, his thoughts stayed with Joan. He thought it was strange, that he could be in love with two women at the same time. What he thought was even more strange, however, was that it felt right. He couldn't imagine giving either one of them up.

What he hadn't expected was that they were in love with him too. He knew neither one of them wanted to let him go. That's why he had to get out. He looked at Linger. Her arm was in a sling, she wasn't so lucky in her last fight. He couldn't let this go on.

Is it ready yet? Fractal asked.

Yes, Writer responded. *It'll be today.*

Good, he looked at Linger. *The sooner the better.*

"Linger?" he asked.

"Yes?"

"Have I ever told you what I did before this?"

"No. I didn't think it was any of my business."

"I was an assassin," Fractal said. "A marksman, actually. Cold and calculating. I stayed with a traveling carnival troop. We were all gifted. Black Joker didn't know that. I exposed myself so that he wouldn't catch the others; it was my sister that I was really worried about."

"I... I had no idea." Linger said. She really hadn't.

"That was the point," Fractal said looking at his hands. She was the Gifter. The one of them that was able to unlock the recessive genes. For Fractal it was the hypnosis. She awakened the parts of his brain that he had never used. He promised that he would do whatever it took to keep her safe. Including getting caught. That was why he had to get out; he had to get back to her.

The chimes dinged; Fractal looked up; his jaw dropped.

Fractal vs Joan Saint Special Bout

"Special bout?" Fractal asked.

"I've only seen that once," Linger said. "It wasn't pretty."

Fractal stood up and walked towards the giant stone door. This wasn't going to be pretty. He walked towards the center of the ring, and facing him was Joan. Her body was covered with bruises and he couldn't understand that look in her eyes. It was as though there was nothing left in there.

"Joan?" he said. "Are you all right?"

"No, Fractal," Joan said, her eyes piercing him. "I will never be all right."

"Hello there, fans," Black Joker said over the intercom. "Today we have a special match up. Our favorite, Joan Saint, and the newly healed Fractal."

Fractal gritted his teeth; the Black Joker knew.

"The best part? This one is to the death," The Black Joker laughed. "I've even made it more interesting. I gave Miss Joan some weapons. It's only fair the woman get the advantage."

Joan Saint looked at Fractal. Then she threw a rock like a knife blade, Fractal barely saw it coming.

"That was a warning," Joan said. "Get your doppelgangers out now or you *will* die."

"I really don't want to fight you."

"You don't have a choice," she said, drawing a sword.

"I don't plan on dying here, Joan. I have too much to live for." His thoughts were of his sister. He crossed his fingers.

He made eye contact with her. He knew she had allowed him; he knew she wanted to fight him at his best. He was healed now, and with six months of practicing, of honing his skill, before her she saw 512 Fractals.

"Impressive; you've been holding back," she said as she pulled out a knife and held it close, "but I have too."

Fractal attacked, and as soon as she felt his first punch connect she trapped it, slicing into his arm with the knife.

"Damn it!" he yelled, kicking at her knee; he was aiming to dislocate it.

She jumped back, letting go. "I will not be as forgiving as I was, Fractal."

Her eyes looked around, searching constantly. She looked totally lost as the Fractals jumped around her. With a flash and a sickening wet sound, she slid a blade into Fractal's stomach.

"All your training, all your power, and you still have that weakness: you always forget to add the shadows," Joan said, twisting her short sword further into Fractal.

"Grk," he gurgled. Blood came pooling out of his mouth. He jumped back. He was aware, painfully so, that his technique was not going to work.

Any time, he thought to Writer. *Sooner is better.*

He said he'd let us know, Writer said.

Fractal flipped backwards. He knew he shouldn't be jumping around like a gymnast, but he couldn't stay still. If he did, it would kill him. He rolled on the ground and grabbed a handful of dirt. He flung it at her face, and she blocked with her forearm before the dirt could get in her eye. She punched his stomach, with everything she could.

He flew across the arena and landed in the dirt. She drew her sword again and approached him.

I'm going to die, Fractal thought to the others, *in the dirt.*

The lights went out. Fractal rolled away, then he ran. He heard the door open and he ran towards it.

Fractal! Duck! he heard Linger say in his head.

He slid to his knees. He heard the sickening crack of bone breaking and Joan's shout as the wave Linger sent radiating outward hit her.

"Damn it, Fractal!" Joan shouted; her nose was broken.

Fractal got under the safety of Linger's force field and the rest did as well. All of them gathered together.

"Stop!" a guard said, waving a gun.

Ash looked up and threw a fireball at the guard, blinding him. Fractal pushed the head of the guard into the rock wall. He was unconscious.

"Reader, come over here," Fractal said.

Reader approached and read the man's memories of the floor plans; she looked at Fractal. "I know how to get us out. Operator, deliver it."

Operator shot the memories to everyone. For everyone it was like they'd walked the halls for years themselves.

They made their way to the exit, emergency trail lights coming on.

NightCard had guards; most of whom Writer's investor's personal troops had already killed.

The last door was the hardest. Standing between it and them was Joan Saint.

"Okay, you bastard," Joan said, covering her broken nose and looking pissed. "I'm going to kill you, then that little bitch that hit me with the force field."

Linger looked at Joan. "Okay, I'm taking the whore down," Linger drew another circle with her fingers.

Joan looked at Fractal and frowned.

Fractal locked eyes and the second he made contact with her gaze he crossed his fingers. He duplicated everyone. Thousands of them were milling around; this time the copies had shadows.

They made it out and were running into the forest. Fractal looked back at Joan.

"I'll be right back," he said to Linger. "I've got to try and save her." He ran back to Joan. "Joan!" he shouted. "Come with us!"

"Fractal! You did this?"

"For us! Come on! Let's leave this behind! You don't need to be here anymore!"

Joan walked up and held him. She looked up and kissed him. "I can't go, Fractal. This is my family."

"No, Joan! I am your family." His voice weakened. "I chose you."

Joan looked him in the eyes. For a moment she believed that. Then she shook herself back to reality.

"No!" She shook her head. "No! The Black Joker told me you would do this! You'd try to ruin my family! You're messing around in my head all over again! Fuck you!"

Fractal didn't see the knife coming at his face until it was too late. She sliced into his face deeply. The blow nearly gorged out his eye. As it was, it reached all the way from chin to forehead, blinding him.

"You leave, Fractal," Joan said, speaking slowly and her body shaking. "Leave and don't come back. I never want to see you again. If I do, I will kill you."

Fractal walked away, covering his face. He met the group and looked at them. They were looking at a bleeding man. One that they looked to for guidance, who had saved all of them at one point or another. They were looking to him.

* * *

Joan Saint went to the Black Joker's Playroom. She sat in the chair and waited for him. He walked in ten minutes later.

Hearts looked on in the corner.

"Miss Saint? I wasn't sure that you were still here. What made you come back?"

"I came back because this is my family. You showed me that."

Black Joker smiled. "You've graduated, my dear." Black Joker moved to the corner of the room and grabbed Hearts. The mask of the King of Hearts reflected the light off it's ceramic-metal smile. Black Joker had been looking for a candidate to wear it. He found his champion in Joan. He placed the mask on Joan. "Well, Miss Hearts, I can't believe this. You're the first King that will be treated like a queen, and I've already gotten your first assignment. Our cameras picked up Fractal talking about something special. I need you to go to a carnival and pick up a special woman for me."

"Will this hurt Fractal?"

"It should. She's his sister."

"Then I would be delighted," Hearts said, her trademark wicked smile spreading across her face for the first time.

~Arc III: Daybreak~

Chapter 58: Pheromones & Flames

Faceless ran down the black corridor of Fractal's underground hideout. He heard laughing. He ripped the door open and he saw Victoria laughing with another woman; both were sitting at a table. The woman's hair was a fire red, and her nose sprinkled with freckles. She was fit, a woman that was in constant action, yet she remained sensual. Sex appeal radiated off of her without a hint of effort in doing so.

"Hey," Victoria said, smiling and feeling a rush of relief.

"Victoria!" Faceless shouted, running to her. He gave her a deep, passionate kiss and held her close. "I was worried Hearts had..."

"I'm fine," Victoria smiled, kissing him back. For a moment, they just held each other. There was something magical in the embrace; it was the kind of embrace that happened because Faceless didn't think it ever could have again. Victoria returned it. Eventually, however, there was a coughing that brought them back to the world. "Oh! Meet my new friend."

Victoria gestured to the woman that was sitting with her at the table.

* * *

"Hey," she said, standing up. "I'm Pheromone."

"All right?" Faceless said, extending his hand to Pheromone.

"So you're the famous Faceless," Pheromone said, smiling at him and looking him up and down.

Faceless frowned. "I wouldn't say famous. In fact, I've been going out of my way to not be famous."

He turned back towards Victoria, placing a kiss on her lips. Pheromone watched; her lip twitched.

"So what can you do?" Victoria asked.

"I'll show you," Pheromone said.

She grabbed Faceless and put him in front of her. She closed her eyes and Victoria saw from a distance that Pheromone radiated a pink cloud. It hung in the air, like morning mist.

"Now kiss me," Pheromone said.

Faceless looked at her. His eyes droopy.

He sneezed.

"Augh. What the hell? You produce hay-fever?" he coughed.

Her eyes spread wide. No one was above her influence. That cloud of pheromones should have made him a dribbling mass of putty in her hands. He should be begging for her body.

"This is... strange," she said.

"Yeah, it is," Faceless sneezed again.

He walked out the door, trying to escape the allergen.

"That wasn't cool," Victoria said, glaring. "Simply saying you could make him sneeze would have been enough."

"It wasn't supposed to," Pheromone said distantly.

Victoria didn't hear her. She was already out the door.

* * *

Pheromone looked at the pink cloud that was still hovering around her. That was triple the strength; he should have literally been licking her feet. She needed to try again; now it was a challenge.

She walked over to Ash's room. She knocked. "Come in," he shouted from inside. She entered the room. Strolled over to him, and grabbed his shirt.

"Tell me I'm pretty," Pheromone demanded. Suddenly a pink cloud like before exploded out from her, misting everything within its reach.

"I think you're damn sexy," Ash said, the mist around him sizzled as his body heat exuded.

Both of them were very special. Pheromone was bred to seduce. Her body created and stored highly potent pheromones and hormones that it can release in a cloud of mist sweat. The effect was a mind-numbing euphoria, and instant arousal. Long term exposure can leave the victim permanently addicted.

Pheromone was strictly warned by Fractal not to do it. He said he knew exactly what relationships in the family can bring. He was both definitive and vague at the same time. Still, Ash was dating Redux, so it could be fun. "You know, I shouldn't be doing this," she said, kissing him.

"You have to. I need it."

"Shut up, handsome; I'm leading up to something," she said, shushing him. "It's wrong of me to take advantage of you like this. It's wrong, it's naughty, and I love it. It's forbidden."

"Yes. You should do it. Take me."

"Handsome, when you talk I just can't get excited." She slapped his face.

"Ow," he said, his voice monotone.

"Damn it. I can't believe it. There's a literally hot body right in front of me, and I can't stop thinking about how easy it was. I want a challenge." She thought about Faceless. She looked once more at the man in front of her and with a grimace walked away.

Ash was left there, in a haze.

Chapter 59: Something to Fight For

A blond, petite woman, one that was shorter than Victoria – and who looked like she would barely be able to lift a gun – much less be an experiment like Faceless, walked up to the pair. "Excuse me," the woman said, walking up to Faceless and Victoria. "I need to see the princess real quick."

"And who are you?" Faceless asked. He was wary of anyone approaching Victoria.

"My name is Redux. I'm assistant to Dust. He wants to examine Victoria to make sure she doesn't have any hidden injuries or anything."

Faceless relented. "All right."

Redux led Victoria to a room that looked like a doctor's office, and to some extent it was. Dust was the researcher and lead doctor for Fractal; he has been a doctor before

NightCard got their hands on him. He was able to break salt bonds, spewing poisonous chlorine gas.

Victoria walked in. Standing at the desk was a Black man, bald with a gray and black goatee. He walked with a cane. He used it expertly, as though he had been for a while. "I'm Dust," the doctor said, extending his hand. Victoria shook it.

"Nice to meet you."

"The reason I called for you is because as we were going over Faceless's clothes, we found a mixture of his blood and Hearts's. We managed, in our escape from NightCard, to grab a few vials of BloodWine." He lifted one up to his face, showing it to Victoria. It was a healthy blood color, the size of a shot. "Between the two of them there was enough blood on the clothes for one vial. Their abilities were close enough. This vial would give you the abilities of Hearts. You'd be able to have hyper-reflexes, super-strength, and the ability to see something once and remember it. You'd finally not have to be just some thing Faceless lugs behind him; you could be his partner, his equal."

She looked at the vial, tempted. She wouldn't be some worthless luggage like she was now. She took the vial from his hands. Just out of her field of vision Redux frowned. Victoria opened the lid, and looked down the opening to the

BloodWine. She thought about Faceless one more time and knocked it back like a shot.

"Ugh!" she said, "That's some nasty stuff! You didn't have grape flavor or something?"

Dust frowned. "Sorry, I'm all out. I was too busy making it taste like a miracle."

"Well, I'm sorry I just expected—" she cut off mid-sentence and fell over, unconscious.

Redux looked at Dust. "This was all for the plan right?" she said, frowning.

"Yes, Redux; it had to be done. It gives him a stake in this, and I can fix it." Redux looked at Victoria laying on the ground, starting to spasm. Redux hoped he was right.

* * *

Fractal and Faceless were sitting in what Faceless assumed was the common area; it was the same room he woke up in. Linger had brought them coffee and then Fractal excused her. He said that her presence caused undo stress to the conversation.

"I grabbed you guys for a reason, Faceless," Fractal said, looking at him. "I need your help."

Faceless took a sip of his coffee and looked at Fractal. He wasn't sure. The last time a group tried to help him he was forced to play twelve hours of "Match This Face." They did keep Victoria safe; he supposed he owed them at least hearing them out. "Why did you grab me?" Faceless asked.

Fractal put his coffee down on the table and leaned back in his chair, opening up his body language. Faceless noticed; Fractal was trying to open up his body language, and seem more trusting; he had done this before.

"NightCard has a special vault they keep their BloodWine samples in. They're currently just storing them, never using them since BloodWine is so hard to manufacture, and taking the samples almost kills the donors, but now, something's changed."

Faceless looked at Fractal. The man had earned his full attention. Why didn't he know this before? "What's changed?"

"They found her," Fractal looked like he was getting past a lump in his throat.

"Who's her?"

"This girl. We called her the Gifter. She had the ability to bring out the dormant chromosomes in our bodies, to release everyone's – anyone's special abilities. I'd kept her hidden, but now they figured out where she was, and now they're synthesizing her blood, harvesting it. Because it can be used to make BloodWine." Faceless was horrified. "Soon every agent of NightCard from the fucking parking attendant on up will have our powers. Then it's only a matter of time before they send an entire army after us."

Faceless's first thoughts were of Victoria. "That's not good," Faceless said.

"No," Fractal spat. "It's worse than you could guess. The Gifter? She's my sister."

Faceless's eyes widened.

* * *

Redux burst into the room, in a panic. "Fractal! I told her not to, but she did it anyways!" Redux was crying.

Fractal's eyes narrowed. He knew what this was, and he had told Dust not to do it.

"Not to do what?" he said, having to play dumb.

"She... Dust was giving her a check up and Victoria asked about the BloodWine," Redux sniffed, "He told her it wasn't ready."

Redux's words turned to gibberish. Faceless looked at her. "What happened to Victoria?"

"She drank Hearts' BloodWine. But it wasn't... it wasn't stable. She's in a coma."

Faceless jumped up and ran to the door. Fractal stepped in his way.

"Calm down. I know how to—"

Faceless grabbed Fractal by the collar and threw him across the room. He crashed into the wall, denting it in.

"Out of my way," Faceless growled. He grabbed Redux by her throat. "Take me to her. Now." All compassion in his voice was gone. Instead all that was left was an unbelievable, crippling pressure that scared Redux. He dragged her to the door with a grip that surprised her. He ripped the door off its hinges. "Run or be dragged," he growled, his face inches from hers.

* * *

Redux and Faceless ran down the corridor to Dust's office. He burst into the door.

"Explain. Now," Faceless said, dropping Redux. Fractal came into the room shortly after.

"I was just about to," Dust said. "She drank the BloodWine. But it wasn't stable. I told her it could be hers if she wanted it, but that it wasn't ready yet. But she took it anyways. The only way I can fix this is to stabilize the BloodWine. Meanwhile, I've put her in a coma to slow the process."

"What can stabilize the BloodWine?"

"The blood of the Gifter," Dust said.

Fractal glared at him. Dust looked away, avoiding eye contact..

It was the only way. Dust thought to Fractal and Redux. Operator sent his message.

"I guess I'll be coming with you," Faceless said. "Which of you was the one that told her about the BloodWine?"

"That was me," Dust said.

Faceless used his right hand to grab Dust by his face and his left to grab his shirt. He flipped him over onto the office's bed. Faceless hefted one fist back and slammed it into Dust's jaw, shattering it.

"That was twenty percent of what my fist can do," he said emotionless.

"Hrgk," Dust gurgled, spitting up blood.

"You'd better hope she lives, or you'll see one hundred percent." Faceless turned and walked out. Dust looked at Fractal.

I gave him something to fight for, Fractal. Dust said, defending himself from the look of disappointment in Fractal's eyes.

Chapter 60: A Plan and Rice Cakes

Fractal was in the common room, a place with which Faceless was becoming increasingly familiar. With Fractal at the center, the others filed in, surrounding him.

"All right guys, we've got a problem," Fractal said, making eye contact with the others.

"A problem?" Linger asked.

"Yes, a very pressing one."

"It's pressing and choking," Redux said, rubbing her throat. She gave Faceless a piercing glare. Only Ash was allowed to do that to her.

"Shut up," Fractal said sharply. He knew very well that she deserved to be choked.

Dust wasn't there. Fractal smiled. He admired Faceless's restraint. If it were him, he would have done a lot more than just shatter Dust's jaw.

Ash walked in with rice cakes and set them down. Linger knew there was a problem. Fractal only served rice cakes when they were about to do something stupid or dangerous – usually both.

"Shit," she said, grabbing one delicately with two fingers and looking at it.

Then Fractal explained the plan.

* * *

"Now I want everyone to understand that you don't have to go. I know none of us want to go back to NightCard."

Ash laughed. "Really? Because I just love the thought of getting back at them." He smiled, leaning back in his chair, his arms crossed behind his head.

Fractal smiled. "If you want to come, that'll be great; if you don't, I get it." He looked at Reader and Writer.

"Don't worry about us," Writer said. "We both think that this is worth it."

"I just understand you aren't as equipped to fight as say, Crux."

Crux looked at him. He was a tall man, slender, with the body of a runner. He had sandy hair and his skin was pale. His body was sinewy, and his hands had different tattoos on the top of them. He was in his forties, but he still looked twenty-five. His cells automatically slowed the oxidization process; it was a side effect of his power. They preserved the elasticity of the skin, and left him in a perpetual state of youth. The left hand had the left half of a black circle tattooed on it. The right hand had the right half of a white circle tattooed on it. Crux had the ability to grab two objects and combine them into one, bending their atomic bonds and creating a strong alloy of both, which he used to make weapons. Fractal had seen him in action before. He was very adept at surviving.

"Let them come with us, Fractal," Crux smiled. "They have just as much right to get back at NightCard as we do."

Fractal relented. "Fine," he said, smiling. He was proud. It seemed to him that it wasn't just the urge to survive that kept them together. They had loyalty to each other.

He looked from Crux to the rest of his team. Then he looked at Faceless. The man seemed the most motivated out of all of them.

"First we need to rest. We'll need to go get some reinforcements in the morning,"

"Reinforcements?" Linger asked, her arm on his shoulder. "Where the hell are we going to get reinforcements from?"

Fractal looked at her, happy he could still surprise her after all these years. "It's about time I introduced you to my family."

Chapter 61: Carnies

There was an old-fashioned carnival that travelled around Europe, known for their spectacular feats – magic tricks that seemed they could only be supernatural.

The Carnival was in Spain that week, and it was night; the sky was clear, and the stars were twinkling in the Spanish sky. The master circus tent sheltered everyone, stretching the length of three football fields. There were lights inside the tent, making it glow with a multicolored radiance, giving it the feel of the magic it promised.

Faceless was at Fractal's left-hand side, Linger was at his right. They approached the Carnival's master tent, the others followed in tow.

"I always thought you came from circus people," Crux laughed from behind them.

They entered the tent and Faceless's jaw dropped. There was something incredible about this place. The lights were shining and were coming in every direction; everything seemed to be rich and vibrant; the crowd there was laughing and having fun; the smell of popcorn and nachos filled the air. A man stood in the center stage, wearing a top hat and a masquerade mask. He grabbed a microphone and spoke into it.

"Hello patrons!" he shouted, his voice boomed around the tent, amplified by speakers. Faceless looked around.

"I don't see any speakers," Faceless whispered to Fractal.

"There aren't any," Fractal said, unsurprised.

Faceless looked closer. The microphone had no cable, and Faceless could see that it wasn't even on. He looked at the man; he was the one amplifying his own voice.

"Ladies, gentlemen, we have something very special for you here tonight! One of our brothers has returned; it is our one, our only, Fractal, the Million Man!"

Faceless looked at Fractal, and saw the Million Man's face tighten.

"Haven't done this in years," he growled; a smile played on his lips.

He walked up, taking off his coat. Underneath was a black crew neck shirt, fitted and showing that even out of his prime, he was still in shape.

"Watch this; it may be important later," he called back to Faceless. Fractal approached the center of the ring. The ringleader laughed, his voice a boom.

"I even got you a new lion," the ringleader said to Fractal.

"Good," the retired carny said. "Maybe this one can keep up."

The lion, young and full of vigor was carted into the ring. The beast glared at Fractal, hungry. Fractal glared back. For the briefest moment, what could have been fear crossed the lion's face.

"Now! It's time for the Million Man to Dance with The Lions!"

Fractal looked at every person in the room. He made eye contact with each individual one, then he looked at Faceless. The lion's cage door opened. As it walked out, it was surrounded by a haze. The lion split in half. Then it changed a different direction and split in two. The next two splits happened.

Fractal walked forward, splitting himself into two, then he backed off, bounding backwards, leaving a trail of Fractals with him.

The ring was soon full of Fractals fighting lions: jumping over them, evading, and wrestling. It was like a parade of them. All of them were twisting and turning, and jumping around. Faceless squinted, concentrating hard, and he could see the real Fractal and the real lion. Fractal had pinned the lion, tied his feet together, and was sitting cross-legged. He stared right at Faceless. He smiled.

To the crowd, it was the most amazing thing they'd ever collectively seen. The lions started to run into each other, becoming one. The Fractals did the same; slowly the two of them remained, and then they saw the facade of a brilliant fight scene where Fractal punched out the lion. Then he lassoed it and stood next to it. Faceless watched as the haze Fractal ebbed into the standing one.

"What did I tell you?" the ringleader boomed. "A great show!"

The performer acted in true fashion, throwing his arms out and accepting the deafening applause. Everyone's eyes were on the center ring. Everyone's, except for Crux's. Crux's eyes were stage right.

"We're going to take a short intermission! Please, feel free to partake of our expensive foods and our over-priced gift shop!" He threw down the mike and walked off-stage with Fractal. "What did you think?" the ringmaster asked, looking at Faceless and the group.

"Eh, I've seen him do that before," Linger said.

"You're no fun," the man said.

"Let's go talk somewhere more private. It's about Delilah," Fractal said.

The smile disappeared from the performer's face. "I thought that was why you were here. All right, let's go backstage." The group migrated, following Fractal and the carny backstage.

They entered the backstage room, littered with costumes and trinkets, candies and flowers, and all what you'd expect from an actor and performer's life. There were masks on the walls and on the shelves. Pictures of places they'd traveled together were pinned to the dresser mirrors.

"Now before you get mad," the performer began, "I did everything in my power—" Fractal punched him across the jaw; the man's head shot down.

"That was my sister," Fractal said. "You promised me, Soprano, that she would be safe here."

Soprano, the ringmaster looked up at him, rubbing his jaw. "She was. It's not my fault that you had to go blab about your circus life in the damned Gene Coliseum. I hid her, Fractal. I even sent her away, shifting her from safe house to safe house for years. I did my part. If you had kept quiet she'd still be here, and the rest of the world wouldn't be fucked."

"You can't blame him for that!" Linger interrupted. "He thought he was going to die. He was trying to make sure I knew the real him."

"And your knowing the real him got his real sister in real trouble."

Linger made a move, but Faceless stood in her way. He made eye contact with each of them in turns. "We can all do this; we can talk about stupid shit that neither of you could really control, or we could get serious. The woman I love is in a coma. The Gifter is the only one who can cure her; I need to get into NightCard. We need your help."

Linger calmed down. Soprano looked at him. "So you're the famous Faceless." It wasn't a question.

"I hate that adjective," Faceless sighed. "I have been trying so very hard not to be famous – or known."

"We come from different worlds," the carny said. "You choose to hide your uniqueness. We choose to boast ours, hiding the real truth behind smoke and mirrors. Everyone thinks it's an act, and it is, but the act is the act." Faceless thought about it. "And when you're done playing 'Save the Princess,' you should consider coming with us." He looked into Faceless's eyes. "You could see the world, just like Fractal did."

Faceless's mind went back to the Gene Coliseum. He recalled every memory Fractal had of traveling the world, every memory he held dear. He could have all of those memories for himself. Living his own life, with Victoria, but that was for later. Right now all Faceless could afford to think about was Victoria.

"What I'm curious about, Million Man," Soprano said, turning his attention back to Fractal, "is how you're going to get in."

Fractal smiled and opened his mouth.

* * *

Dust looked at the unconscious woman on the bed in his office. He inhaled. The air smelled like bleach in his doctor's office. He was used to it of course. He had patched up all of their group at one point or another. Doing so was part of his job. He owed Fractal his life, and this is what Fractal had asked him to do.

He came out of his thoughts, still looking at Victoria. Fractal had specifically asked him not to do this, though. He comforted himself thinking that sometimes he had to make the hard choices, choices that Fractal wasn't willing to make; he had to do things that needed to be done. He just prayed he had made the right decision.

"I don't know if you can hear me," he said, "but I want you to know I only did what I did because I thought it was right." He rubbed his jaw. Braced around it was a metal bar. It was the only thing allowing him to talk. He wasn't about to allow this kind of injury to happen again. That metal bar was staying there. He didn't relish in the thought of another of Faceless's punches. Faceless's power, even at twenty percent, was enough to shatter it in seven places. He only prayed that the woman didn't die. He really didn't want to feel a hundred. They wouldn't know for another two days.

Chapter 62: Bound

Faceless's jaw was open. He could only stare at Fractal. This was insane. His plan, while brilliant, had way too many variables. So many things could go wrong.

"I love it," Soprano smiled devilishly. "Sounds exciting."

"Are you serious?" Faceless said.

"Of course," Soprano said. "It wouldn't be worth my time if it was too safe; now, remember our deal, Fractal?"

Fractal grimaced. "I remember. If you help me—"

"Then you and all of the people you have come and join the Carnival."

"I can't speak for them. But you will have me," Fractal said.

"Like we'd let you go alone," Redux said. "You're the reason we're all here in the first place. Why we're all free, I mean."

"Yeah, man," Crux chimed in. "We're in for the long haul."

"Then you have yourself a deal," Fractal said, extending his hand to Soprano.

"Not just yet," Soprano said.

He stood up, crossed the room and grabbed a woman from the other side of the door. She entered. She was curvaceous and tall. An amazon build, with blue and black hair. Piercings adorned her body. Everything about her seemed to be eccentric. Like a real carny.

"This is Binder," Soprano said. "She is one of our more special Carnies. She makes me able to trust the word of just about anyone."

Binder inclined her head slowly, acknowledging his words.

"I remember Binder," Fractal said, "You've got the ability to bind people to their promises."

"Bullshit," Faceless said, smiling.

"Seriously," Soprano said, "try."

Faceless approached her. She took off his shirt. He was surprised, but Soprano nodded that it was okay. Binder pressed her hand to his chest.

"Promise you'll touch your nose in one minute."

"I promise," Faceless laughed.

There was a jolt to his chest and his body stiffened. She removed her hand. "Now in 60 seconds, I recommend you touch your nose." The group waited.

"Told you man, this was just—" Faceless began. He cut off mid sentence. He gripped his chest. He was having a heart attack. He dropped to his knees.

"You have 45 seconds, before it kills you," Binder said.

"Faceless, I'd recommend touching your nose," Soprano said.

He touched his nose. Immediately the pain subsided. He fell to the ground. Faceless gasped. Rocking back and forth on the floor, trying to remove the kinks from his body.

"That's a hell of a trick," Crux said, staring at the collapsed Faceless.

"Yep," Soprano said. He looked down at Faceless. "Shake it off, guy. Come on, put your big boy pants on." Faceless glared upwards at him. With a cringe he stood up. "So do we have a deal?"

"I think we do," Fractal said, extending his hand to Binder. "I hope I don't regret that," Fractal said, flexing his hand and looking at it. Faceless just watched in awe.

"Tomorrow we go," Soprano said. "So tonight, everyone try and get some sleep."

They separated, each going to the section of the tent that they were assigned. All except Crux. Faceless watched Crux wander outside of the tent.

"It's normal," Linger said, "He does that before every mission. Poor guy can't sleep."

Chapter 63: Hush

Crux was wandering around the center ring. He stood in the middle of it, imagining there were faces in the crowd. His eyes glanced around the rest of the stage; if they didn't die on this mission, then standing in this ring would be his future. He didn't want to admit it, but he was there for another reason. When everyone else had been paying attention to Fractal, Crux had been focusing on the surroundings.

When he was focusing, he found something that caught his attention: a woman. She was a brunette with amber hair, and hazel eyes. He didn't know why, but she made his heart race; and it was strange; as soon as his heart started beating faster, her glance went to him. She looked at him in the eyes, and she smiled.

Now he was looking at where she used to be. It was dark, only a few sparse lights that made the ring just barely more than pitch black. The lights were dim, but they cast stark shadows against the canvas of the tent. They were unnerving. Crux looked at where she used to be, and his eyes softened; the action was hard for a war-hardened fighter like himself; as surprising as it was, his heart began to speed up again.

Then he heard a rustle behind him. He turned, slowly. He wasn't unduly afraid. He could handle most things that came his way. When he turned though, he found he was wrong. It was the girl. His breath caught in his throat; it was another first.

"I... I'm Crux," he said, immediately feeling infantile. Surely he could do a better opening line than that.

The woman cocked her head to the side. She looked at his eyes. Then she touched her forefinger on her right hand to her chin, then to her ear.

I'm Deaf. Crux read her sign language; he was the only one of the few of Fractal's group who could speak American Sign Language, a side effect of being an American college student who never made it back to America.

Crux pointed to himself. Then he spelled C-R-U-X with his hand.

I Crux, he said. Again, he felt stupid. He had a perfectly good second chance and he ruined it.

The girl smiled; it was a warm, friendly smile. It made Crux's heart begin to beat faster again.

I Hush, she said. *You Sign?*

Yes, Crux said, nodding his fist in agreement, the sign for yes.

I happy, she said. *I no think you sign. I want meet you.*

It took Crux a moment to decipher the sentence structure. ASL was different than English, and he was rusty. However the U.S.A. and the U.S.S.R. had intervened, making ASL the universal sign language.

I wanted to meet you too, Crux said, completely honest. He wasn't used to ASL sentence structure, resigning to English grammar.

I know, Hush smiled. *I feel your heartbeat.*

Crux knit his eyebrows together, the universal sign for confused was the same in ASL.

I feel your heartbeat. I no hear. But I feel. Soprano my brother. I feel sound. I send out sound. I feel your heartbeat. It faster when you look at me. Hush smiled at him.

Crux blushed red. Another first. *I'm sorry,* he said, not really sure what he was apologizing for.

I no hear. I born Deaf, but I feel sound. This, she said while approaching Crux, *this is first time heartbeat feel like yours. It three-times heartbeat.*

Crux frowned. She had noticed his heartbeat was special. He had a triple heartbeat. His heart was built by NightCard to have three chambers, to improve physical activity and stamina.

I born same. Heart m-u-r-m-u-r. My heart three-times same you. It good, she signed. *I can feel everyone heartbeat. But special your heartbeat. It tell me what you thinking.*

Really? Then what is my heart telling you right now? he signed.

That it happy to meet me too, she said. *It sound same like my heart now.*

* * *

Soprano looked on in the corner, watching his sister and Crux communicate. It had been a long time since he had seen Hush smile like that, and it had been even longer since she had anyone else to talk to, other than himself; not many people knew ASL in the Carnival. He lifted the curtain to go backstage; he spared one last moment to glance at his sister.

Soprano went to the still-awake Fractal.

"Fractal," Soprano said.

"Yes?"

"I was thinking," Soprano said. "Do all of us really need to go on the first step of this mission?"

"Why?"

"Because I was thinking it would slow us down." He shifted, shrugging. "Maybe just you, I, Operator, and Faceless should go."

Fractal looked at him, considering what he had just heard. "Crux is crushing on your sister?"

"W-what?" Soprano stuttered, surprised.

"You're giving that crooked smile you always have on your face when you're keeping something from me, but there's that special look in your eyes; you get it when you try and do things for your sister."

"And?"

"And you're removing yourself from the picture, but even if you want to limit the people that go, Crux is my right hand. And you know that. Leaving him here means that you want him here for some special reason. Add that to the fact that he knows Sign Language, it means they like each other,"

"I had no idea that he knew ASL."

"Bullshit you didn't," Fractal scoffed. "You're the only one that knows Sign Language here. You're taking Operator; you wouldn't leave your sister here without someone that can help communicate. That means you know Crux speaks Sign Language."

"I forgot how crafty you are. I never was able to get anything past you."

"But as long as I have Faceless and you, that's fine," Fractal said. Then he looked at Soprano sharply. "But I swear to God, this better not be some ploy to make me keep my promise by pairing those two up."

"I swear it isn't." Although the thought had crossed his mind.

"I'm sure the thought crossed your mind."

"Damn, you're good."

Chapter 64: Ditzy

Fractal, Faceless, Soprano, and Operator were on a train, the least secure form of transportation in Europe, save for a car.

Fractal wasn't happy with where they were going, but he knew they had no choice.

DayBreak, Inc. was a Europe-wide weapons manufacturing corporation. They sent everything from automatic weapons to hand grenades to whoever would pay for them. It was their president, actually, that Writer had brainwashed. They were one of the few companies with resources enough to help them. It was Fractal's thought process that if they could get him out, they could get him back in. It was their fight too. NightCard's super-agents were making DayBreak's offering of regular soldiers and weapons less and less appealing.

They walked into the front doors of DayBreak's main office, a towering building of tinted, reinforced glass and polished steel.

They walked up to the receptionist, a stereotypical blond chewing bubble gum.

Even I know this is cliché. Faceless thought to Operator. The woman smiled.

"Can I help you's?" The woman said in a mock Jersey accent.

"No fucking way," Faceless smiled.

"Wha?" she said, pausing in her gum chewing, mouth slacked open and giving him a confused look, which to Fractal hardly was distinguishable from her usual one.

God, I hope Crux is having better luck than us, Fractal and Soprano thought at the same time. Operator chuckled to herself quietly.

Chapter 65: Silent Love

Crux wasn't sure how, but the woman in front of him was able to get him to open up effortlessly. That was another first. Crux and Hush were in her tent. The light from her lamp lit the tent completely.

I alone, she signed. *Only Soprano talk to me.*

That must be hard, Crux frowned.

Was hard, she said looking at him smiling. *It not hard now.*

Hush touched her hand to his chest.

Different, she said, *feel sound close, feel sound far. Close sound feel... special. Real.*

Crux wished desperately that she could feel his thoughts as well.

Soon you go right? Hush asked.

Yes, but I promise: I will come back. Crux signed.

I feel you will, Hush said. *Because together with you, I want.*

Same, Crux said. Then he put her hand back on his heart. *Because only you make my heart do this.* Crux signed. *What it say now?*

It think same like me, she smiled.

Crux tipped her chin up and locked eyes with her. He pulled her in close and kissed her. Their chests touched. They felt each other's heartbeats, and they both smiled. Crux laid down and pulled her on top of him; he wanted to make their hearts race one more time before he left.

Chapter 66: Help

Fractal, Faceless, and Soprano found themselves in the CEO's office at DayBreak Inc.

They were being given 'the wait', as Soprano referred to it. He often did the same. By making them wait, he would make himself seem important. This was a psychological tactic. None of them were impressed. Finally, the door opened and in walked a man in a blue suit.

"How may I help you gentlemen?" the man said. He had the beginnings of facial scruff. His hair was cropped short and had hints of gray.

"We're here because we think we can help you, actually," Fractal said.

The man's eyebrow raised. "How can you do that?" the President said, crossing his arms. Soprano assumed he was still bitter; Fractal had told him how Writer had never called him back; apparently it was him who had broken them out of the Gene Coliseum all those years ago.

"I think you'll like our proposal, CEO Green," Soprano chimed in. "We will allow you to let us use your weapons and give us transport to go and take out NightCard for you."

"Really," CEO Green said. His face betrayed nothing.

"Really. As an added bonus, we won't even charge you," Soprano said.

"Well, gentlemen, as much as I fear the answer to this, I have to ask, why would I want to get rid of NightCard?"

"Because they are steadily taking your business."

"How's that?"

"Because they're breeding super soldiers. I know this from personal experience," Faceless said.

"The fact that they are doing this means that your regular soldiers and weapons orders must be going down," Fractal included.

"Actually, you're wrong," Green said, leaning against his oak desk. "People are fearing NightCard. Everyone wants our protection. Our sales orders actually went up." He looked Soprano in the eyes. "So no, I won't be supplying you with soldiers to help take down the one that carved us this little niche market, but thank you for the opportunity."

Soprano did not like being challenged. "I would think on that a little more," Soprano said.

"I think I've spent enough time thinking over this frivolity," Green said, pursing his lips into a thin line. "Now get out of my office."

The group were out the front door before Soprano broke his silence.

"This is not over," he growled, looking back at the building.

* * *

Combust sat in the crowd; around her were the remains of the troupe, and Soprano stood before them. Combust followed his eyes to Hush, who was sitting in Crux's lap; a small smile danced across his lips, then he surveyed the rest of them.

"Well, they said no," he said, over-exaggerating his sigh.

"And?" Combust said, all too familiar with her boss. She knew that he wouldn't leave it at that. He never took no for an answer. His pride wouldn't allow it.

"Well, naturally we're going to break in," he said, as though that were the only rational course of action. "Tonight."

He looked at Combust.

"I'll probably need your help," he said, smiling.

"I figured that." She frowned. Something was going to explode.

His gaze shifted over to Crux. "I'm going to need you to take your hand off of my sister's ass," he said. Crux lowered his hand, seemingly ashamed. "At least until after we get the weapons. Then you have my permission to smack that ass," Soprano said.

Hush tapped his shoulder, pointing at Soprano and asking Crux to sign what he said. Combust looked at Crux squirm a little, unsure how to tell his girlfriend that her brother wanted him to spank her.

Soprano told them his plan and they got ready to go. It wasn't that long of a trip; DayBreak's storage warehouse was within an hour's ride.

* * *

Soprano was looking at DayBreak's warehouse; he had no choice but to be impressed by the building. It was only three floors tall, but it was wide, and encompassed by an electrified fence.

"You know…" Soprano said, looking at the fence. "It probably would have been a good idea to have one of us that could channel electricity."

"Man, I'm having enough trouble keeping you bastards straight without adding anyone else," Faceless said.

"I'm just saying, it would have made sense."

They all stared at the fence for a moment, then Faceless broke the silence. "Okay, this is going to hurt, but I have an idea."

"What's your idea?" Ash asked.

Faceless threw Ash against the electric fence. Ash stifled his yell, but his body caught fire in self-defense, within seconds he was burning hot enough to melt through the metal. He fell through to the other side, leaving an Ash-shaped hole in the fence.

"Wouldn't it have been easier to just have him throw a fireball at it?" Fractal asked.

"Look I just make plans. You want a good plan, think of one yourself," Faceless pouted.

"I like this guy," Soprano said, patting Faceless on the back as he copied Ash's shape through the fence, trying to pose himself like a man being electrocuted. He found the experience fun; he couldn't help but hope Faceless stayed around for a while after all this was over.

* * *

They approached the building, Faceless taking the lead. He ran around the building, sticking to the shadows. Ash couldn't help be impressed at the agility the asshole had.

Faceless crept over to a window, looking inside. There were three minimum-wage guards playing poker. Faceless took note that one was cheating, having an ace in his lap, and then walked back to the group.

"Okay, so there are only three, one of which cheats. I could knock them out," Faceless said.

"Let's not follow another one of your ideas," Ash said, still bitter and burnt.

"Let's go with one of mine," Soprano offered.

"Why do I get the feeling this is going to be just as bad?" Fractal said, frowning.

"Do I get electrocuted?" Ash asked.

"Nope."

Ash looked at Fractal. "Then I say we try it."

Soprano grabbed Combust and whispered in her ear. She cringed and looked at him in disbelief.

"Now," Soprano said, his voice having more iron in it than usual.

"Fine."

Combust walked up to the door, rubbed some dirt on her face and tore some of the clothes she was wearing. She paid extra attention to the front of her blouse, tearing enough to expose just the right amount of cleavage. She went up to the door, knocking on it like a woman in panic.

"Watch this," Soprano whispered, nudging Ash in the ribs with his elbow. "She's an amazing actress."

Ash winced in pain. It was only slightly, but he was burnt on that particular rib. An experience he'd not had before. It seemed to only be on that rib and a little on his right cheek and eyebrow. Anyone else would have died. Maybe Faceless's plan wasn't the worst after all. Then Ash felt for his eyebrow; it wasn't there; damn that Faceless.

Another sharp rib nudge brought his attention back to the dramatic scene in front of them. The door opened.

"What?" the cheating poker player said. Having been about to win that round, he wasn't wanting to tolerate a lot of distraction.

Then he saw Combust's perky, full breasts in front of his face.

"How can I help you?" the guard said. Ash watched the asshole slide off his wedding ring and pocket it.

"My car broke down. I need you to come look at it. I crashed and I'm so scared," she rushed him, teary eyed and seeking his embrace, which he gladly provided. Embracing her, his left hand a little too low for her comfort.

"Will you come help?" she asked, her request garnished with puppy dog eyes and pouty lips.

"Yeah," he said, grabbing his flashlight. "I'll be right back guys."

Their response was that they muttered that he forfeited that round and they'd split his winnings.

* * *

Combust led him out the door and into the forest.

"It's just beyond here, on the road," Combust said.

"Wait," the guard said. "There is no road here."

Soprano swung around from behind a tree and knocked him over the head with a log.

"What would be a good line here?" Soprano asked, looking at the group. In unison, they shrugged.

"You aren't the only one with wood?" Faceless offered.

"Oh dude. That works," Soprano said, smiling.

He looked at Combust. "Next," he said, gesturing with his head to the door again. She turned to go. "Wait. Wait!" he whispered loudly. "Come back!"

Combust returned.

"You've got something on your back."

She turned. Soprano groped her ass and smacked it, pushing her forward with a jump. The others looked at him as he watched her go.

"What?" he said, looking at the others in self-defense. "That was like, the perfect amount of cleavage. I'm only human."

Combust sighed and went back to the door. "The other guard said he needed another one of your guys' help with this."

The two looked at her. "Johnny needed our help?" One in a blue jumpsuit said, suspicious. "That doesn't sound like Johnny."

Combust had to improvise. "Yes, but he said 'don't get the douchy one, get the cool one. They know which is which.'" She bit her lip, hoping that sounded more Johnny-like.

"Yeah, that sounds about right," Blue Jumpsuit said, standing up.

"Dude, what makes you think he was talking about you?" Red jumpsuit responded, flustered.

"Dude, come on," he said, bobbing his head and acting like that was the most obvious and only choice.

"Whatever, dick," the offended guard said, throwing his cards on the table, then crossing his arms.

The jumpsuit guard followed Combust into the forest, equally aroused as her previous victim had been. He was staring at her ass when he felt a blow across the back of his head that, while it hurt, failed to knock him out.

"Ow!"

"Sorry, man. You moved at the last second," Soprano apologized.

"What were you planning on doing?"

"Hitting you, knocking you out, and then saying 'You aren't the only one with wood,'" Soprano said the last with a weak laugh.

"Hah, that would have been good," the dizzy, bleeding guard said.

Then he received another blow to the back of his head. This one was by Faceless and was well placed enough to knock him out.

"You aren't—" Faceless started.

"Dude!" Soprano shouted, cutting Faceless off. "That's mine. Don't you take that from me." He looked at Combust. "Get the next one."

Combust sighed and walked back. Three minutes later, another aroused man was walking behind her, the one who had thrown his cards on the table.

"They can't possibly both be this—" His sentence was cut off by a blow to the back of the head; it was a little harder than necessary, but Soprano would prefer it did the job.

"You aren't the only one with wood!" he crowed.

Faceless let out a single laugh.

* * *

The group had tied their captives in their poker room. They were each tied to their individual chairs. Combust was left with them, Soprano saying it would be nice if she helped them continue their game. She was shifting cards and moving chips on the table for them. Each thought it was the nicest they'd ever been held against their will.

"Oh, sweet Baby Jesus," Soprano said, when the group walked into the holding bay.

There were weapons everywhere. Swords, stun guns, automatic weapons – everything the aspiring conqueror could hope for. There were even ATVs to help them carry it in.

Faceless whistled. "You've gotta love the Baby Jesus," he said.

The group gathered as much as three ATVs could carry and made their way back home.

Faceless looked out the rearview mirror and saw the factory, filled with dynamite and C4, explode behind him.

He slammed on the brakes, trailing behind the others, it took them a few moments to come to a stop.

"Who did that?" Faceless roared. "We had won! We had what we wanted! Who the fuck did that?"

"I did," Soprano said loudly, getting out of the car. "Now they know who they're fucking with."

Faceless picked him up and slammed him against the side of the car, denting it in. A gasp of air escaped Soprano.

"You didn't have to kill them," Faceless said, keeping his tone even. His eyes burned with fury.

"That's the truth of war," Soprano said, "and you may not want to admit it, but we are at war. You're a soldier. If you don't use that gun on that shoulder strap of yours to kill, then you need to get the fuck out of the way."

Faceless picked him up in the air then pitched him fifty feet.

"You... fucking... you," Faceless said, unable to form a proper sentence.

"He's right, Faceless," Fractal said, patting his shoulder. "He chose to show you in the wrong way, but he was right. If it was between them and Victoria, who would you pick?"

Faceless looked at him. "Victoria loved me," he said, "for my view of the world – not yours."

Chapter 67: Reasons to Fight

Hush looked at Crux. She was desperate for him to stay.

Stay, she signed. *Stay with me.*

I can't, he signed. *I want most to stay with you. But Fractal need me. I need go.*

Stupid. Stupid. Stupid, she signed, allowing the fist shape to hit her forehead repeatedly. It was the sign for stupid, as well as an emotional reaction.

Crux grabbed her hand away. The look in his eye was that of a pleading man. He kissed her forehead, where there was a red mark now forming.

You no hurt yourself because of me, he signed; he tried to seem angry, but his eyes betrayed his emotions. All he could feel was sadness.

I love you, she signed. Her eyes just barely held the tears.

Same, he signed back with a smile. *That why I go. If I no go, then maybe NightCard find us. Maybe they take you from me. I won't allow that.*

She looked at him. She understood why he was doing what he was. It was true; NightCard would find them eventually. He was going off to fight so that she wouldn't have to; everyone was.

Faceless looked at the photo strip of Victoria and him. The same one he'd brought to his fight with the Kings. He ran his fingertip along a picture of them sharing a kiss. He was coming back. He thought of Victoria, just hoping she would hold on a few more days. Faceless hoped she was dreaming of him.

Back at the base, Dust was watching over Victoria. He noticed a spike in her brainwaves. "You're dreaming," he said, looking at her unconscious body. "I just hope that Gifter blood works. I don't want to be the reason you died."

Fractal was under the tent, lying down with Linger, having just made love, they were sharing what could be their last moment of peace together.

"Fractal?" Linger said, turning over onto her lover. The blanket still covered them.

"Yes?" he said, looking her in the eyes. She was being very strange.

"I know," she looked at his muscular chest to avoid his eyes.

"Know?"

"About Joan. I know that you two were... involved." Fractal didn't know what to say. He just froze. "It's okay," she said, nuzzling into his chest. "I mean, it wasn't okay for a while, but, I forgave you a long time ago. You are the man I love. Do you love me?" She looked at him in the eyes, her eyes pleading.

"Of course I do." He did.

"Then I won," she said, laying on his chest. "I didn't want us to go into tomorrow without your knowing." Fractal stroked some hair behind Linger's ear. He had to come back, for her.

Ash sat across from Redux. She was treating his burn wounds, and as she was touching an ice-pack to his burnt off eyebrow, he winced.

"Sorry," she said.

"You know I have never been good at this emotional crap," Ash said, a rare moment where his stone facade slipped.

Redux looked at him with a sweet, forgiving smile. Her husband was never the emotional type. But on the rare occasions when he was emotional he always said the right thing.

"I know," she said, "but it's just a burn."

"That's not what I meant," Ash said. "You... you have always meant the world to me. I've never been able to say it in a way that you deserve, but you do."

"You've never had to say it."

"I was blessed with the most amazing woman in the world," Ash said, looking into her eyes as she held the ice pack to his forehead.

"No," she said. She kissed him. "I thought we'd agreed on this before. I'm the luckiest woman in the world. That's why I ended up with you."

She laid down next to him, choosing to relax. His ribs didn't hurt so bad, as long as it was her pressed up against them.

Pheromone walked into Faceless's area. Looking at him, she couldn't stand that he had told her no.

"Hey," she said, looking at him.

Faceless looked up from the photo strip and processed who it was.

"Oh, you're that girl I'm allergic to," he said, forcing a smile. "Pheromone, right?"

"Yeah," she said, "and what I don't get is how you told me no."

"What do you mean?"

"I've seduced every man I've wanted from here to Sweden. You shouldn't have been able to escape me."

"Well, maybe it's my genetic makeup," he said, "or maybe I just had someone else I cared about more." His eyes drifted back to the photo strip.

"Maybe," she said. She could see why Spade wanted to take care of him. His was a love that defied logic, reason, and temptation. It was... intriguing; and she wanted it. "I'm going to make sure you come back, because I want to test that."

He wasn't sure he understood.

"I want to see if that woman is really so special, but I want it on a fair playing field, with her conscious." She leaned forward and kissed him. He had forgotten what a woman's kiss felt like. He pushed her off, immediately. "That was to even the playing field a little." She walked away.

"I will never understand women," Faceless said, wishing Spade was alive. "Crap. I just made myself sad."

Operator was lying with Reader and Writer. When they had learned that, in a world where they were more special than the others they needed to rely on each other. They had started out as best friends, but slowly, as they began to understand they were more unique and they were the only ones truly capable of being honest with each other, Operator fell in love. The sisters who shared one mind knew that Operator loved both of them. They accepted the pure love and ever since they had been polyfidelous: lovers and partners both.

We'll be all right, won't we? Reader asked.

We'll be fine, Writer said.

We will, Operator thought to them. *We've got these others to look after us.*

What makes you think they'll look after us? Reader asked.

Because I've felt it, Operator responded. *Would you like to?*

Show her, Writer said, kissing her sister's forehead.

Operator probed into each and every one of their adopted family's minds. She gathered all the love and loyalty they felt for each other. Every drive they had for making it out alive on the other side. The last that she gathered was Fractal's. His love for them had more warmth in it than all the others' combined. With his alone, Reader felt safe. She smiled and snuggled in between Writer and Operator, content. Operator looked at Reader, protective, and kissed her lover. Writer smiled.

I think everyone needs to feel this, Writer said, referencing the warmth of everyone's loyalty to each other.

I think you're right, Operator smiled.

With another thought, she sent all those good feelings to everyone. There was a wave of relief that spread among them. Operator felt that wave and smiled. They were going to be just fine.

I'm proud of you, Writer said, kissing Operator goodnight.

The wave of relief spread among all of them, and everyone in the room wore smiles as they drifted off to sleep.

Chapter 68: A Train Ride & Raw Sewage

In order to get to NightCard, the group had to ride an intercontinental train. The Railway had been constructed after World War II; it created a link from the Scandinavian Peninsula to mainland Europe.

The group took up a train car by themselves. It was easier on a train, Fractal and Soprano had said. They could sneak weapons on easier. It also had fewer cameras. Having done that, the group collectively looked out the windows, wondering if the Swedish landscape was going to be the last they ever saw. The ocean was visible, and the sea air was refreshing.

The sun was only about an hour from setting as they disembarked the train in Stockholm. There was an aura that emanated from the group. People moved, getting out of their way, sensing the group's fortitude. The group ordered cheap take out and checked into a shady motel room on what they unanimously decided was the wrong side of town.

They weren't exactly excited about trying to break into Fati. It was its own fortress, on the edge of Stockholm.

"Any last regrets?" Soprano asked, sitting next to Faceless and offering him a beer.

Faceless took the beer and drank some. "Only making love twice," he said, chuckling. His lips still on the rim of the beer bottle; the action made a soft whistling noise.

"We're in Stockholm," Soprano said. "That isn't a problem."

"It is when the only woman I love is in a coma," Faceless said, sighing at his forced celibacy.

"Oh right. I forgot you were all like, monogamous and shit," Soprano sighed, taking a swig of his own beer. "Well, then I guess you have something worth living for."

"All right, everyone," Fractal said, gathering them around him. "Tonight we are going to NightCard. We were thinking about breaking into two teams, but then we realized that's how bad shit happens."

Everyone nodded in agreement. It was true.

"So instead this is what we're going to do..."

* * *

Faceless could not stand the smell. The most reliable, quick way to get into NightCard had been the exit grates of the sewage system. The ventilation shaft, his preferred method of entry and exit, wouldn't have worked. Fati was different than the other base; its ventilation system was enclosed completely. Their only remaining option was the one NightCard thought people would never choose.

"Whose shitty idea was this again?" Faceless hissed, trying hard not to breathe through his nose. Combust laughed.

"It was our fearless leader's," Soprano said. If Linger's shields gave out, Faceless knew Soprano would have been after Fractal. Soprano was wearing his nice suit. Soprano had found the most amazing things in DayBreak: bulletproof suits. He'd decided he needed to wear one. In case he met his maker, he might as well be dressed for the occasion. Faceless had adopted the same idea; that was before realizing they would be trekking their nice, black suits through sewage.

They finally reached their destination. They had received a crude drawing of the inner workings of Fati from a janitor that Writer had persuaded was in love with her. They had climbed through two hundred yards of sewage to reach the men's bathroom, one of the few places the workers had demanded there be no cameras.

Combust put her hand on the wall, causing it's chemical bonds to loosen. The wall fell apart, crumbling to pieces in front her. They walked through and entered a stall. Combust placed her hand on the wall behind the toilet, delivering the same treatment to it. It fell apart, allowing them access to the surveillance room.

"All right guys," Fractal said, authority in his voice. "This is where Linger, Reader, Writer, Pheromone, and Operator stay. Redux, Ash, go with Crux to the experiment level there," He pointed to the computer screen. "I want those experiments freed and ready to join us. Our exit is going to be messy. We'll need a full list of their powers, which I need Operator to send to us. Operator, can you talk to them from here?"

"No, something's blocking me," she frowned.

"It's all right. We just lost an advantage I hadn't expected to have in the first place," Fractal said. The group looked at him frowning. Every advantage they could get would have been a welcome one. Fractal took his group and led them left out the corridor; Crux led his group right.

"Make it back alive," he shouted at Crux.

"Worry about yourself, old man," Crux called back.

Chapter 69: Stairs Again

"Tell me again why we're climbing stairs?" Faceless said.

"Because we can't afford for them to trap us in an elevator," Fractal said for the fourth time.

"It would be dramatic though," Soprano noted.

"Come on now, you really think that'd happen?" Faceless asked. They exited the stairs, entering the 40th floor quietly. They had just passed the elevator they could have used.

Fractal. Operator said in his head. *There are thirty extremely well-armed guards coming up that elevator.* Fractal had Faceless help him wrench open the elevator doors. They looked at the shaft cables trailing up. Fractal shot the cables, and the elevator detached, speeding to its very explosive, very dramatic death thirty-nine floors below.

"That's why we don't use elevators," Fractal said. Fractal looked at Faceless, who shrugged in agreement. Soprano and Combust laughed.

Chapter 70: Taking One for the Team

The guard on duty had heard the elevator crash; the explosion had spilled out of the elevator, into the main lobby. "Hey!" he said knocking on the locked surveillance room door. "What the fuck happened?"

The door opened and Pheromone's cloud emanated from the room. "Don't say I never took one for the team," she laughed, looking at Operator. She looked back at the guard. "So stud, you have any STDs?"

The guard shook his head. Pheromone looked at Operator. "Oh. Yeah, he's telling the truth," Operator said.

Pheromone pulled the man on top of her with a growl, about to take one for the team.

Writer put her hand over Reader's eyes.

Chapter 71: Hallway Melee

Crux was shooting at fifty-or-so well-armed guards that NightCard had sent their way. He was comfortable shooting his semi-automatic, but there was something therapeutic about using his sword. Although a sword wouldn't be very realistic, given their current situation. They were pinned down in a hallway. He and Redux were on one side of the intersection, while Ash was on the other.

"Tell me again why my woman is on your side of the hallway?" Ash asked, half playfully; the other half had a twinge of jealousy.

"Because I find the people she's around tend to die less," Crux shouted laughing.

"You're using your skills on another guy?" Ash said. "I'm betrayed."

Redux stood up and walked in the middle of the walkway. It was at that exact moment every one of the guards ran out of bullets.

The guards looked at each other.

"I call bullshit," Crux said.

"Call it all you want; it just happened."

Redux rushed them, pulling out her sake bottle.

"Oh, you're going to like this," Ash said to Crux.

Crux looked on, and then he realized the style. Redux was trained in Zui Quan – Drunken Fist. She downed the bottle and then smacked it on a guard's head. Crux thought that wasn't exactly a traditional move, but certainly effective. One of them threw a punch and her upper body flew backwards, bending and shifting her center of gravity lower. She threw a Drunken Fist punch, hitting with the outside of her wrist. The blow struck the man in his throat and he gasped for air, then she threw another to his jaw, breaking it. She stumbled left, avoiding an attack from behind. Then she dropped to her knees, wrist-punching her attacker in his balls. The man fell. Redux rolled, slamming him with the heel of her fist and breaking his nose.

Crux had joined in. He abandoned his gun, pulling cement from the floor and metal from the walls. When he pulled the materials away it was as though it flowed; it left teardrop-like branches from the material. He combined them together, making a sledgehammer, which in one swift movement he used to break a guard's skull.

Ash concentrated, allowing his naturally-combustible sweat to pour from his body. Then with a flick from his lighter he lit himself. He punched the first man, leaving a third degree burn on him, effectively taking him out. He assumed a boxer's stance, throwing punches at every guard within reach. One hit him from behind with an empty gun. Ash looked at him, hurt; then he gave the man a lethal bear-hug of forgiveness. Within two minutes the guards lay before them. Most of them were dead; some were just broken.

"Damn, baby, I love you," Ash said, pulling Redux in to an embrace and planting a sizzling kiss on her lips.

"Gross," Crux said, slightly jealous Ash's woman was within dramatic victory-kissing's distance.

Chapter 72: Separation Anxiety

Faceless, Soprano, and Fractal ran down their own hallway. At the end of the hall was an elevator that led directly to the BloodWine Cellar, most likely where Fractal's sister was. Combust was trailing behind, not built for running.

Combust was still running when one of the guards shot her in the leg. She fell, and Fractal turned to go back for her.

The blast doors fell, trapping Combust on the other side. She stared at the thirty plus horde of armed security personnel that rounded the corner. She pushed her hands to the walls and used her powers to loosen their bonds. The walls began to creak and bend. The guards looked at her, confused and scared. They shot at her and she felt each one of the bullets plug into her. her arms began to sag, and her blood dripped onto the concrete floors. Soon pieces of the ceiling were falling into the blood pools, splashing it. As the walls buckled and as the ceiling began to cave in she looked at the door where Soprano was.

There are worse deaths, she smiled. Operator heard her.

Back in the operations room, Operator felt the life leave Combust.

The lights dimmed a little over Faceless, Soprano, and Fractal – and the Black Joker walked in.

"Sorry, but the dear shouldn't have been so slow. Besides, we should weed out the unnecessary company; I wanted a little privacy anyways. I've been looking forward to this, Fractal," he said, holding out a gauntlet; it trailed wires to a harness on his back. "I even came up with something exciting to deal with that ability of yours."

He pressed a button and the lights went out.

"Aw crap," Faceless groaned in the dark. "See, I told you bad shit happens when you separate."

* * *

Crux, Ash, and a not-as-of-yet-sober Redux had finally reached the door to the lab.

All right, Crux thought, *after we finish here we'll bring them to you in the surveillance room.*

Please hurry. Pheromone is about to go into round three. Operator thought with disgust, looking at Pheromone and her new lover.

What do you mean? Crux asked.

This, Operator said, sending him a mental picture.

Ugh! Why would you show me that? Crux said, physically pitching his head back.

"Ash just blow the damn door," Crux said, rubbing his eyes, as though that would help.

Ash wasn't sure why Crux was upset, but he wasn't going to ask. Instead, he tried very hard to blow the damn door.

The door flew inward, a trail of smoke and fire following it. The experiments looked at it, panicking. They were all wearing white scrubs, with various numbers spray-painted on them, not even names, just numbers. None of them had the collars that were typical. It was as though NightCard didn't worry about their escaping.

"All right, everyone. We're here to save yooouuu!" an inebriated Redux said, tripping inward and landing face-down.

"This will go well," someone shouted from the crowd.

* * *

Crux's group had rejoined Operator, Linger, Pheromone, Reader, and Writer. Together they made it out of Fati through the sewage system. None of them had met any resistance. And they didn't know it, but that was for the best. Every one of them was vulnerable. All they knew was that this time they noticed the sewage around them.

"Operator, send a line to Fractal. Tell him where we're at."

Operator nodded. She tried hard, grunting and straining. "I... I can't," she said, stunned.

"It's him," one of the experiments said. "Neutralizer." He, gestured to the one in the corner that had been bleeding out, and hadn't made it. "They stuck him with us so we couldn't use our powers. He's dead, but it still takes about an hour for it to wear off." Crux's eyes widened. They were out of contact with everyone. He prayed they would last an hour.

* * *

Fractal tried once more to get a hold of anyone; he couldn't. The Black Joker was giving some inane speech about how Fractal knew this day was coming. Fractal was ignoring him.

"This is fine," Fractal whispered to Soprano. "Everyone knows their jobs."

"I'm more worried about us," Faceless said. "Joan's told me stories of the Black Joker. None of them were happy stories."

"Don't be too worried. You'll be sitting this one out," Fractal said, pulling out a sword.

"That won't do you much good," Black Joker said at the sound.

"Blah-blah, you'll kill me, blah-blah, you have a big penis. Just fight already," Fractal said.

"Thanks for letting me know where you are," Black Joker said, aiming the gauntlet, "and, for the record, my penis is very big."

He pressed a button and a piton shot from the gauntlet, one which Fractal almost caught in the face. It slid by, hitting the wall next to his head, anchoring into the wall.

"That's not what I was expecting," he said. The Joker sent out five more, each one anchoring in the wall. "You kinda suck at your aim," Fractal said, walking forward. His cheek tore open. "Damn it!" Fractal shouted, moving away. He hadn't even heard that shot.

"Surprise, motherfucker," Black Joker laughed from the dark.

Chapter 73: Playing with Fire

Ash hated waiting; it sucked, and what he hated more was waiting powerless. He stared at the dead body of Neutralizer, wondering if anything could be salvaged from this.

"Hey you," Ash said, looking at the experiment that had told them about Neutralizer.

"Y-Yes?" he asked, stuttering in his nervousness.

"Can the blood neutralize us?"

"Not directly."

"What do you mean directly?"

"Y-you'd have to drink it."

Ideas began to rattle around in Ash's brain. Ash pulled out the baggie he carried his matches in. He emptied it and scooped up some blood. He ran back towards the sewer, into a maximum security base filled with people that were already trying to kill him—without his powers.

"The crap I go through for this guy," he said, wading into the sewage.

Chapter 74: Razor Wires and Stunning Improvisation

Fractal was cut again from the dark; he was unable to move in yet another direction. He heard another piton and cord fire off. He ducked, avoiding a piton aimed for his eye; instead it was another one anchored into the wall, limiting his movements even further.

Faceless wanted to help. He wanted to intervene. But he wasn't allowed; Fractal had made that perfectly clear. Faceless had just to wait. He stared into the dark. Hoping he was doing the right thing. Soprano touched Faceless's shoulder.

"He'll be all right," Soprano said. "Remember, he used to fight lions; this guy is no problem."

"Come now, I expect more from the man that took my eye," the Black Joker said, presenting his most vicious smile to the dark void.

"It doesn't mean anything unless it's me," Fractal said, wiping the blood from his face.

He knocked his sword sideways. He touched something. Something that was stopping his movements, cutting him. Then he touched one with his hand, getting cut; it was thin, and it was angled. They were wires.

The wires all led back to the Black Joker. They were letting the Joker know where Fractal was. That was the secret. Fractal smiled.

"I'd stop using the wire and face me like a man," Fractal said. "For your own good."

"I'll risk it," Black Joker's voice echoed out in the darkness.

Faceless knew the plan at that moment. He took out the stun gun he had picked up from DayBreak. He slid it on the ground, in the direction he heard Fractal's voice come from. Fractal heard it slide and picked it up.

"Fuck you," Fractal said, touching the stun gun to the wire that had cut his face.

The electricity ran along the wire, tracing all the way back to the Black Joker. The Black Joker writhed in pain, an almost lethal voltage making every muscle in his body contract. The electricity made the darkness light up in bursts. Fractal could see his enemy thrash during the flashes of light.

The electricity of the stun gun finally ran out. The Black Joker dropped in the darkness.

"HAHAHAHAHAHAHA!" Black Joker laughed. "You got me, you bastard." He rolled over, trying to drag himself away.

Fractal was able to see the wires when the electricity was running through them. He knew his way in the dark. He dodged them, finding his way to the Black Joker.

"You've hunted me," he said, tired and stumbling. "You've locked up my sister. Turned the woman I fell in love with into a monster."

Black Joker let out a weak chuckle. It was some of his prouder work.

"But you changed me from a mindless assassin into a leader," Fractal said, picking his sword up from the ground. The tip trailed on the ground, making a scraping sound. "I'm not who I could have been, because of you. Now I have purpose. I should thank you for that, and right now I'm about to fulfill some of that purpose you gave me."

He bitch-slapped Joker with the flat side of the sword. Then he pointed the blade at Black Joker's heart. "I suppose I should beg for my life?"

"No. Begging won't help."

"Then you're finally the man I tried to make you out to be," the Black Joker said. "So I'll give you your graduation gift. The BloodWine Cellar, where your dear sister is being kept, is protected by my brother, the Red Joker."

"Well fuck," Faceless said, hearing one more piece of bad news.

"He's on the top floor, the penthouse, and he'll be a lot harder to kill than I."

"It'll be a lot less gratifying; of that I'm sure," Fractal said, slamming the sword into the Black Joker's heart. Fractal wiped some of the blood splatter off of his face. He looked at them; there were still splatter marks of blood on his right side and there were still smears of blood on his left. "You guys want to take the elevator or the stairs?"

They shook their heads and avoided his wild eyes.

Chapter 75: Elevators and Penthouses

The three were in the elevator, the only way to get to the penthouse.

"I thought you had said taking an elevator was a bad idea," Faceless said, stating the obvious question that was lingering in the air.

"Did you see any stairs?" Fractal asked.

"No," Faceless admitted.

"Then shut the fuck up."

Soprano laughed. The door opened and they cautiously walked into the room.

"Hello," a man said from a leather chair near the wall of windows showing off the Swedish skyline. "The BloodWine Cellar you're looking for is over there in that vault. Along with the girl." The man in the black suit gestured to his right.

"And you are?" Faceless asked.

"Ah, see that's the tricky part," the man said, standing up and walking over to the liquor table, pouring himself another drink. "I don't really exist, at least not as far as the government is concerned. I died a long time ago. About thirty years."

Soprano was not in the mood for games. He was tired, and his new bulletproof suit was ruined. "I don't have time for riddles. Just tell us who the fuck you are or we'll just kill you."

"See that's where you're wrong. You won't."

In a flash the man was on top of Soprano. Soprano shouted, his booming voice threw the man back. The man flew back, into his liquor table. He stayed there for a second, then stood up.

"That wasn't very nice," the man said. "You see, I don't hate you. I'm not like my brother, whom you so thoroughly killed. I'm not a psycho, nor do I enjoy killing." He dusted some broken glass off. "But…" he said, looking at Soprano. "I am a business man. My name is Morgan and you've been fucking around in my building. You came in here, killed one hundred and fifty-seven employees, freed the experiments, and killed my brother. You three have been very bad for business."

He was gone, faster than before, and grabbed Soprano by his throat. Soprano tried to scream, but Red Joker crushed his grip, collapsing Soprano's throat. Soprano tried to use his voice to defend himself, but his crushed, torn windpipe only drowned him in blood; his voice only came to a gurgling sound. Soprano could tell he was dying; his last act was a spit in the face of the Red Joker; the look in his eyes out, and his face's last look was that of a drowning man still trying to be smug. Red Joker dropped Soprano and flexed his hand.

"That's one annoyance out of the way," he said. "Just so you know, I have a very special ability. I can absorb your powers, if I drink enough of your blood. They only stay in my system for about six months, but that's six months I think is well used. That woman…"

He pointed at the broken alcohol stand; a bottle of BloodWine had shattered on the floor.

"That woman was a very special case. We had to freeze her before we could cut her. She had the ability to absorb kinetic energy, and she was kind enough to pass that on to me." He turned his neck to the side, popping it. "So let's see if you can find yourself at the same loss we were." Red Joker sped to Fractal, then with one hand flung him across the room. Fractal hit the wall: the shock sent cracks up it and caved part of it in.

Red Joker came for Faceless next, who bent back, avoiding the first blow. Red stepped on Faceless's foot, planting him. Faceless caught a fist to the stomach, flying across the room and against the bulletproof window; his body cracked it all the way up the pane.

The Red Joker heard a ding, and the elevator door opened. A fire extinguisher came through the door, flying at Red Joker's head. A bullet followed, exploding the fire extinguisher, and making the foam shoot out. It blinded the Red Joker.

"Fractal! Here!" Ash said, running towards Fractal. "This stuff will neutralize him!"

Red Joker recovered and slammed his fist into Ash. His fist went all the way through and barely missed Ash's heart.

Ash looked at his chest. Red Joker's fist was still inside Ash's chest cavity, and a red patch was beginning to spread along his shirt, blossoming from the center.

"Man," he said, chuckling. "I knew coming up here without powers was a bad idea, but I had to play the hero." He dropped Neutralizer's blood and fell to his knees. He thought about Redux. "Wasn't so lucky after all, babe," he smiled, then fell forward. His smile stayed on as Ash's flame went out.

Faceless came up with his sword and slashed at Red Joker, who swatted away the blade.

"What did I just tell you?" Red Joker said, bitch-slapping Faceless, knocking him against a column.

"I wasn't trying to cut you," Faceless said. "I was trying to buy Fractal some time."

Red Joker turned around, as Fractal touched the stun gun to him, electrocuting him. The stun gun ran out, and Red was still standing.

"That would have been smart, if you'd had a full battery," Red said. He looked left. Faceless was reaching for the neutralizer. "Oh, hell no!" Red shouted, running at him with Faceless's sword.

Faceless closed his fingers around the neutralizer, then turned to see the blade coming at his face. He knew he couldn't move fast enough.

Fractal dove, trying to save Faceless.

Outside the group saw the penthouse explode.

Chapter 76: Going Home

Fractal walked out of the sewer system. He had Soprano's body on his back, and was leading his sister with one hand.

He met the group and looked at them. They were looking at a bleeding man. One that they looked to for guidance, who had saved all of them at one point or another. They were looking to him, again.

"Let's go home," he said to them.

* * *

Fractal gave Victoria the antidote. He had Dust move her to the Carnival. She took the antidote in her veins but still didn't wake.

"How long?" Fractal asked.

"There could be no telling," Dust said. "But you know who the first person is she will want to see when she wakes up, right?"

Fractal looked at Victoria. His eyes showed complete, utter sadness. "I failed you," he whispered.

Chapter 77: The Truth

The next morning Fractal went to visit Victoria in her trailer. She was awake and asking for Faceless. The carnies thought it best Fractal break the news to her.

When he entered, she was sitting, looking out the window. Her glasses rested on the window sill. She didn't need them anymore. One of the many parting gifts of Faceless. Fractal's mouth formed a frown and he sat down across from her.

"I imagine you want to know what happened," Fractal said.

"I couldn't not know," she said.

* * *

Fractal landed a few feet short, and watched as Faceless was run through with the blade.

"Hhhgk," Faceless said, looking at Red in the eyes.

"I take you with me," he smiled, running himself higher up with the sword. He punched the vial into Red's mouth, breaking it, and causing the blood to pour into his mouth.

Red pitched back with a cry of pain. Fractal looked at the Red Joker's face, and the glass vial had cut his lips.

"No!" he screeched, becoming a normal man again.

Fractal pulled out his gun, up to now useless against Red's impenetrable skin, and pointed the barrel at Red. Red showed fear on his face for the first time. Red looked up the barrel, feeling his own mortality.

"Go to hell," Fractal said as he pulled the trigger.

The bullet went into Red, splatting out the back of his skull. Red's gore and brains showered the floor. He was not getting back up. They had won. Fractal dropped the gun and slumped over to his backpack and fell to his knees. He was exhausted. But there was one more job to do. Fractal looked at the BloodWine Cellar. Then he reached into his backpack and took out the C4 charges. After his sister was safe, he was blowing this place to hell.

* * *

"That's what happened," Fractal said. "Your man died a hero. You would have been proud."

"I am proud," Victoria said, not looking at him. "I was always proud of my Boy in the Rain."

Fractal stood up, and left the room. Operator was waiting for him in the hallway. "That's not how I heard it," Operator said. She looked him in the eyes.

Fractal frowned. "Then tell me what you heard." Fractal closed his eyes and listened.

* * *

Faceless closed his fingers around the neutralizer, then turned to see the blade coming at his face. He knew he couldn't move fast enough. Fractal dove, trying to save Faceless. He made it, sliding in front of the blade meant for Faceless.

"Hhhgk," Fractal said, looking at Red in the eyes. "I take you with me," he smiled, grabbing the vial from Faceless. He ran himself higher up on the sword. He punched the vial into Red's mouth, breaking it and causing the blood to pour into his mouth.

Red pitched back in pain, and shouted out in pain. Faceless saw the glass cut Red Joker's lips. Faceless pulled out his gun, up to now useless against Red's impenetrable skin, and pointed the barrel at Red. Red showed fear on his face for the first time. Red looked up the barrel, feeling his own mortality.

"Go to hell," Faceless said as he pulled the trigger. The bullet went into Red, exploding out the back of his skull.

Red's gore and brains showered the floor. He was not getting back up. They had won. Faceless looked at Fractal.

"God, that was stupid," Fractal said, spitting up blood.

"You saved me, Fractal."

"Yeah, I kinda noticed that."

"I can't... I can't ever repay you," Faceless said. "On account of the dying thing."

Fractal chuckled. "Yes you can," he said. He pulled out a vial of BloodWine. "Dip this in my blood and drink it."

"What?" Faceless asked, shocked.

"You want to repay me? Then you become me," he said, staring Faceless in the eyes. "I need you to look after everyone when I'm gone. They need a leader, especially now."

"I can't do this," Faceless said, still trying to stop the bleeding.

"You're the only one that can," Fractal said, removing Faceless's hand and putting his BloodWine into it.

"But I'm not you. I'm not as smart or as clever."

"That's where you're wrong," Fractal smiled. "You are a lot more intelligent than you give yourself credit for. Consider it another challenge. Like the one I gave you all those years ago. As I recall, you met that one."

"But you're old. I don't want to be an old man for the rest of my life," Faceless said, trying to ease the tension.

"I'm only forty-one, asshole," Fractal laughed. "Just, promise me you'll take care of Linger; you've got an anniversary tomorrow." With that final retort, he chuckled and then fell silent. He spared a thought to Operator.

Go to Plan C, Fractal thought to Operator.

Fractal's last thoughts before he died in Faceless's arms were of Joan Saint, and the day he fell in love with her.

"Are we in love?" Joan had asked, holding Fractal after one of their workout sessions. They were both naked, and Fractal was running his fingertips around on her stomach.

"I think we are. Do you?"

"Yes," Joan said, giving him a smile that Fractal would never forget. "We are definitely in love."

"I thought so."

"So tell me. Tell me you choose me over Linger."

He closed his eyes to rest a moment and watched Joan, the last thing he saw before his eyes closed. A tear fell down Fractal's cheek as he lay bleeding in Faceless's arms. "I chose you," he whispered. Then Fractal passed away.

Faceless looked at the BloodWine Cellar. Then he reached into his backpack and took out the C4 charges. After Fractal's sister was safe, he was blowing this place to hell.

Chapter 78: On the Horizon

"Come with us," Operator said aloud. Faceless followed her to Reader and Writer's room. "Fractal had a contingency plan. As soon as he heard you had escaped, he designed it. He said that if anything should ever happen to him, you were the only one that could take his place."

Writer came up to him. "What I am about to do is upload you with all of his memories. You will still retain yours, of course, but you will have his too. You will have lived his life, and felt every emotion he has."

Writer pressed her head against his. Faceless could feel every memory of his being pushed aside, and another of Fractal's pressed next to it. It was impossible. It was as though for each memory he had, he had another memory of what was happening to Fractal at the same time.

He crossed the room to the mirror. He thought of every memory he had of Victoria. He thought of every thought Fractal had of how much he wanted to protect his adopted family. Then he thought about the fifty or sixty people, Carnies and freed experiments, that were waiting outside the room. All of them were expecting Fractal to walk out of the room.

"One last mask," he said, touching Fractal's face, accepting his final role. A tear rolled down the back of his hand. "I'm sorry, Victoria," he said in Fractal's gruff voice.

Operator watched Faceless's back as he walked out of the room. It was the strongest back she had ever seen. It held the hopes of everyone. The night had finally ended. Daybreak was finally on the horizon. She walked up and placed a hand on his strong shoulder. "If you don't experience the sad endings, you won't appreciate the happy one," she said, "and I promise, it is coming."

Chapter 79: So Close/So Far

There was an easel in the corner of the room. It was covered haphazardly, as though in a rush to save it from Fractal's notice while he was in Victoria's room.

"Stop staring at it," Victoria said.

"I was more so just wondering what it was."

"Let's get back to what we were talking about," Victoria said.

"I'm just telling you, Victoria, that I want you safe. You need to stay here, not go out in the field," Fractal said.

"Faceless went out in the field. Why the hell won't you let me?"

"Because as he died in my arms I promised I'd keep you safe."

"If you let him die what makes you think you'll do any better with me?" Victoria said callously.

"What is that supposed to mean?" Fractal/Faceless said.

"It means you let the man that I love die. You promised me you'd bring him back. You broke that promise, why should you keep this one?" She pushed him out the door and closed it on his face.

Faceless slammed his fist on the door. He pressed his head to the door and a tear rolled down Fractal's face.

"She's gone," he whispered to himself. He felt the tear roll down a cheek that had never been his, but now it forever was.

"He's gone." Victoria slid down the other side of the door. She looked at the easel. It was one last picture, but this time the man had a face.

"I miss you," they both said in sync.

Only a door separated them, but it could have been an eternity. The two lovers stayed, frozen in time for a few moments, leaning against the door, tears rolling down their cheeks.

Chapter 80: Aces up Their Sleeve

Patterson walked into the room. It was dark, with the only light coming from the giant stasis vat in front of him. He was in Terra, the underground retreat option for NightCard. In the vat at the center of the room was the Red Joker.

He was suspended in clear liquid. Attached to his face was a mask, a tube leading from it supplied him with air. His body was cut and the vat was slowly healing him. When he spoke, his voice, mechanical, came over speakers.

"Were they evacuated in time?" Red said.

"Of course," Patterson said. "I made sure at the first explosion."

"Where are they now?"

"They are in transit, along with her; they're on their way here now."

"She ask any questions?"

"I had Hearts be the one to ask her. She and that guy are best friends. Besides, remember? She thinks we're the good guys."

"Ah, Hearts, he was always my favorite."

"I was a fan of Clubs myself. She has more class."

"Either way, 1344 is safe. Keep Hearts watching her for a while. I want those other three hunting 1343. I want that bastard killed."

Patterson's eyes grew large. "Faceless is alive?" Patterson asked, his voice slipping emotion.

"Now I know I heard that wrong. It must be the glass. It sounded like you actually cared about that face-peeling bastard."

"N-no sir," Patterson bowed his head, a sign of respect. It was, however, secretly to hide his look of joy. A look even he didn't understand why he was wearing.

"Good. Now I want that woman taken care of."

"I'll let the Aces know," Patterson said.

Chapter 81: Freedom in Spades

A man with a fresh buzz cut and a five o' clock shadow walked into an Anime shop in New York City. He saw a nerdy, slightly overweight shopkeeper stood behind the counter. The man went into the adult section.

"Hey man, what's your poison? We have tentacles, she-males, schoolgirls—?"

"No, thanks."

"Schoolboys?"

"No…thanks. Just give me a game that's a quick play, and be sure it has a lot of romance."

"Oh. Sure, man, I have just the thing."

The store clerk turned to pick the game and the customer scratched his forearm. The clerk turned back around and noticed the tattoo.

"Dude that's awesome. I always thought about getting that kind of tattoo. What made you pick that?"

The man stopped scratching. There was a symbol of a spade etched out in slightly faded black ink. There was a fresh scar gash that was cut right through its center. "I had to get it for work," he laughed.

He paid for his game and turned to walk out the door. As the man walked into the sunlight he smiled. He breathed in the free air. He stretched and smiled, thinking he would never get tired of the way freedom felt. He rubbed his neck, where there was a tan line the width of a dog collar; sometimes the absence of things was worth enjoying as well.

He pulled out a worn photo from his pocket. One that looked like it had lived through war. It was from a photo booth. It was one single frame; it was of a couple he once knew.

He swung his bag over his shoulder and shoved the photo back into his pocket. As he walked away, he hummed the opening bars to a Beethoven song; it was a melody a friend had taught him.

ABOUT THE AUTHOR

Dustin Sanchez graduated Lamar University with an English degree; he plans on teaching English at the high school level. He is a fan of anime and comic books. He is working on the sequel of this book, as he has been for the last few years—although he promises that it is coming, eventually. He hopes the book wasn't too offensive, but dislikes the ideas of refunds; he finds them remnants of a patriarchal society, therefore do not expect any.

Have a great day.